<u>Reviews for *Vampire]*</u>

Vampire Dawn is a new look a_
Written from the point of view of bou_ _
human, it doesn't immediately assume that all va.._ ,
evil. As the story progresses it becomes less clear who is un_
hero and who is the villain.

Vampire Dawn is a superb story of good versus evil. Original,
well crafted and compelling – a must-read for any vampire fan.

Lesley Mazey - The Eternal Night

Henry has a genuine talent for telling a good joke, and you'll
find plenty of them scattered throughout *Vampire Dawn*. The
story also gets very serious in places; particularly near in the
end, where there are some jaw-droppingly unpredictable
moments. It takes some unexpected turns and keeps the reader
on his toes, never sure what to expect. Best of all, I found my
interest level gaining the further I got into the story. This
one's definitely for those who prefer Joss Whedon to Bram
Stoker. It's a worthy first novel, and Philip Henry is one to
watch.

Darryl Sloan - The Alien Online

Vampire Dawn is a wonderful tale. The knowledge of just who
the bad guys and who the good guys are gets murky as roles
interchange and morality lines are crossed by all.

Vampire Dawn is a fast paced, exciting read with revenge, fear,
romance both lost and found, and justice deserved for the true
monster of the tale. I highly recommend *Vampire Dawn* for
both a horror and a romance genre reader; Mr. Henry has
captured both exquisitely.

Catherine McHenry - Romance Reviews Today

Vampire Dawn is a terrific tale that provides a fresh look at the vampire-human "relationship". The story line is told from the varying perspectives of Claire, Xavier, and Christian without regard to who is the real hero as none of the three are totally saints or sinners. Fans will appreciate this superb action-packed horror drama in which author Philip Henry leads his audience into a one sitting read that ends with the reader wondering who is the good guy for the means is as important as the ends.

Harriet Klausner - Amazon.com

MIND'S EYE

PHILIP HENRY

Philip Henry

CORAL MOON BOOKS
In association with
EXPOSURE PUBLISHING

www.philiphenry.com

Coral Moon Books
In association with Exposure Publishing,
An Imprint of Diggory Press
Three Rivers, Minions, Liskeard, Cornwall, PL14 5LE
www.diggorypress.com

British Library Cataloguing In Publication Data
A Record of this Publication is available
from the British Library

ISBN: 1846852978
978-1-84685-297-8

Cover art by Philip Henry

10 9 8 7 6 5 4 3 2 1

Supported by The Arts Council of Northern Ireland

Fifteen years ago, the town of Portstewart was the scene of a series of strange deaths. You may remember reading about it, or seeing it on the news. Speculation was rife concerning the culprit(s), motive, and method. Everyone had a theory, and everyone felt their theory was more plausible than anyone else's. I can tell you now, everyone was wrong. Only three people knew the whole story of what really happened. I am one of those three. You are about to learn the truth.

Chapter I - Everyone's Favourite Nobody

Someone once said, "Everyone will be famous for fifteen minutes"... I forget who.

Imogen Collins, *Art Beat*

- September, 1989 -

1.

There's a kid like Johnny Knox in every high school. He's the one who walks around the playground by himself, gazing at the different cliques but never daring to approach them. He's the guy who's no good at sports and consequently gets called lazy (by the P.E. teacher who follows in his golf cart) and gay (by the athletes frolicking in the showers). His clothes are hand-me-downs that kids hiding behind designer labels laugh at. He enjoys the creative aspects of school and usually excels at one (in Johnny's case Art). He's the quiet, sensitive type who American movies tell us the best looking girl in the school will eventually fall for, when she realises that his inner beauty far outweighs the good looks and muscles of the football star. But we all know that doesn't really happen. Kids like Johnny Knox go through high school largely unnoticed. The most popular kids at our school would never even have known his name if he hadn't been murdered.

Of course, as soon as the TV news cameras arrived, everyone claimed to have had some relationship with the dead teenager. It was thought at first to be suicide. I remember feeling really uneasy that this explanation was so readily accepted. "He was a loner" was a popular sound-bite. The immaculately dressed Imogen Collins—local TV's ubiquitous star—nodded sympathetically as she talked to the 'friends' of Johnny Knox, but after several repetitious interviews she stopped and picked the most photogenic pupils for the six o'clock news report. I'll never forget the look on her face after the third pupil had given her pretty much the same opinion of Johnny as the first two; she looked like she'd heard it all before. This kind of kid committing suicide made sense to her; maybe she had even reported a similar story before and by changing a

1

few names she could use a lot of the same material. She nodded to her cameraman and her empathy was immediately switched off as she checked her face in a pocket mirror, to be sure that all the nodding and brow-furrowing hadn't upset her make-up. Everyone thought she was gorgeous on TV, but when I saw her up close it reminded me of the time I painted my bedroom without filling the cracks in the wall first. My Dad had told me a good job was all in the preparation, but I figured if I slapped enough paint on, it would cover the cracks—Imogen Collins seemed to have the same philosophy about her face. We were both wrong.

I wasn't standing in the queue of 'friends' waiting to speak to her, so I wasn't disappointed when she picked perfect complexions over acne. I didn't want my fifteen minutes of fame at the expense of Johnny's suicide. I wasn't his friend, but unlike the seventeen pupils in the queue, I had at least spoken to him.

It was at the Prize Day at the end of last term. Our school gave out awards at the end of each year for the students who had distinguished themselves. He was being awarded the prize for Art, and I was getting the prize for English. A lot of guys teased Johnny about being gay, but he wasn't. That day, sitting backstage, he turned to me and said, "What do you think of Miss Crabtree?" By my instant smile, he knew that I thought the same as he did…and maybe a few more things besides.

Miss Crabtree, the new science teacher, was a true gift from the gods. Fresh out of teacher training college, she was slim, pretty and, for such a small waist, had huge boobs. For the past month the weather had been blinding, and she had taken to wearing flimsy little summer dresses and no bras. Never in the history of education had so many teenage boys been so interested in convection currents, capillary action and anything else that might rise of its own accord. It was a toss-up (no pun intended) how she was best viewed: calling Miss Crabtree—or Miss Cocktease, as she had been renamed—to your desk and getting a good eyeful when she leaned over to answer your question, or just watching her stand at the front of the classroom. Standing at the front was always my personal favourite because it had a double advantage; 1) She stood with her back to the window and you could see every curve of her body through her dress! And 2) the fan was at the front of the room and, if God was smiling, the cold air would hit her dress and reveal the location and shape of her nipples. Calling her to your desk was OK for a quick fix, but for a sustained appreciation of her, standing at the front of the room always won in my book. Still, the debate continued after every class. Johnny had never joined in or offered an opinion, as far as I can remember, but it was clear to me now that he had thought about it.

Johnny took a piece of folded paper from his pocket and handed it to me. I unfolded the A4 page and my eyes nearly popped out of my head. He had drawn Miss Crabtree stark naked! I glanced at him and then returned to the drawing. It was incredibly detailed and I wanted to remember as much as possible for a more convenient time.

"How did you do this?" I finally said.

He smiled. "You've seen her in Science class—I just filled in the blanks."

I looked at the detail intensely. I knew I only had a few more seconds before I would have to hand it back and I *had* to remember this picture. With a feigned attempt at nonchalance, I folded the paper and handed it back.

He looked at the paper for a moment and then looked at me. "You hang on to it. I've got lots more stashed under the window-sill in my bedroom."

With restraint that I could barely believe myself capable of, I nodded and slowly put the drawing in my hip pocket. We talked for the next half-hour, mostly about girls—his other unwitting models. I was surprised to find we had the same taste in women. Not just the girls who had blossomed and were stretching their pullovers, but some of the quiet, interesting girls who took Drama and weren't going to be filling a bra anytime soon. He even mentioned that he thought my girlfriend, Rachel, was very attractive. The conversation stopped there. I'm sure it was out of his mouth before he even thought about what he was saying. I guessed from his silence that maybe Rachel was part of his private art collection, too. He looked embarrassed. I felt sorry for him; he didn't have any

3

friends and his family life was no picnic either. If he wanted to imagine my girlfriend naked, that was fine with me. After all, it's what I'd been doing for the last six months. Maybe that was another reason I never pursued the matter; if he had shown me a drawing of Rachel, I wouldn't have been able to tell him how accurate it was. That, above all, was something that no boyfriend should ever have to admit.

"You, boy," Imogen Collins said, snapping her fingers at me. "Go and get me a bottle of mineral water." She looked at me as if she was doing me a favour by incorporating me in her world. She was puzzled that I didn't leap at her command. She snapped her fingers again. "Now, please." I'd never heard the word please said with such disregard for its meaning.

I walked slowly over to her. "Not blood?"

"What?" she said, proving her mouth could snap as well.

"I thought you fucking leeches only drank blood," I said, calmly. I stayed just long enough to see her true face, the one all the make-up in the world couldn't hide. It wasn't pretty.

Classes were strange that day. No one felt much like doing anything, not even the teachers. The end of every class brought with it a new series of rumours and theories about Johnny's death, everything from accidental overdose to autoerotic asphyxiation. The only fact that remained constant was he was found lying on his driveway that morning still in his pyjamas. No one seemed to know for sure how he had died and I decided the only way to find out was to watch Imogen Collins's report that night.

Even the popular kids were making a stab at being upset. They were like the politicians that everyone looks to in a time of crisis for how to react.

Obviously we're upset at this terrible tragedy, but life must go on.

Drew Dillon, the school's alpha male, paused for a minute's silence as a sign of respect before the kick-off of the first match of the season. His female equivalent, Maxine Dawson (the undisputed sex-symbol of the school), spent the afternoon comforting weeping girls who felt bad that they had either never got to know Johnny, or had ridiculed and

4

humiliated him when they caught him stealing a glance at their legs or breasts.

While the memorial football game and Maxine's love-in were going on, the rest of us, who didn't fit in either group, were left to our own thoughts. It was only the second week of the new school year and the teachers realised we weren't going to be able to concentrate, so giving us a day's indulgence seemed the only thing to do. It was during my last class of the day that a note arrived summoning me to the headmaster's office. Usually this wouldn't have bothered me; I wasn't one of those kids who were always in trouble. When I got called to see Mr Reese, it was nearly always to commend me on an essay I'd written, or some competition he wanted me to enter on the school's behalf. This time I was nervous. I had the terrible feeling that Imogen Collins had told him what I had said to her.

On the long walk to his office, I looked around for anything that might slow me down. *A visitor arrived and I had to show them out to the football field; a pupil was sick and I had to stay with him*—something like that, but no excuse presented itself and before I knew it I was at the door of Mr Reese's office. I was sure he'd had the door made disproportionately big just to make it more foreboding. There was no way anyone would ever need a door *that* tall or *that* wide. I knocked timidly.

I knocked on your door, sir, but there was no answer.

The huge door swung open almost immediately and the headmaster motioned me to come inside. There were two seats set out facing the desk; one was empty and the other held the divine form of Maxine Dawson. She turned and smiled her "It's terrible, but I'm being brave" smile. I sat down beside her (really close to her) and tried to focus my attention on the headmaster.

"Well, Steve, how are you holding up?" he said, fidgeting nervously.

"I'm OK, sir," I said; wondering why, out of all the pupils in the school, he should be asking me.

Maxine Dawson put her hand on my leg and squeezed. "It's all right to be upset, you know." She smiled right at me. God, she was beautiful. Of course she had a boyfriend: Doug

5

Winters. I sometimes think girls like Maxine are born with boyfriends. Not that I would ever have dared to ask her out; she was way out of my league. Still, if you held a poll of who most of the boys in our school fantasised about, Maxine would win hands down (still no pun intended). Her big brown eyes, her lightly tanned skin and her long chestnut hair hanging around her breasts. Her body was athletic, but not too athletic; she still had generous curves and she sat with the confidence and ease of a woman, not a girl. She had an allure that was just irresistible. I had to stop looking at her or it was going to become apparent to everyone in the room just how sexy I thought she was. I turned quickly and looked at Reese. He was staring at Maxine's legs. His head snapped up and he momentarily looked guilty. He regained his composure and continued.

"I spoke to Johnny's father this afternoon and I understand you were one of his best friends."

Maxine took my hand. Maxine Dawson was holding my hand and there was no one around to see it. I turned to Reese again. Surely even *he* must have known that I wasn't friendly with Johnny Knox. What had given Johnny's father the idea that we were friends? I didn't want to tell Reese that I had only spoken to Johnny once. I didn't want it to get back to his grieving parents that Johnny didn't actually *have* any friends. And, OK, if I'm honest, I didn't want Maxine to take her hand away just yet.

"Yes, I suppose I was," I said, glancing at both of them to see if they believed me.

"Yes, well, Miss Dawson is organising a collection for some flowers and a condolence card and we thought you might take it round to his house on behalf of the school."

Go to Johnny's house? Walk up the driveway where he had died? There was something very ghoulish about that, I thought.

"Not today, of course," Reese added. "But, before the funeral I think. Maybe tomorrow afternoon?" He turned to Maxine. "Will that be enough time for you, Miss Dawson?"

Maxine nodded pleasantly and stood up, removing her touch from my hand but leaving it forever in my mind. I stood up and followed her out the door.

"Steve?" Reese called as I was closing the door. I looked back. "Thank you," he said, nodding. I nodded and closed the door.

Maxine was waiting for me outside the door. I stopped dead, completely out of my depth in such a social situation. I mean, what do you say to a goddess?

She stepped close to me and whispered in my ear, "That was a really nice thing you just did, Steve." She stepped back and smiled that incredible smile of hers. She walked off down the corridor. I stood there, still smelling her perfume lingering around my neck, watching until she disappeared round a corner.

She *knew* that I didn't know Johnny. Was that what Reese's thanks were about? Did he know, too? I walked slowly back to class with my mind still thinking about how close I had got to Maxine Dawson. Then I felt guilty that I should be so happy on a day like this.

Johnny was lying on a cold slab somewhere.

2.

The bus ride home was the only normal part of the day. Everyone seemed to use it as a breathing space from thinking about death. At school, the students were forced to confront their fear and mortality, and when they got home they would be bombarded with the questions and concerns of their parents; once again putting the uneasy thought in their heads that life was fragile and could be taken away at any time. On the bus ride we allowed ourselves to forget. Boys chatted-up girls, with varying degrees of success; girls giggled at the boys clumsy attempts at being suave; Joey Turner lit farts on the backseat to rapturous laughter that was fifty percent amazement, fifty percent revulsion, and Ted 'Boggy' Marsh did his famous tripping in the aisle and falling into an unsuspecting bosom routine. It was a refreshing change from the sombre six and a half hours that had gone before.

I didn't join in. There was nothing that could top my exchange with Maxine. No matter what happened, today would stand out first and foremost as the day I met Maxine Dawson. Guilt protested again inside my chest. If Johnny hadn't died I never would have met her. It was a horrible situation to be in; I was too happy to be sad, and yet something inside me wouldn't let me be fully happy either.

The further we got from town the emptier the bus became. My house was one of the last stops and the raucous behaviour had calmed to silence. I stepped off the bus and looked at my house, preparing myself for the questioning which would ensue as soon as I walked in the door.

"There, he's home now," my mother shrieked into the phone.

"Hi, ma."

"Are you all right? What was it like at school? Did you know the boy? Do you know why he did it?" she said and angled the phone so my responses would be heard.

"I'm fine and I don't know anything," I said, hoping that would put an end to it.

"He's very upset," she whispered into the phone.

"Before I forget, I'll be home late tomorrow; I have to drop off flowers and a condolence card..."

"To the dead boy's house?" she asked.

I nodded. The thought of doing it was making me queasy and I began to wonder if I would have agreed to it if Maxine hadn't been there.

"Did the headmaster ask you?" I only got halfway to completing a nod before she continued, "The headmaster asked him personally," she whispered excitedly down the phone. I walked off to my bedroom while my mother tried to improve her social standing further.

Usually after school, I went into my bedroom, put on some music and lay down on the bed. It was my way of unwinding from the day. That day I just lay in silence. I had a lot to think about and I also didn't want to forever associate my favourite music with this feeling. No matter how much I tried to think about what a tragedy Johnny's death had been, my thoughts always led me back to Maxine; to that innocent touch of my hand. In a perfect world we would be together; she would be my... Rachel! I had totally forgotten about my girlfriend. I was

8

supposed to meet her after school. We met every day behind the curtains in the Assembly Hall to kiss and cuddle for ten minutes before my bus was called. Damn. I jumped from my bed, opened my door and heard my Mum was still yakking on the phone. I closed the door and dropped onto my bed. There was no doubt I had been in a euphoric daze since I had been in Reese's office, but to totally forget about Rachel...

It was all I needed. Not only did I have the unpleasant job of delivering flowers to Johnny's parents to think about and the confusion about how to act when I saw Maxine next (could I speak to her about non-Johnny matters?), but now I would have to take shit from Rachel for standing her up.

I had been going out with Rachel for over six months now (she could probably tell you in days, hours and minutes). We seemed to have survived the summer break that destroys so many school romances, but there was something different about her since we had returned to school. We had started going out together in March and she had deflected every attempt my hands made to explore, but the first week of school after the holidays my hands had made significant progress. Breasts are just fantastic, in a way that magazines and movies just can't do justice, and for the first week I enjoyed my newfound pastime with an air of quiet smugness. Then I started to think about why. Why had my hands, which had so long been locked out, now been given visiting privileges? My suspicions were further aroused when she told me about the two weeks she had spent with her aunt in Newcastle. Details were sparse about what she had done while she was there, but she had come back with a more open mind and a more open blouse. Still, my suspicion was minor compared to my lust so I kept quiet.

I didn't even realise my dad was home until he called up the stairs to me. As I descended, I could smell the dinner from the kitchen; I had been lying on my bed for two hours. I walked into the living room. My dad was balancing his plate on his knees and sitting in front of the telly.

"Watch this, it's on next," he said through a mouthful of potato.

9

Sure enough, Imogen Collins appeared on screen and began her report from the playground. She started off by interviewing Danielle Rhodes (who I can safely say never gave Johnny the time of day) and Julia Parkhill (who I'd never even noticed before). They both gave what sounded like rehearsed testimonies to Johnny's quiet and gentle nature that no doubt made Imogen Collins happy; they were pretty and acne-free and I guess that's what mattered.

It was the end of the report that was most interesting though, when she said, "What was at first thought to be a suicide, is now looking more like death from natural causes. I spoke to the pathologist in charge and he said he could find no external trauma to the boy's body. The most likely possibility now is that Johnny Knox was the victim of an aneurysm or similar neurological episode. A full autopsy is planned for tomorrow." A tear welled in her eye. "From William Hutchinson Memorial School, I'm Imogen Collins, reporting on this dark day when a young man was cut down in his prime." Before the camera cut away the tear rolled down her cheek and she brushed it aside.

Yeah, right, I thought. How many takes did you have to do before you got that on cue? Bitch.

"She's some bit of stuff, that one," my dad said, nodding at the screen.

I said nothing.

After dinner I went back up to my room and lay on the bed. The news that Johnny's death might have been from natural causes somehow made me feel better. I don't know why, after all he was still dead at fifteen years old. I guess I just didn't feel as guilty. Like everyone, I had spent the whole day wondering if he would have committed suicide if I'd taken a greater interest in him. Now they were saying it wasn't suicide—no one was to blame. No one could have done anything; it still would have happened if he had been the most popular boy in school.

My mother shouted up to tell me that Rachel was on the phone. Damn, she had slipped my mind again. I ran down the stairs and lifted the phone in the hall. As usual, we both waited for my mother to put down the kitchen extension before speaking.

"Hi, Rach," I said, sounding really depressed (laying the groundwork for my excuse).

"Hi," she replied, sympathetically. "I'm sorry I missed you today—you didn't wait too long, I hope."

She hadn't been there—a break. The tables were turned now and *she* would have to make it up to *me*. "What happened to you?" I said.

"Well, you'll never believe this, but I was talking to Maxine Dawson." The girls regarded her as something of a role model and they all wanted to be her friend.

Panic hit me. *Rachel, your boyfriend was flirting with me.*

"Maxine Dawson? What were you talking to her about?" I asked innocently.

"About you, actually."

"Me? What did she say about me?" I asked, growing ever more nervous. What I had to be nervous about I don't know. I hadn't said anything suggestive to Maxine—I wouldn't dare. Still, I was scared that Rachel would know that I desired Maxine as much, if not more, than every other guy in the school. Looking back I should have changed the subject, but I guess I wanted to know what she had said; what she thought of me.

"She's something of a fan of yours," Rachel said, proudly. I don't want to sound arrogant, but I got the feeling that Rachel was enjoying the fact that Maxine—the most beautiful girl in the school—liked me, but *she* had me. "She told me about Reese asking you to go round to Johnny's tomorrow. She said you were really sweet for pretending that you were close to him. She said I was lucky to have you."

Maxine Dawson thought about me. I think it was the happiest I'd ever felt; even better than unclipping an occupied bra for the first time. Maxine Dawson admired me. A huge grin broke on my face and I was glad Rachel couldn't see how happy she had unwittingly made me. I had to get a grip on myself. I played it cool with a joke. "Well, I've been telling you that for ages." She laughed and continued to talk.

She talked about school; who had burst into tears and who had said what, but I was only half-listening. I was desperate for her to tell me more of what Maxine had said but I knew I couldn't ask without arousing her suspicion. The last few minutes of the phone call were filled with sweet-nothings that seemed oddly insincere for the first time.

Despite going to bed thinking about Maxine and all the possible ways we could get together, I had a troubled night's sleep. I had hoped my dreams might have reflected the fantasies I had been having. You know the sort of thing:

Steve, what are you doing in the girls changing rooms?

Hi, Maxine. Mister Reese said there was a loose coat-hook in here. I just came in to fix it.

Well I hope you don't mind if I have a shower.

No, Maxine, you go right ahead.

And so on...

Unfortunately, I did not have dreams scripted like a bad porno-movie. I had strange, dark nightmares. I couldn't even remember anything specific in the morning, but I woke up feeling a cold dread, like the feeling you get when you've done something wrong and know you're going to be found out any second. Sweat was running down my forehead. I had been scared—really scared. Still, all I could remember was the dark.

3.

On the way to school I rationalised my nightmare. I was fifteen, full of raging, uncontrollable hormones, and someone I knew had just died—it was OK to have a nightmare. More than OK—it was natural. My explanation made perfect sense but I was still uneasy; something inside me was not satisfied.

Mornings on the bus were more sedate than the afternoons. There was only a quiet mumbling when the bus was full, but combined with the fettered cigarette smoke it made my stomach turn. If I distracted myself it didn't bother me as much, but I had nothing to think about. Not even thoughts of Maxine could grow in this hostile environment. I looked at the empty seat next to me and wished Gary was still around.

Gary Richards and I had been friends since we were three years old. He had lived in the house two hundred yards down the road from mine. We started school at the same time and had grown up experiencing everything together; from collecting Star Wars action figures to investigating the curvy-bits that girls had. His dad had a secret stash of adult videos that we watched when his parents were out. It was quite a harsh introduction to sex, now that I think about it. We weren't told in any sugarcoated terms about the Birds and the Bees. Instead, we watched a whipped-cream-coated German woman paired with a pot-bellied man with a big perm and moustache, show us where everything went. It still makes me laugh to think of us sitting there watching it, wondering what, besides seeing a woman naked, made sex so pleasurable?

Gary had been a tryer where women were concerned. He never had a girlfriend for more than a few hours, but he always approached them with confidence and a wisecracking attitude that got him more than his fair share of one-night stands. He even had the balls to ask Maxine Dawson for a dance at last year's school disco. She had turned him down, but politely. I think he was quite charming and she was flattered, but her boyfriend was having none of it. Gary would be jealous as hell if he knew how close I'd got to Maxine yesterday. I'd have to ring him.

During the summer his family had moved away. His dad was offered some great job in Dublin and as soon as the school holidays had started they packed everything up and moved down there. I missed him. I could talk to Gary about absolutely anything. Now I had no one to talk to. Except Rachel, I keep forgetting. My girlfriend, her name is Rachel—I can talk to her. Maybe I *could* talk to her...but I didn't.

School was back to normal, more or less. Rumours still abounded about Johnny—the latest was that he was a heroin addict—but the teachers didn't let us indulge as they had the previous day. They forged ahead trying to get us excited about trigonometry, the Cavaliers and the Roundheads, tectonic plates, and fucking Dickens. I thought with this being my final year we might get to read something good in English class but no, out came Oliver Twist like a dose of The Plague. I know that as an avid student of English and an aspiring writer I should have loved this opportunity, but Dickens was so boring to me. Like most nineteenth century writers, the language is so filled with multi-syllable words that the story gets lost. I had argued this point with Mrs Wilton last term and I thought she would have picked something better for us. I told her it was, 'Stilted, unemotional, and read like an insurance policy.' Mrs Wilton had gone off on maternity leave now though and her replacement, Mr Kawaji, didn't look like he was up for a discussion on the merits of classic literature.

Even science class was a let-down that day. The cold autumn air had brought with it cardigans, trousers and thick pullovers. Miss Crabtree's body had gone into hibernation—we wouldn't see it again until spring.

There was an excitement tickling my stomach all day and in the last class of the day, *it* happened. Maxine came into Science class. I remember it like it happened in slow-motion. As she walked over to Miss Crabtree with a note in her hand she turned, looked at me, and smiled. Not a big smile, but if you were watching every millimetre of her face (like I was) you would have seen it. Miss Crabtree looked at me but my gaze was fixed elsewhere. Miss Crabtree coughed discreetly, trying to attract my attention.

Steve, there's a coat-hook in the girls changing room that needs fixed.

"What?" I said, turning my stare from the pretty student to the pretty teacher.

"I said, you're to report to the office. What is the matter with you, Steven?"

"All the blood's rushed from his head, Miss," Boggy Marsh shouted. The classroom erupted with laughter. I could feel my face getting redder and redder.

"That's enough," she shouted, calming the class. She turned to me again. "Take your schoolbag; you won't be back."

I walked up and joined Maxine, and the two of us walked out to a mixture of wolf-whistles and a hummed version of the Wedding March. It was that bastard Boggy that started it again; hadn't the fucker ever heard of subtlety?

We stepped outside the classroom and I closed the door. "Sorry about that," I said.

"Don't worry about it," she said with a little smile.

God, she was gorgeous!

We walked up the corridor and she told me about what kind of flowers she had got, and everyone who had signed the card. Her voice was like music to me. More than that, I just loved being in her company.

We collected the flowers from the office and she handed me the card to sign. I couldn't believe how many signatures were on it, but then if Maxine had asked the boys in the school to jump into Portstewart Harbour, they would probably have trampled each other to get there first. I signed the card as close to Maxine's signature as I could—because we had done this together it felt right.

I put the card in my bag and hooked it over my shoulder. Maxine handed me the flowers and then something happened that I couldn't believe. She leaned in and kissed my cheek. It must have only lasted a second, but it was a second I could have lived in forever (and one I would replay many times). She pulled back and looked at me. I'm sure my face was contorted with surprise, joy and confusion. I didn't know what to say.

"Good luck," she said and turned and walked away. I stood there stunned for a moment by the enormity of what had just happened. She was halfway down the corridor when she turned and shouted, "Find me tomorrow and tell me how it went."

"OK," I shouted, much too loudly for the distance I had to cover. She smiled and walked on. "OK," I repeated quietly to myself.

4.

As I walked to Johnny's house, I tried desperately to wipe the grin off my face, but it was hard. I was ecstatic. I didn't even feel stupid—like I thought I would—carrying a bunch of flowers through town. Instead of feeling like an idiot, I felt like a grown-up; the kind of guy who wasn't ashamed to deliver flowers, the kind of guy who beautiful girls kissed. It should have been a sombre journey but no matter how I tried I couldn't get my head into that frame of mind. I was drunk on that kiss and I didn't sober until Johnny's driveway came into view.

I guessed which was his house without looking at the address the school office had given me. All the other houses on the block looked like their owners took pride in them, but the one on the end looked run down. The lawn looked like it hadn't been mown since the seventies and there was a rusted Ford Cortina sitting in the front garden, stripped to its shell. A lanky looking Red Setter was tethered to the Cortina with a piece of rope. It lay on the bonnet of the car and looked at me lazily for a moment then went back to sleep. Even the streetlight outside the house was the only one on the block that appeared to be broken. The glass of the front door had also been broken at some point and a rectangle of plywood covered the opening; 14 was spray painted on it. I pulled out the piece of paper and confirmed that I was at the right address.

I walked reluctantly up the driveway, avoiding the dog-shit, but it was something worse that stopped me in my tracks: the faint impression of chalk on the ground. Chalk that on closer inspection made out the shape of a person; the shape of Johnny Knox. A shiver crept up my spine and that same feeling I had woken up with filled me. I shouldn't be here; I wasn't his friend. How was I supposed to talk to his parents? I didn't know anything about him. I should leave the card and the flowers on the doorstep and go. They're in mourning; they don't want visitors, especially not impostor friends.

Find me tomorrow and tell me how it went.

And what would I tell Maxine? 'I chickened out and legged it. Want to go out sometime?' I looked again at the ghostly outline, which had been mostly washed away by last night's rain. I could almost imagine Johnny's eyes set in that crude circle, staring up at me. The dark feeling chilled me again.

I took a deep breath and walked up to the door and knocked the loose plywood. Johnny's father answered the door. He was wearing trousers but no socks and he still had his pyjama-jacket on. His hair looked like it had been hastily patted down but it was his eyes that really struck me. The sockets were red, his eyes bloodshot—cried until they were raw.

"Hello, Mr Knox. My name is Steve Norton; I was a friend of Johnny's. The school would like you to have these with our sincere condolences." I'm sure I said it too quickly. I just wanted to get it over with and get out of there. He took the flowers and silently beckoned me in. The hallway smelled of cigarettes and stale alcohol. He looked at the flowers and touched the petals gently. I thought he was going to start crying again. "There's a card as well," I added to distract his grief. I rummaged in my bag and handed it to him.

He opened the card and tears began to well in his eyes when he saw all the names. "His mother would like to see this," he said, rubbing his eyes. He nodded down the hall. "Maybe you should wait in Johnny's room." He turned and walked into the room behind him. For the few seconds the door was open I saw that the living-room was destroyed; it looked like they had been burgled. Then I saw Mrs Knox sitting on the floor in the middle of the debris with bleeding knuckles and I knew she had done it herself. She was staring vacantly into space and didn't acknowledge her husband entering the room. The door closed and I saw no more. I wandered down the hall to Johnny's room to save Mr Knox embarrassment if his wife lashed out again.

Johnny's room was unlike the rest of the house. He had made it his own. There was no wallpaper that was twenty years out of style or threadbare carpets; he had painted the whole room to his taste. The floorboards were painted blue. The walls were various shades of purple and blue all expertly blended into each other in giant swirls. It looked amazing; like a little galaxy. Examples of Johnny's artwork were stuck to the walls and for the first time I realised just how talented the guy had been. He had experimented with a lot of different styles like Van Gogh, Picasso, Dali and lots of others that I didn't recognize.

I walked over and looked out the window at the front garden. For such an uninspiring view the guy sure did some imaginative work. I looked down and saw the window-sill and thought of the drawing of Miss Crabtree.

You hang on to it. I've got lots more stashed under the window-sill in my bedroom.

I could rationalise what I did by saying I didn't want his parents to find the drawings and remember their son as some kind of pervert, but I did want to see the other drawings as well. The motivation was 50/ 50…maybe. I grabbed the wooden ledge and it lifted up quite easily. There was a cardboard folder with maybe a hundred pages inside it. I quickly stuffed it into my bag and replaced the window-sill. I walked out to the hall again. It was very quiet up there. Mr Knox had been in such a daze I wouldn't have put it past him to forget about me. I walked up the hall and listened at the door. There was no sound. I knocked gently and said, "Mr Knox?" There was no answer. "I have to go now; my Dad's picking me up in town." Still no answer. I opened the front door and left, being careful to avoid the outline of Johnny on the ground.

It was almost half-past four when I reached my Dad's work. He owned a shop called More Than Gardens—it sold gardening and DIY stuff. The shop was supposed to be open until five o'clock but unless there were a lot of customers in (which there never were) he was usually locked-up and out by a quarter to five. It was fifteen minutes I would usually have spent sitting in the car listening to the radio, but not today. I patted my bag ensuring the valuable cargo was still there and went off to buy a lock for my bedroom door.

5.

The news report that night told us that the medical examiner couldn't find a specific cause for Johnny's death, but there was evidence of neurological problems. The case had been closed with a verdict of Death By Natural Causes. They also said he had just been accepted on a full scholarship to a very prestigious art school in London. Imogen Collins was standing outside his house while she said that. The little boy who had almost made it from rags to riches—I'm sure she thought it made great TV. Bitch.

After dinner I went upstairs to my room and began screwing my new lock onto the inside of my door. I was trying to do it quietly so my parents wouldn't hear. I knew if they saw me doing it I would be in for a million questions, so it was better to just put it on and hopefully they wouldn't notice. My parents rarely came into my bedroom, they mostly just shouted up the stairs if they wanted me, but now I had things in my possession that had to remain private and I felt the added security was justified. I fitted the lock in about ten minutes and slid the bar across into its companion. Safe now. I walked over and opened my bag and took out the cardboard folder. I just sat staring at it for a few moments, my heart beating like a pneumatic drill in my chest. I looked over at the lock once more, making doubly sure the door was secure, and opened the folder.

At first glance I thought I was out of luck. The first drawing was of a demon or a monster or something. It had a long head with small, bony protrusions along its jaw and two small horns at the top of its forehead. Its eyes were black and without emotion; like a shark's, and its body was shaped like a muscular hard shell. I thought I'd stumbled across Johnny's ideas for a comic book, but the pages underneath changed my mind.

It was better than I could have expected. Not only did he have every good-looking girl in the school in there, but there were other teachers besides Miss Crabtree as well, and women from TV and film—all undressed by Johnny's imagination. There *was* a drawing of my girlfriend, Rachel. The picture looked straight down on her from above as she was lying in a meadow. Her hands were playing with the stalks of wheat and her eyes were squinting, presumably from the sun above her. Damn, that guy had a good imagination!

The pictures weren't the depraved sexual imagery that I had imagined; they were artistic. Every girl was put in a background that reflected her personality. Debbie Wallace— school superbitch, but really tasty—stood before a background of flames, with her face grinning wickedly. She was wearing nothing but elbow-length gloves and knee-high boots. While Anne Porter—Miss goody-two-shoes—stood under a waterfall with her arms outstretched, laughing as the water ran down her body.

It was near the back that I found what I had been hoping for—Maxine. And not just one drawing of her either; there were three. The first showed her lying on an altar with vampire versions of her boyfriend and her three closest girlfriends drinking blood from her hands and feet. That was pretty weird. The second showed her standing by the roadside wearing nothing but a pair of cowboy boots and sunglasses. Behind her was a sign saying: You Are Now Leaving Mediocre. She had her arm extended and her thumb raised, trying to hitch a lift. The final, and surprisingly my favourite, was a simple portrait of her face. I looked at it closely; it was so detailed. Johnny must have spent hours secretly looking at her to get this level of accuracy. He had captured her essence perfectly. She was smiling but her eyes showed a hint of sadness like I always imagined they did. She was more than just a sex-symbol and a clothes horse; behind those eyes were thoughts and ideas. I looked over at the lock again.

By ten-thirty I was physically exhausted 'looking' at the drawings. I went to bed after hiding the folder at the back of my cupboard behind some old UFO magazines.

In the darkness my thoughts turned again to Maxine. Maybe it wasn't such a crazy idea that we would get together. She *had* kissed me. Doug Winters was an asshole anyway, how could she be happy with him? Yes, it all made sense; she had grown tired of watching Doug chase a ball around a patch of grass—she needed intellectual stimulation. She needed me. We would be good for each other. She would make me more popular and I would introduce her to great writers and make her sexy *and* learned.

We would just click as soon as we started going out together. We would be best friends as well as boyfriend and girlfriend. We would be the perfect couple for the remainder of the school year and then apply to the same universities so we could stay together. When we both left Oxford with our degrees in Literature, we would get jobs on magazines or newspapers while we wrote our novels in the evenings. We would live in a little cottage by the sea, far from the town and free of distractions. Our surroundings and ourselves would be all the inspiration we would need. When we were both published and successful novelists we would travel the world together, experiencing all the different cultures and incorporating them into our lives and our books. We would be wealthy, healthy, and above all, happy. I wrapped my arms around my pillow imagining those days ahead when it would be Maxine lying beside me in my arms. I fell asleep smiling.

I sat up in bed quickly. It was still dark outside. I looked at my clock; it read 3:31. I glanced around my room wondering what had woken me. I hadn't been having a nightmare that I could remember. There was light drizzle falling outside. Maybe it had been raining harder and that had woken me. I lay down again and pulled the covers under my chin.

"Steve," a voice called softly.

I sat up again. At first I thought it was my mother but then I realised it had come from outside. I got up and walked to the window. Maxine was standing in the middle of my garden in her pyjamas looking up at me. She smiled when she saw me. The wind was blowing the drizzle into her face and her eyes were squinting to stay open. The breeze blew her hair over her shoulders and, combined with the rain, was hugging her navy-blue silk pyjamas tight to her body.

I opened the window and leaned out. "Maxine? What are you doing here?"

"I have to talk to you, Steve. Can you come down?"

"Of course. I'll be right there." I hastily put on my dressing gown and my slippers. I grabbed my bedroom door, as I had done a thousand times before, and flung myself forward. I forgot about the lock and slammed into the door. I yelped. I stood motionless, wondering if I'd woken my parents. Seconds passed and I heard nothing, so I released the lock and walked out onto the landing. On my way past the airing cupboard I reached in and grabbed a towel for Maxine, thinking she must be soaked to the skin. I charged down the stairs, again making too much noise, but caring less and less as I got closer to Maxine. I ran into the kitchen and looked out at the back garden. She was walking towards the kitchen door. I grabbed the handle and found it was locked. Where did my mother put the key at night? I rummaged through the drawers frantically. I looked over at the door. Maxine was looking through the glass at me. I smiled apologetically and kept looking for the back-door key. Then I spied it hanging on a hook on the side of the cupboard. I grabbed it and ran over to the door.

She looked so distressed and sad. She was upset and she had come to me—not Doug. I put the key in the door and instinctively my other hand raised and flipped the outside light on. As soon as the light came on Maxine was no longer there. In her place stood a huge black monster. *The* monster from Johnny's drawing. I screamed and stepped backwards. The creature, realising it had been exposed, punched through the back-door glass and reached inside with its long, muscular arm and lunged at me with its large, claw-like hands. It grabbed my pyjama-top around the neck and pulled me close to the door. It lifted me from the floor and brought me to its face. There was only a cracked pane of glass between us. I saw its breath mist the window inches from my face. The unreality of the whole incident seemed to have paralysed me momentarily, but now I struggled. The creature's grip was strong but my pyjama-top wasn't and ripped easily. I dropped from its grasp and my back slammed hard on the cold tiles below me. Without turning over I raised myself onto all fours and scuttled backwards. When I was sure I was beyond its grasp I stopped and looked at the monster in awe. This wasn't a guy in a rubber suit or a special-effect; this was a real monster! My reverie was broken as it crashed into the door, shattering more of the glass and some of the frame. It slammed the door again and I could see the lock was going to give. I lifted one of the shards of broken glass and approached the door. The creature shot its arm in quickly to grab me and I drove the glass dagger into its claw as hard as I could. It roared and pulled its hand back. It fell silent and glared at me with those dead, black eyes.

The hall light came on and my mother shouted, "Steve? Is that you down there?"

The monster's head turned sharply to the voice and then it ran. I watched through the broken pane as the creature moved out of the light and I could just make out long brown hair and navy-blue silk pyjamas containing a beautiful ass, running off into the night.

6.

"Sleepwalking?" I heard my mother say to the doctor.

She had refused to let me go to school after I had told her truthfully what had happened. She had called Doctor

McKendry first thing, and after giving me a quick examination and bandaging the cut on my hand (where I had gripped the shard of glass) he had gone downstairs to speak to my mother in private. I'd followed him out and listened from the top of the stairs. He was convinced that the trauma of losing a friend had invaded my sleep and caused me to sleepwalk down to the kitchen and break the window.

"What about the boy's funeral tomorrow," my mother asked, "Should I let him go?"

The doctor cleared his throat. "That's really up to you Mrs Norton. On the one hand it could give the boy a sense of closure on the whole incident, or it could escalate his anxiety. There's really no way to tell." I heard shuffling as he put his coat back on. "At the end of the day, you know your son better than I do; I'm sure whichever course of action you choose will be for the best. Give him a few days off school and call me again if you have any problems. I can recommend a counsellor who specialises in this sort of thing."

"Is it that serious?" my mother asked.

"Not yet, but it may become so." The door clicked open. "Anyway, you'll stay in touch and keep me informed of any developments."

"Yes, doctor. Thank you." My mother closed the door and I quickly tiptoed back into my room and into bed.

Sleepwalking. What a crock of shit. I know when I'm awake and when I'm asleep. I knew what I saw and I knew it was real. My mother stepped cautiously into my room with a cup of tea (her answer to everything) in her hand. She handed me the tea and sat on the edge of my bed.

"I think you should stay off school until Monday; get some rest," she said smiling.

"Rest from what? I haven't anything to rest from." I said, trying to stay calm.

"You're under pressure, that's all that's wrong, it's stress. And I think you should give that boy's funeral a miss as well— like you said, you didn't really know him."

Maxine: dressed in her Sunday best...I could only imagine.

"Mum, I want to go to the funeral. I think it would be good for me," I pleaded.

"Sorry, Steve." She rubbed my hair and pulled the covers up to my neck. "Are you warm enough?"

"Mum, I'm not sick!"

"You stay there and rest. Listen to your music or something. I'll come and check on you in a while." She walked out of the room and closed the door behind her.

I was so angry I was shaking. Looking back now, I know I shouldn't have been. My mum was only trying to help in circumstances that she was totally out of her depth in. Tea and lying in bed all day would cure sleepwalking—that was one for the medical journals.

No, I had watched enough horror movies and read enough Stephen King books to come up with a better theory than that. This…thing, monster, whatever it was, had the ability to alter my perception of it. It had made me think it was Maxine to lure me outside but the light had exposed it for what it really was. Johnny! Could that have been what happened to him as well? He was found lying on his driveway. There were no signs of a struggle inside his bedroom and, most importantly of all; he had a picture of the beast. So, he must have seen it at least once before it got him. Now I'd seen it once. I began to worry that maybe my escape hadn't been so lucky; maybe this thing didn't give up that easily. It all made sense; what had happened to Johnny was now happening to me and unless I found a way to stop it, it would surely kill me as well.

That night I kept the light on and a torch by the window. I tried to stay awake all night but fell asleep sometime after five. Thankfully, I slept uninterrupted.

I awoke at eleven the next morning. The time of Johnny's funeral. I wondered who was standing at the graveside and who was crying? Was Maxine crying?

My mother brought me some soup at dinnertime (same principal as tea—hot and wet, so it must be good for you) and she told me Rachel had phoned to ask how I was.

I would usually have been paranoid as hell about what my mother might have said to Rachel, but I didn't care that day. "I'll call her later," I mumbled. I would have to have a long talk with Rachel soon and tell her how things were with Maxine and I. It wasn't a conversation I was looking forward to, but it had to be done.

That night I watched Imogen Collins milk the last drops of dignity from Johnny's death by doing her news report from his funeral. I kept an eager eye on the background for Maxine, but I couldn't see her. Imogen Collins was dressed in a black suit with silver trim. Silver! She looked like a magician's assistant. Dumb bitch. Then, against all odds, she said something interesting:

"The medical examiner has retained samples of Johnny Knox's blood. It appears that this young lad may have been a victim of a, as yet unidentified, disease. This is Imogen Collins at Portstewart Cemetery."

They could shake their test-tubes all they wanted, I knew what had killed Johnny and it was far from being microscopic.

7.

As each night passed without event, I got a little more sleep. I spent that whole weekend thinking about what to do. I'd watched enough movies to know that trying to convince disbelieving townsfolk was only going to get me a straightjacket, a shitload of Thorazine and a stay in Sycamore Acres. Still, that thing was huge and I didn't know if I could defeat it myself. I needed help, but who could I trust? I needed someone who would believe me even in the absence of proof. I wished Gary were still around. Maybe I could tell Maxine. It was quite exciting, if a little life-threatening. She might be quite intrigued to be invited into such a mystery. That was the other thing I spent the weekend thinking about; what I was going to say to her when I saw her? By Sunday evening I had composed an opening statement, anticipated every response she could give to it, and had a response for that as well. I was prepared.

I was back at school on Monday and after reassuring a lot of people that I hadn't had a nervous breakdown, I went looking for Maxine. I couldn't see her in the morning or at break-time. By the end of seventh period I was beginning to think she wasn't at school, then I saw her through a window talking to Mr Sloan. He was the new Careers Advisor and all the girls thought he was dreamy or some such shit. I wondered what Maxine was doing with him so early in the year. They were probably just discussing her options; she was quite intelligent as well as beautiful.

I knew where she went at the end of school to meet up with her friends and the superfluous Doug. I waited within walking distance of her friends, nodding as they looked over— it was only polite, soon they'd be my friends, too. Maxine finally arrived with Doug in tow. I took a deep breath and walked towards her. I wasn't going to babble. I wasn't going to stutter. I had been working on it all weekend and I knew exactly what to say and how to say it.

"Hi, Maxine." She turned and looked surprised. "How was the funeral?" God, that sounded stupid now that it was out of my mouth. I felt my face begin to redden. "I didn't make it; I was home sick." Shut up you fool! "Was it, you know…cool?" Cool? Was a funeral cool? What are you saying you *idiot?*

Her three girlfriends and Doug were staring at me as if I was insane. Maxine smiled at me, but it was a different kind of smile. It was a smile of sympathy, not affection. "It was fine, Steve. I'm glad to see you're OK."

The five of them shuffled off together and I heard one of her friends say, "I heard he had a breakdown." Doug looked back at me over his shoulder and slid his hand onto Maxine's ass. He smirked at me and they walked on down the corridor.

As I waited behind the curtains in the Assembly Hall for Rachel, I felt like crawling into a hole and never coming out again. Not even breasts were going to cheer me up today (though I would give them every opportunity to try). I had totally blown it. If I had ever stood a chance with Maxine Dawson, that chance was gone now.

She never spoke to me again.

Chapter II - Wasted Love

I love children, but I never seem to get pregnant at a convenient time. It always happens when I have too much work on my plate, or when my money is all tied up with other things; thank God there are still some abortion clinics that take credit cards.

*One to One with...*Imogen Collins

- October, 1989 -

1.

I was something of a laughing stock for the next few weeks. I think it was more down to Doug than Maxine. I'd dared to challenge him and lost, but it wasn't enough for him that I'd fallen flat on my face—he needed to grind me into the ground completely. I heard fragments of stories ranging from me sending Maxine roses every day, to booking us into a hotel in Donegal without her knowing anything about it. None of it was true. I was beaten and I had given up.

I wrote a story about our, or should I say *my*, ill-fated attraction. In the story everything had worked out just as I'd imagined. The quintessential happy ending. It's why I loved writing; things always turned out how I wanted. Material things like money or sporting prowess didn't sway girls. The girls in my stories saw beyond the thin veneer of sincerity that guys like Doug owed their success to. I read and re-read my story taking comfort in it and wishing it was true, but knowing in my heart that the happy ending was the one thing that made it so false.

I turned my attention to trying to track down the beast that had attacked me. It occurred to me that if I had escaped its clutches, other pupils might have as well. I took Johnny's drawing to school and photocopied it. I stuck the posters up on notice boards all over the school with just my name and class printed at the bottom of each one. It was getting close to Halloween so I figured that any casual observers would just see it as a decoration for the forthcoming holiday. Two days passed and I began to think I was truly alone in my pursuit of this creature, and then a student approached me with the poster in their hand.

2.

I'd never spoken to Emily Matthews before that day. She was in my year but not in any of my classes, and she was quiet. I had her pegged as something of a wallflower. She hung around with Danielle Rhodes and Debbie Wallace who were very pretty, but they liked to be very loud, flamboyant and occasionally cruel, to draw attention to themselves, whereas Emily was quiet and reserved. She was pretty but it was understated—she didn't wear make-up or jewellery, she didn't have her hair done in some outrageous style or piercings in every conceivable place—she was just a naturally pretty girl. Unfortunately, this was not a quality that got you noticed at high school. Ask anyone who Debbie and Danielle hung around with and you would probably be faced with a blank stare. If Debbie and Danielle were a painting, Emily would have been the frame. She really didn't fit in with those two but by the last year of school it was too late to find other friends (something I knew only too well since Gary had moved away).

Emily had become even more quiet and withdrawn in the last few weeks. She had had a big falling out with Danielle and Debbie over something that the whole school knew about (and we'll get to later). She sat alone in class and on her breaks. She was rarely seen in the playground and no one knew (or cared) where she went or what she did. High school girls can hold a grudge better than anyone and Danielle and Debbie, her oldest friends, weren't going to forgive her anytime soon.

When Emily approached me, she showed me the drawing and nodded me to follow her. We walked outside to one of the mobile classrooms. She led me round to the back of it. We pushed through the hedges and trees that had grown out to meet two sides of the classroom. At the corner of the wooden structure there was a small clearing maybe six feet in diameter. I knew immediately that this is where Emily must hide. This was her private little sanctuary. There was a milk crate turned upside down (her seat) and dozens of cigarette butts lying on the ground. She sat down on the crate and pulled out a cigarette and lit it.

"Sorry I can't offer you a seat, I don't do much entertaining," she said nervously. "You don't smoke, do you?"

"No, I don't," I said and sat down cross-legged on the ground. We sat in an uncomfortable silence for a moment.

"I hope you don't mind coming in here. I didn't want the whole school to start hating you too; guilty by association, you know." She took a long drag on her cigarette. "I suppose you know why I'm getting the leper treatment?"

I paused for a moment then nodded.

She smiled and nodded. It was such a painful looking smile, like she was smiling just to stop herself crying. "Of course you do, everyone does."

I needed to change the subject. "Why did you come to me with that drawing, Emily?"

She locked eyes with me. She obviously had something to say but was weighing up whether or not she could trust me. "Did you draw it?"

"No."

"Who did?" she asked suspiciously.

Now it was my turn to be cautious. Would she believe me if I told her my theory? I decided to give her the same facts I had and see if she came up with the same conclusion. "Johnny Knox drew it."

Fear blossomed in her eyes. She dropped her cigarette and twisted it into the ground with her shoe. "Why did you put it up with your name on it?"

She knew something. One of us had to make the first gesture of trust, so I looked at her with my most serious expression and said, "Because I've seen it, in the flesh. It tried to kill me. I think it killed Johnny as well". She looked shocked, but somehow not surprised. She didn't speak and I wondered if she was going to exploit me to regain some acceptance with the other students.

Norton's gone mental. You'll never guess what he told me...

Cover it, quickly. Make something up. A story I'm working on. I wanted to see how people would react. "Emily, I..."

"Steve," she interrupted. "I've seen it, too."

3.

The bell had rung shortly after Emily's revelation and she had asked me to come over to her house that night and she would tell me everything. She lived about two miles from me with her father. Her mother had run off with a charismatic bingo-caller when she was seven and since then it had been just the two of them. Bill Matthews worked nights at a factory in Coleraine— 7pm to 7am—so Emily said to come over anytime after he had gone.

My mother was wary about letting me go out without ample amounts of tea, but she eventually yielded. I told her I was going out for a bike ride to get some exercise. With a warning that the nights were drawing in and the clocks would soon be going back (how long did she think I was going out for?), she waved me on my way.

It was a nice evening and the ride to Emily's was mostly downhill, so I wasn't too exhausted when I got there. I checked my watch: half-past seven, her father would be long gone. I leant my bike against the front of her house and knocked the door. The bungalow was in a small group of a dozen houses, a couple of miles from town. As I waited for the door to be answered I glanced over at the next house. I was met with an icy stare from a guy about my age kicking a football listlessly around his lawn. I nodded "hello" at him and he turned his back on me. Emily opened the door and stood back to let me in. She was wearing jeans and a white shirt that you could see her bra through. Her feet were bare and her dirty-blonde hair hung around her shoulders. She looked a lot more relaxed than I had ever seen her at school, and prettier.

The house was neat but functional. It was obvious that Mr Matthews was single. Everything was there that the house needed; furniture, carpets, appliances, but there were none of the telltale signs of a wife. The little ornaments and *objets d'art* that no man would ever dream of buying were notable by their absence. The furniture gave him away as well because, although it was all new and quality stuff, none of it matched. It would drive most women crazy to have two bookcases—one pine and one teak—sitting next to each other, but Mr

Matthews (and most men) could live with them on condition that they held books.

Emily led me down to her bedroom where she perched herself on the window-sill and opened the window. She nodded at the bed. "Sit down, make yourself comfortable."

I somehow repressed the porno screenplay that was writing itself in my head and sat down. I couldn't help thinking about sex; it was the first time I had ever been in a girl's bedroom (Rachel's mother wouldn't let me near hers). The main thing I noticed was the smell; it smelled nice and not just from residual sprays of perfume but there were little baskets of pot-pourri and scented candles sitting around everywhere. I never even thought about what my room smelt like—it most probably reeked. Everything else in the room was just the girlie equivalent of what I had; my model of the queen from *Aliens*, her stuffed animals; my posters of Princess Leia in her slave costume, her posters of Jon Bon Jovi with his shirt open; my Stephen King collection, her Mills & Boon romantic novels; my photo of Rachel on my mirror, her photo of a guy who looked a lot like the guy who had snubbed me outside her house.

"Is that the guy who lives next door?" I asked, pointing at the photo.

She took a pack of cigarettes out of her shirt pocket. "Yeah, do you know Colin?" she said, mildly interested.

"No, I don't know him. I saw him outside and he was a bit frosty to me."

"Yeah," she said, putting a cigarette in her mouth and lighting it. She inhaled deeply and blew the evidence of her habit out the open window. "You'll understand why when I tell you my story."

"That guy has something to do with the monster?"

"I have a story and a theory. You have to hear the first to understand the second."

There was a long silence and I just sat and watched her smoke. I was sitting on the edge of her bed like I had an ironing-board down the back of my shirt. Would it be too presumptuous to lie back on the bed? This sounded like it was going to take a while and holding this rigid posture would get really uncomfortable, really quickly.

"I've thought a lot about where to begin," she said, "and I think I have to start with the day I moved into this house when I was seven years old."

This *was* going to take a while. I took out my pocket tape-recorder that I had got for Christmas the year before, and began recording. She looked at me suspiciously. "I want to get everything straight," I said. She weighed me up for a few seconds and then nodded.

"We were unloading stuff from our car," she began. "My mum left us in '81 and we had to move to a smaller house. I didn't want to move out here in the middle of nowhere; I had friends back where we used to live, but I understand now my dad couldn't afford the other house by himself." She smiled briefly, remembering. "I was being a real pain; doing everything as slowly as I could, as if that might make my dad change his mind. Then from down the street came this little boy wearing shorts and a dirty T-shirt. That was the first time I saw Colin. He offered to help me carry any stuff that was too heavy for a girl. That afternoon he told me that this wasn't such a bad place to live, and he was right. We were the only two kids our age on this estate and that summer we became best friends. He got a lot of stick from other boys for playing with a girl, but it never stopped him. We went fishing, built huts in fields and hedges, and raced our bikes down Franklin's Hill...it was a really good time. At the end of the summer— just before we started back to school—I had my eighth birthday party. My first birthday without my mum. There weren't many people there; I'd left most of my friends behind, it was really just cousins and aunts and uncles. Colin was quiet around my family, but after I'd blown out the candles and made my wish—that my mum would come back—he took me by the hand and led me to the barley field behind our houses. He had flattened a large circle and laid out two packets of crisps and a bottle of lemonade on a rug. We sat down and he fumbled in his pocket and brought out a little ring. He got onto one knee—said he saw it on TV—and put it on my finger." She laughed, with tears in her eyes. "My forefinger. I was overjoyed. I hugged him and then I kissed him on the lips. It's funny, that kiss was so bad now that I think of it. We both just held our tightly pursed lips together with our eyes closed. Neither of us moving, neither of us knowing what to do or how long we were supposed to stay like this. Somehow we prised ourselves apart and smiled at each other. Then we just sat down and ate our crisps and drank our lemonade. I said that kiss was really bad, and it was. But there hasn't been a kiss since that's even come close to feeling that good. Do you know what I mean?"

I nodded. "Of course I do." I didn't, and I suspected Mills & Boon were playing a considerable role in the telling of this story.

"We remained best friends when I started school. He got even more stick for spending his breaks with a girl but he didn't care. Those three years—despite a few arguments—we were inseparable. Then he went to Dalriada (the local grammar school) and I went to Hutchinson High. We'd still see each other every night and talk about our days...it was like we were married. But he never once said or did anything to make me think he was interested in me romantically. We were just best friends. Then, three weeks ago, everything changed." She flicked her cigarette butt out the window.

Three weeks ago Emily had been the hottest story in the school and I hadn't been sure how much of it to believe, so I was glad that I was now going to hear what had really happened.

She took a deep breath and continued: "It all started in seventh period, Religious Education. I'd been reading Carrie by Stephen King—do you know it?"

I nodded, smiling. Emily had just risen in my estimation and was now even more attractive.

"It's not really my type of book, but Colin loaned it to me and suggested that I might like it, so I read it. Miss Betts was late getting to class after lunch and I was reading it while we waited outside the classroom. She got there fifteen minutes late and we all filed into the room and I left the book sitting on my desk. Everything was normal: she set us work and we were doing it. Near the end of class she began to circle the

33

classroom looking over everyone's shoulders; making sure they had completed enough of the work to satisfy her. When she got to my desk she froze with horror. You know what old Betts is like, don't you?"

Indeed I did. Two years before I had caught her wrath by suggesting—just as a joke—that Abraham had worked in a video shop at weekends. She didn't find this funny at all, which was strange because the rest of the class did. Old Betts was in her sixties, never married, didn't drink, smoke or swear and yet she seemed to spend the whole time in penance for something. She had had her sense of humour removed some time prior to arriving at Hutchinson High, but, like an appendix, I don't think she missed it when it was gone. "Yeah, I know what she's like."

"She grabbed the book and thrust it in my face. 'What's this filth?' she screamed. Talk about judging a book by its cover…I'm sure she had no idea what the book was about but seeing Carrie White's face dripping with blood and the piercing stare of her wide eyes on the cover was enough to send her batshit. I told her it was just a book. She said, 'The devil has many voices.' She marched up to the front of the room and hurled the book in the waste-paper bin. The whole class was silent—no one had ever seen her flip to this extent. She stomped back to her desk and began reading her Bible again. No one was working; everyone was still in a daze, so when one chair screeched back everyone jumped. Billy Love got up and walked to the front of the room and took the book out of the bin. He walked over and set it back on my desk. He smiled at me and I smiled back. It was a nice moment, until Betts screamed at him to put it back in the bin. Billy told her to fuck off. She told him to get out and go to Mr Reese and tell him what he did. Billy said, 'What's that, postponed your invasion of Poland for another day?' Betts got up and dragged him down to Reese. I don't think he got in much trouble for it."

"All the teachers know Betts is mental," I said.

"I guess," she said, taking another cigarette out and lighting it. "I started to see Billy Love in a different light after that. I sort of fancied him, and I thought he fancied me too. He'd catch me looking at him in class and I caught him looking at me too. I mentioned it to Danielle who told Debbie immediately; they both thought he was bad news."

Incredible as it seems I actually agreed with Debbie and Danielle on this one. Billy Love—an ironic misnomer—was a fucking dickhead. He wasn't a bully as such, more like an overgrown child who thought he could do what he wanted and damn the consequences. At the parent/ teacher meeting last term he had brought a hammer with him and smashed in the sunroof of the geography teacher's car and then pissed all over the insides of it. He never got pinched for that, but everyone knew it was him. He had been nabbed for other things; gambling, graffiti, etc., but he was always careful when it came to a major stunt.

Emily continued, "Debbie had a party that weekend. Her parents were away and Billy and a couple of his mates showed up uninvited. Debbie wanted to throw them out but I convinced her that they were OK and weren't doing any harm. They brought some vodka and Billy shared it with me. We talked for nearly an hour and I was amazed how much we had in common and how many things we agreed on. Anyway, after a while I went upstairs to the toilet and when I came out he was standing waiting for me. He nodded me into a bedroom and I went with him." She stopped and looked outside at the sky. She stared out there for a long time and I thought she was going to change her mind and not tell me the story, but then she carried on, "We didn't...you know. We just lay on the bed and kissed. His drunken hands wandered, but I didn't let him touch—God, this is embarrassing—he didn't reach his desired destinations, is what I'm trying to say. OK?"

I nodded. Poor old Billy, I thought to myself. Rachel had willingly shown me the sights and I visited them regularly. I could write a goddamn travel guide.

"Then Debbie burst in on us and imagined the worst. Apparently it was her parents' bed and she was a bit freaked. She threw us both out and Billy gave me a lift home on his motorbike. I know that wasn't too smart, him having no license and being drunk, but I just wanted to get home. I was feeling quite sick when he dropped me off but we kissed and he said he'd like to see me again and he'd speak to me at school. I went to bed that night happy. Billy wasn't as bad as everyone thought." She inhaled hard on the cigarette and blew the smoke into the garden. "Of course, by the time I got to school on Monday you would think that Debbie had caught us half-way through the Kama Sutra. She told everyone what a whore I was and her and Danielle stopped talking to me."

She said that final statement with a brave face on, but I could tell that it had hurt her more than she was telling. Girls have such an insidious way of hurting each other. If two guys at school fell out there was a scuffle, maybe a punch or two, and that was it, but girls took a long-term approach to revenge. They spread stories, told lies, and made sure that no one offered sympathy to the girl that had stole another's boyfriend or wore the same dress out twice.

"Billy was the only one who spoke to me that week. We arranged to meet again on Friday night. He picked me up on his bike and we rode out to the sand dunes on The Strand." Her head lowered and her voice softened. "And I let him…" Tears were welling in her eyes.

I couldn't understand why she was so sad. Sex was the prize that all teenagers sought, wasn't it? And unless I had misunderstood completely, it was supposed to be enjoyable (certainly all evidence and my own private experiments backed-up that assumption).

She sniffed hard and continued, "It was mercifully brief at least. Afterwards we lay there for a long time and that bit was nice. I felt loved. I had a boyfriend and a grown-up relationship. I had tamed the wild boy and I thought of all the things we would do together. I could forget about Debbie and Danielle now because I had a boyfriend. The next day," she said and flicked her cigarette outside, "I was lying on my bed and…I need a drink. Do you want a beer?"

"A beer? Sure, I'll have a beer," I said nervously. She walked out of the bedroom and I followed her to the kitchen.

4.

I wasn't quite sure how to hold a beer and make it look natural. I imagined there must be a grip that seasoned beer drinkers used to enhance the experience, but I didn't know it. The beer can felt awkward in my hands (I don't know why; its dimensions were exactly the same as a soft-drink can). Of course the key would have been to ignore what the can contained and treat it like any other drink, but my exaggerated movements just made me look like the 1st year students holding cigarettes and trying to tell their peers they had been smoking for years. I looked inexperienced. Emily was much more at ease with her beer and drank at a leisurely pace from it. I watched her closely; how she held her can, how much she drank in each swig and what she did with it when she wasn't drinking, then I aped her as best as I could. She finished her can (and I finished mine) and she got two more from the fridge.

She sat opposite me at the kitchen table and looked at me in a way no girl had ever looked at me before. Maybe it was attraction. Maybe it was relief at telling the true facts of her story to someone. Maybe it was sexual arousal. Maybe it was camaraderie. Or maybe it was just the beer.

I have to admit the beer was having an effect on me. I wasn't dancing naked on the table or anything, but I was making eye contact with Emily a lot more. It's what they call Dutch courage, I believe. She was less inhibited, too, and continued her story with fewer pauses.

"OK, so where was I?" she pondered. "Oh yes, my first day as a non-virgin. Well what can I say about that? I thought about the night before a lot and frankly I didn't see what all the fuss was about. It really didn't feel very good. I don't know why the actresses on TV do these huge flailing motions and moan in ecstasy. It's not like that at all. Anyway, I'm sure you know what I mean."

I was so shocked I didn't really hear her last statement. Sex—not that good? It was like finding out the Holy Grail was a paper cup. That which I had believed in all my life was torn to shreds; my theory of sexual evolution: *In the beginning there was man. Then, roughly thirteen years after the beginning, man discovered the true purpose of his right hand, and lo the union provided many years of happiness. Then came woman with bountiful treasures and man was interested and he did salivate. And it came to pass that man went on a quest to discover these treasures and surviving many trials and weird moods he did attain sexual coupling. And he went forth and ordered Pizza and did not brag to his mates, because his smug contentment was its own reward.*

"Steve? Did you hear me?"

"What?"

"I said you must know; you and Rachel have been going out together forever. You must have...you know."

What do I say to that? If I say yes and it gets back to Rachel the gates will close on the fun-park, but if I say no I'll look like a total dork. Muddy the water—that's the answer—admit nothing, but imply everything. "Well," I said coyly, "we *have* been going out for over six months."

Emily smiled and nodded. "Of course."

I'm a genius.

"So it was mid-afternoon and Colin—my friend from next door—came to my bedroom window. He said he had overheard Billy talking to his mates in the café. He said one of Billy's mates asked him who he had on the back of his bike last night. Colin said Billy replied: 'Emily Matthews. Just some ol' slut I'm bangin'.' I didn't believe him, but he said he heard their whole conversation about me and said Billy was just trying to get his score up on Three Hole Golf."

I should explain Three Hole Golf at this point, for those of you who don't know what it is. It was a game that single guys played at our school. At the start of the school year whoever wanted in signed up and put £1 each in the kitty every week. Now, kissing a girl every week would keep you Par for the Course, if you kissed two different girls in the same week you would go to one under par and if you didn't get a kiss you would fall to one over par. This is why only single guys were allowed to play; anyone with a girlfriend—like me—would win too easily.

The full scoring system was this:

Kiss.................... 1 point
Touching breast(s)....1½ points
Slippin' the hand...... 2 points
Oral.................... 2½ points
Sex..................... 3 points
Sex with a virgin...... 4 points
Threesome............ 5 points

I think there were more which got higher points, but that was a specialist market which few, or possibly none, ever went to. To be honest, getting 3 points was pretty much unheard of. The winners of the previous two years had won and collected the kitty (over £500) without ever having sex. Last year the Golf Club had chipped in and bought Ken Armstrong an inflatable woman for coming last—an incredible 32 over par. He didn't join this year.

"Do you know what Three Hole Golf is?" Emily asked.

I nodded slowly, hoping that she did too and she didn't want me to explain it to her.

She nodded and lit another cigarette. "Of course you do, everyone does. Did you know Billy was in the Golf Club?"

I nodded again. She was getting very agitated. I think she was embarrassed by her misplaced trust.

"Well, I didn't know he was." She opened her second beer and I quickly opened mine. She inhaled slowly on her cigarette. "Colin was so hurt," she said softly. "He asked me to tell him it wasn't true; that I hadn't slept with Billy. Of course I couldn't." She flicked her ash into the sink behind her. "That's when it all came out. Colin told me he'd been in love with me all his life and he couldn't believe I would sleep with someone like Billy Love.

"I was taken aback at first and didn't know what to say, like I said before I never thought Colin had any feelings like that for me. I tried to reason with him to start with, but he got more and more angry and the insults got worse and worse...from both of us. In the end he walked out, but the last thing he said was, 'Emily, I'll never love anyone as much as I love you...but don't ever fuckin' speak to me again.' And then he left." Emily swallowed hard even though she hadn't taken a drink. She stood up, turned her back to me and leaned over the kitchen sink. Her head hung there for a while and then she raised it and looked out the window. Still with her back to me, she carried on: "I never felt as bad in my whole life as I did that Saturday. Then Billy called that evening. I was prepared to give him both barrels but before I could he told me about falling out with his friends earlier in the day because they were bad-mouthing me. He said he could stand to lose his friends but not me. He said he thought he was falling in love with me. With everything else in my life falling apart, I believed him. I believed him because I wanted to. I wanted to feel that he loved me. I wanted Debbie and Danielle...and Colin, to be wrong. And at that point I really thought they were. I was in love again and so happy. Billy said his bike had died so I said I would meet him somewhere. He suggested the boathouse."

The boathouse is another place of local legend. It's not far from the beach but it's miles from anywhere else. It was a place where a lot of virgins walked in, and few walked out. There are other derelict buildings in Portstewart but none of them are as ideal as the boathouse. For one, it was still waterproof; when buildings are deserted for a long time the roof seems to fall into disrepair first, and a love-nest with wet patches that you didn't make yourself isn't that romantic. Another thing the boathouse had going for it was soft(ish) furnishings. There were old tarps (which wipe clean very easily), ropes (if you were that way inclined) and blankets. All these things were dry and reasonably clean and with the soft glow of the old kerosene lamp and a little music from a radio (not supplied) the ambience was perfect for deflowering.

"As soon as dad left for work, I started getting ready," Emily said. "I must have changed half-a-dozen times. Eventually I found the right balance of glamour and practicality—I gave the high-heels a miss, remembering the three-mile walk I had ahead of me. The miles passed quickly. I thought of Billy and the relationship I had that all the other girls at school would envy, whether they'd admit it or not. Who knows? Doing sex might even get better. Thoughts of Danielle, Debbie and Colin all drifted to the back of my mind. There was only Billy and me against the world. Two lost souls who found each other."

She realised her cigarette had burned down to the butt. She stubbed it out in the ashtray and lit another immediately. I could see real fear in her eyes now.

"I was close to the boathouse when I left the main road. You know the little path that cuts through the trees?"

I nodded even though I didn't.

"Billy was standing on the path wearing a suit and tie. I stopped, startled by him. He didn't say anything, but he was staring at me intently. 'Why the suit?' I asked. He said he was going to take me somewhere special. I don't know why I didn't trust him; he didn't seem like himself. There were none of the little winks and grins that Billy probably doesn't even realise he does. I didn't move towards him. He asked what was wrong with me and there was a menace in his voice. He took a step towards me and before I could decide what to do, a pair of car headlights shone through the trees and Billy disappeared and your monster stood in his place."

She was taking short drags on her cigarette and mouthfuls of beer too fast for me to keep up with, as she stuttered out the rest of the story.

"I ran. The boathouse was the closest thing I could think of. The car on the road was already long gone. I charged down the beach. I didn't look back but I could hear it running up behind me. I thought I would feel its claw on my shoulder at any minute but I kept running towards the boathouse hoping Billy—the real Billy—was already there. He would protect me. When I got to within a few yards of the boathouse and saw no lights on I thought my chances of being rescued were slim. Billy had told me how to get into the boathouse—the window at the back."

She glanced at me and I nodded as if I knew.

"I think I was lucky that I tried the right window first. I threw it up and jumped in and slammed it down again. Inside the boathouse, I looked around quickly for something to defend myself with. I ran to the cupboard by the old stove and opened it. There was nothing but a few fishing rods inside. I heard the creature hit the front door. The door was dead-bolted but I didn't think it would take it long to find the window with the broken latch. I stepped into the cupboard and pulled the door closed behind me. I slid to the ground as quietly as I could, pulling my knees up to my chest and hugging them. I don't know how long I sat squashed in that cupboard, crying without a sound. Then I heard the window open and someone come in and pace around. I held my breath.

"'Come on.' It was Billy's voice, but was it Billy? The window rattled again.

"'Stood up, eh?' Came the unmistakably whiney voice of Danny Wells. 'I told you she wouldn't go for a threesome. We'll have to drink this ourselves.'

"Then Billy said he hadn't told the dumb whore about the threesome." Emily looked totally humiliated. "They waited 20 minutes in case 'the ol' slapper turned up.' They chatted about how they had got their golf points so far and who they intended to try next. Then they left. I could cry with sound again...and I did. When I cried myself out, I climbed out of the cupboard and out the window. I reached the trees again and I heard movement up ahead in the bushes. I shouted at it to come out and give me its best shot. I realised I'd started crying again. My taunts at the beast to come and get me were broken as I tried to catch my breath between words. I stomped off towards the road, thinking I was shouting at nothing. Having lost my school-friends, my best friend and my boyfriend; I thought my sanity was the next friend to desert me. But I wasn't crazy. I'd almost reached the road when it stepped out in front of me. It looked just like Johnny's drawing. It must have been at least seven feet tall. It looked at me with those dead eyes. I was wrong about my sanity being the next to desert me; it was actually my bravery. I was terrified. I thought I was going to die. I closed my eyes and tried to remember something from the Bible that might act as a password when I got to Heaven. I opened my eyes, half-remembering Psalm 23 and ready to belt out a chorus in defiance, but it was gone. I looked all around me and it was nowhere in sight. I ran to the road, and most of the way home."

5.

Emily finished her beer and dropped the cigarette butt into the can; it fizzled slightly as the last dribble of beer extinguished it. She looked at me for a long time. It was another strange look that I couldn't quite work out. Whether she intended it or not, when I was staring into her big, vulnerable, brown eyes, she was looking really sexy. But the Dutch courage was short lived and retreated; I thought this must be the reason why Holland had never become a world superpower.

"So that's the story," Emily said. "Now here's the theory..."

"Telepathy," I blurted out. I was the horror and sci-fi expert after all; she didn't have to spoon-feed me a theory, I already had it all worked out. "That's how it made itself look like Billy. It looked inside your mind and took an image that you would trust." I sat back, proudly.

"Oh, yeah. That's obvious. But there was a reason why it was trying to attack me before I went into the boathouse and why it didn't attack me when it had the chance afterwards. That's the real crux of the story. It took me a while to figure it out but if you think about it logically, something must have changed between those two times."

She looked at me like she wanted me to answer. I couldn't think. "Tell me everything you did and touched in the boathouse," I said.

"I walked in, sat in the cupboard for half-an-hour, and left." She was smiling, like she was itching to tell me the answer.

"Were you sweating?" I was thinking pheromones.

"No, it was pretty cold in there." She smiled again and said, "I'll give you a clue: I went into that boathouse with something and came out without it."

A talisman? A crucifix? A lucky rabbit's foot? I shook my head finally, admitting defeat.

She leaned in close to me and whispered, "Hope."

I said nothing while I thought about it. When I had seen the monster, my hope of getting Maxine must have been at its pinnacle. And Johnny—didn't Imogen Collins say that Johnny had just been accepted to some art school or other? It made sense...sort of. But hope isn't something tangible, how could a creature live off something that doesn't physically exist? Although, you could make the argument, I suppose, that some people only go on living because of love, which you can't see, measure or put in a test-tube either. Was hope really so different? "So because you didn't have any hope left when you came out you think you weren't...desirable, to it anymore?" I asked.

"More than that," she answered quickly. "I think I actually repelled it, like Kryptonite to Superman; it couldn't touch me without hurting itself."

"You were really brave, do you realise how big a risk you took? How close to death you might have been?"

"Yeah." She took a deep breath. "In any normal week, any normal life, that would have been the worst part over with," she said. "But when Monday morning came I realised it was just beginning. Billy told everyone about my 'unquenchable sexual appetite.' I don't know who made up that phrase for him. I was...well, you know what it was like."

I really wanted to hug her at that point; she really looked as if she needed it. But big, brave men in Northern Ireland didn't do such things.

"It never even occurred to me," she went on, "that he hadn't used a condom until the other girls told me that I probably had AIDS."

The AIDS epidemic had only recently hit the headlines and the government's Don't Die Of Ignorance campaign was having little effect. Ignorance was the only subject that almost everyone at our school would have passed with flying colours. I remember someone put an unused condom over the handgrip on my bike once, and when I took it off I was told I must have AIDS because I'd touched a condom. This is what we had to deal with. So you can imagine that when someone had sex, and especially unprotected sex, that the idiot scaremongers felt like Christmas had come early. Emily did get a hard time that week, I remember Rachel telling me some of the horrible things the girls were saying about her.

Emily cleared her throat and said, "Of course I didn't think I had AIDS, but I was worried about being pregnant so— stupid me—I went to the school nurse. At first I thought she was going to be as helpful as we'd always been told she would be. She took me to the doctor and I got a pregnancy test that afternoon, which was negative. The doctor and the nurse gave me a hell of a lecture about safe sex. I got back to school and my being excused from all the afternoon classes just added fuel to the fire; everyone was convinced I had AIDS now. Next day, though, they knew the truth, and not from me. Since the nurse was the only other person who knew, I guess it was her. Even the teachers looked at me with disgust that day." Emily hung her head.

I still had half of my beer left and I decided I would finish it, then I walk over, throw the can into the bin, and on the way back to my seat, I would give her a hug. I tried to down it in one, but I couldn't, and Emily had started talking again.

"So then everyone at school thought I was the biggest whore on the planet. No one spoke to me...oh, except for a few other members of the Golf Club who thought I would be an easy lay. I was just glad daddy hadn't found out. Then, on the Friday of that week, Imogen Collins shows up on my doorstep. Thank God daddy was at work. She wanted to do an interview with me on teenage pregnancy to be shown on TV. I told her to fuck off. She said I would be doing the community a service and no one would know it was me. I just wanted her to go away; daddy would be home soon. I slammed the door in her stupid face. She stood outside for ages, pleading with me through the letterbox. She finally left about five minutes before daddy got home. Dumb bitch. She's not even nice-looking up close. Do you think she's pretty?"

"I think you're pretty." It was out before I even thought about it. Emily looked at me suspiciously at first then her face melted into a subtle smile. Maybe that porn scenario in my head wasn't so unlikely after all. She walked slowly towards me. I stood up (with difficulty). She wrapped her arms around my neck and rested her head on my shoulder. I put my arms around her waist and inter-locked my fingers. I could feel the softness of her skin through her flimsy shirt. Her breasts were pressed against my chest; my heart banged rapidly to draw my attention to their proximity. She made a little groan and her head began to rise. This was it. She was going to kiss me, and who knows what else. There were tears in her eyes but she was smiling. Her face, her mouth, was only inches from mine.

Her lips parted slightly and she said, "Rachel's a lucky girl. You're like the big brother I never had."

Ah, fuck.

We exchanged phone numbers and I said I would call her when I had made a plan as to what to do next. She saw me to the door and gave me another of those brotherly hugs. I couldn't even fantasise this time; she'd taken all the fun out of being that close to her body.

The ride home was slow. Not only was it all uphill this time, but I think the fresh air had heightened the beer's effect. My bike was doing a lot of wobbling even on straight sections of road. I stopped a couple of times, fearing I was going to throw up, but, I didn't.

I got home and went straight to my room. I was cold and felt quite dodgy. I lay on my bed thinking about Emily's theory and feeling quite annoyed that I didn't come up with it. I almost wanted to find a hole in it so I could prove her wrong, but I couldn't. I climbed under the covers trying to get warm. My stomach was making weird noises that I felt might go on all night, like noisy neighbours keeping me awake. My mum came in and gave me a cup of tea. I got to sleep quickly after that.

Sometimes, mums are right.

Chapter III - Darkness Comes

A hot body isn't a good reason to date someone. My second husband was a fitness instructor and our marriage was a disaster. I suppose I should have seen the warning signs: he took 45 minutes to shower at the gym, he came home from clubbing with really minty breath and once, during sex, he called me Derek.

Teen Advice, Imogen Collins

- November, 1989 -

1.

The eleventh month stole the long summer evenings from us as it always did. By five o'clock the streetlights were on and children retired to watch *Knight Rider* or *The A-Team*. The sudden shortening of days brought with it cold and (for me at least) a sense of foreboding. That creature was out there somewhere and it could assume any form it pleased in the dark; its potential hunting time had just dramatically increased. I wondered why light so easily penetrated the creature's guise. Then I remembered that two years ago I had spent Halloween at my cousin's house...

My cousin Terry was two years older than me (and still is) and his idea of how to spend Halloween seemed a lot more risqué than mine. My aunt had warned him not to get me into trouble when we left that night, but Terry obviously took no notice of her because he brought a full bag of supplies. It started off harmless enough; we wore our masks and rang doorbells and hid, pouncing out when the door was answered. Terry lived in a little cul-de-sac where everyone knew everyone and got on (mostly). It was the sort of place where the wives spent all day going in and out of each other's houses drinking tea while their husbands mowed lawns, washed cars and drank beer together. It was a nice place to live and after the initial shock of us pouncing out at the neighbours, laughter always followed and then Terry's explanation of who I was. Some of them even gave us sweets or crisps. This was great fun to me but Terry said he had something better in mind, but

I couldn't tell my mum about it. It sounded dangerous, but I didn't want to appear scared so I agreed to go with him.

We walked across two fields and up a lane. The suburban lights had faded into the distance but there was moonlight and our eyes soon became accustomed to it. We came to an old house; a large stone building that in its day was probably very grand. There were stables at the back and a big yard. Terry said the house had been boarded up since the owner, Paddy McCorrin, had hung himself from the upstairs landing with his two Labradors locked inside. He wasn't found for days, by which time the starving dogs had gnawed at his hanging body until it was barely recognisable. The story gave me chills. Terry said no one ever knew why he had killed himself. He also said teenage couples used to drive out here to have sex in their cars but they stopped when things started happening. I had to ask, "What things?" He said his best friend's brother had been up here with a girl and they were in the backseat riding, when they heard something outside. The guy got out, thinking they had been caught in the act, but there was nobody there. He got back into the car and was about to try again with the girl when they heard dogs scratching at the doors. The girl started screaming. The guy looked outside and saw nothing, but still he heard the scratching. The girl was hysterical now and the guy, fearing more for his paintwork than her sanity, jumped into the front and started the car. The wing mirrors showed nothing on either side of the car, but the screeching sound, coupled with the girl's screams, was unbearable. He turned on the headlights and spun the car several times in the yard. There was nothing there so he raced home. I remember Terry, leaning in to tell me the punchline of the story, whispering, "When he looked at the doors, there wasn't a mark on them."

The story scared the life out of me, especially since we were standing on the very spot it had supposedly happened...and on Halloween. Somehow I held the illusion of bravery and followed Terry into the house. It smelt awful; like nothing I had ever experienced before. I thought of the dogs locked in for days, ripping at their owner's flesh and wondered if I was smelling his decaying blood, maybe soaked in to the floorboards, but still pungent after all these years. The house was bare apart from a few spiders that had taken advantage of the shelter and I heard mice scuttling somewhere not far enough away. That could be my way out; I could tell Terry that even though I wasn't scared of any ghost, I didn't want to get rabies. I kept the thought in my head, ready to use on a moment's notice.

Terry asked if I wanted to see where he hung himself. I nodded, even though it was the last thing I wanted to see. I felt like we were in competition; who was going to crack first? We started up the old staircase and something scuttled past my foot. I jumped and slammed my back against the wall. Terry turned and grinned at me. He put a silencing finger to his lips and continued up. I followed because the thought of being alone was worse than anything at that moment. We reached the top of the stairs and he pointed up at six inches of rope with a frayed end. "That's where the cops cut him down," he whispered. I looked at the ground and saw dark stains on the floorboards. A shiver went up my spine. Terry was still smiling and beckoned me to follow him down the landing to a door at the end.

I suppose it was the master bedroom, though it was completely empty. Terry sat opposite the large bay-window and turned to face the wall. He shrugged his backpack off his shoulders and unzipped it. I tentatively sat down beside him. He produced a candle, a lighter, a mirror and a Bible. He asked if I wanted to see a ghost. Strangely, I did, and told him so. We were together after all, what could happen? He rested the mirror against the wall and lit the candle. The candle was only about two inches tall but he placed it just in front of the mirror's surface. The light reflected and I felt safer. Terry opened his Bible and handed me a bookmark with the Lord's Prayer printed on it. He said I had to read it backwards and look in the mirror…and I had to do it alone. Now panic gripped me, but also an excited compulsion to try it. I let Terry leave without objecting. He said he would wait outside the door. He closed the door gently and I looked around the room. The candle was throwing my twitching shadow on the walls and my breathing made clouds before my face.

I looked into the small shaving mirror and began, "Amen. Ever and ever for glory the and power..." It felt really wrong saying the Lord's Prayer backwards. I don't know why; they were just words, I thought as I continued. I wasn't doing anything sacrilegious. "...temptation into not us lead..." I was really uncomfortable now, like something inside me was screaming for me to stop. I carried on, "... Heaven in is it as Earth on done be shall thy..." I could hear something; a creaking noise. My pulse was racing, my heart close to bursting. "Heaven in art who Father our." I finished and looked in the mirror. It reflected the window behind me and I saw a figure revealed by the candlelight. An old man with grey hair and a beard was staring at me, looking directly at my eyes. He raised his arm. I could take no more and jumped to my feet and ran out of the room.

Terry wasn't on the landing, but I didn't stop to look for him, and ran down the stairs. I couldn't remember where we'd come in and ran about in the dark looking for a way out until I saw the back door ajar. I raced at it and slammed it open. Terry was halfway up a ladder with a white sheet on and nearly fell. He taunted that I had chickened out before he had even got to the window. I screamed at him that we had to get out of here, and ran. He eventually caught up with me and we walked back towards the orange glow of streetlights.

I told Terry what I'd saw and he emphatically denied it was him. I knew it wasn't anyway; his white sheet wouldn't have fooled anyone. He tried to make out that he had won our little battle because I had got scared first, but when I suggested he go back and get his mirror, candle and Bible, he said he would get it in the morning.

That night we stayed over at my aunt's house and I didn't get much sleep. Terry was in a bed on the other side of the room and made exaggerated snoring noises occasionally but I knew he wasn't sleeping either.

The next day, I had all but convinced myself that what I saw was nothing more than my own reflection in the window. This explanation never really rang true. When I got home I wrote a short story about it. The facts were all there (except I was a grown-up, had a sexy redhead girlfriend and drove a

Ferrari) and I made up a reason for what happened to the old man (his son had hung him for insurance money and made it look like a suicide). The story wasn't bad and at seven pages, it was the longest thing I had ever written.

When I was thinking about why our monster's true identity was revealed by light, I remembered something from that story and went back and re-read it. This was the part that seemed relevant:

'Darkness is the medium of fear. Fighting fear in the dark is fighting it on its own turf; you cannot prevail. Only light can admit rationality and bring with it a legion of other possibilities. Fear cannot triumph when light is present.'

I know the language is a little pompous but I was fourteen and thought the wordier the better. Sometimes I look at old stories and wonder what the hell I was thinking, but sometimes, mixed in with the Ferraris, sultry redheads and pretentious grammar, there's a nugget of truth.

2.

It's dark in the mornings and the lights are on inside the school bus. It always looked odd to me as I watched it climb the hill to my house; it looked like a room that had broken free of the rest of the house and was making its escape. I always felt exposed as I rode to school; we were visible inside the bus, but outside anything could be watching, perfectly camouflaged by the dark.

I hadn't been seeing much of Rachel recently. It was another disadvantage of the nights drawing in; we couldn't go for walks in the evenings. Not that we ever really did; we walked two-hundred yards from her house to an old barn and spent the next hour putting smiles on each other's faces. It had been a long time since I had smiled. We still met at the end of school but we were severely limited by what we could do in 10 minutes in a place where someone might walk in at any moment. The weekends were no better, we both lived miles from anywhere (and each other) and we were too young to drive. Seeing her was tough. So you can imagine the jubilation when I heard her parents were going away for the weekend

51

and she was having a party. I could spend the night with her...finally! I would have to come up with something to tell my parents, though they were more liberal than Rachel's folks were, they wouldn't let me enjoy myself that much. Still, I was confident I could come up with a plausible story and I did.

It's a technique I call the Plea Bargain. I told my mum I was going over to Boggy Marsh's house for a party. She knew the reputation the Marsh family had and my mum left it to my dad to iron out the finer points.

"What are you going to be doing?" he asked.

"You know, playing Poker, watching videos," I said, feigning innocence.

"Poker for money?"

I shrugged.

"And what *kind* of videos?"

"Erm," I mumbled. It was all he needed. A smile broke on my dad's face and he ruffled my hair.

"Don't tell your mum," he said and winked at me as he left the room.

You see this is the beauty of the Plea Bargain; you admit that you're going to do something wrong—that makes it believable, but you plead guilty to a lesser charge: i.e. having sex becomes watching porn. It works a treat.

Rachel seemed surprised that I knew about the party when I finally caught up with her. She told me there were about fifteen girls and eight guys coming. I was itching to ask were any of them staying over, but I didn't, I played it cool. I had faith that alcohol and sexual desire would prevail. Rachel didn't seem overly excited about the party but that was understandable I guess; not only did she have the worry of things getting broken and people throwing up on her mum's carpet, but she was no doubt nervous about losing her virginity. If I'm honest, I was, too.

I had three days to prepare for the most important night of my life. Condoms were the first problem. Portstewart was a small town; if I bought condoms the entire town would know two hours later. Thankfully our school had a professional for just such occasions. Porno Bill (AKA William Porter, brother of goody-two-shoes Anne) was the guy you went to for any items of a sexual nature. Porn videos, magazines and even condoms were no problem for him to acquire and sell at a reasonable profit. I was going to ask him for condoms, but I heard a rumour that he slid a pin through all the packets he had in stock as a joke. Instead, I opted for an educational and instructional video entitled *Amsterdam Virgins*. It cost me six pounds, which seemed a lot at the time, but considering the years of use I got from it, it really wasn't.

The lock on my door came in handy that night. Even though I knew my mum and dad wouldn't be moving until after *Dallas*, my heart was pounding as I put the tape into the VCR. The tape consisted of implausibly plotted scenarios each lasting about 10 minutes. The writer should have been ashamed of himself, his story-lines were all very similar: a pizza delivery girl comes to the door and has sex with the guy, two mature girl-guides come to the door and have sex with the guy, a TV repair-woman comes to the door and has sex with the guy, a woman selling steak-knives comes to the door...anyone else seeing a pattern here? The girls in the video didn't seem nervous at all and I began to wonder if they really were virgins. The video wasn't much help in preparing me for Friday night, unless getting a perm and growing a moustache would enhance my confidence and sexual prowess, nevertheless, I watched it carefully, several times.

Condoms were still a problem. They're not even the sorts of things you can discreetly browse over and, according to the chat at school, there were dozens of different kinds. How was I to know which kind Rachel would prefer? I could ask her of course, but would she know any more than I did? How was I to choose between different styles, colours and flavours...flavour? She did like banana milkshakes.

Serendipity solved the problem eventually. I was walking down the street and noticed a pub that had its toilets just inside the main door—I remembered someone telling me that they sell condoms in pub toilets; I hoped the man selling them was there today. I ducked in. The toilets were empty and I saw a great white johnny-repository attached to the wall. I ran over and read the instructions. I rummaged in my pockets and counted my money. There were two choices: ribbed and featherlite. I had enough money and decided to get a packet of each. The sweat was running down my forehead, any minute now someone would come in to relieve his bladder—probably a friend of my dad's. I fumbled with the money, dropping it a few times, before getting it in and collecting my purchases. I stuffed the two packets of three into my jacket and walked out.

I got to the pavement and looked around. I didn't see anyone I recognized. I had done it. A smile broke on my face and I walked proudly down the street. In the last three minutes I felt I had grown up a lot.

3.

The days before the party were the slowest that I ever experienced. Rachel and I still met and kissed but mentioned the party in only a passing way. We were both nervous and shy about discussing what Friday night might bring. I held fast to the belief that when the time came the awkwardness would be overcome by instinct and we would have a night as close to magic as reality allowed.

It wasn't surprising then, that when Emily approached me on Friday morning saying she needed to talk to me, I was more than a little distracted. She was whispering something about old newspapers and visiting the library but I really didn't take it in. I was supposed to meet her at morning break, but I took the opportunity to eavesdrop on the latest meeting of the Golf Club.

They met in the cloakroom to brag about what they had done and what they were going to do. I needed to hear an unabridged version of what was involved in the whole sex thing. That night wasn't going to be like TV where we start kissing and make love during a series of well lit dissolves and fades while some power-ballad provided the rhythm in the background. But after listening to the Golf Club I hoped it wasn't going to be as they described either. They talked of girls in pain, of tears...and of blood. I didn't want to hurt Rachel. Blood? Should I bring Band-Aids as well as condoms? I obviously didn't know as much about sex as I thought I did. When Billy Love started describing his romp with Emily, it reminded me that she wanted to talk to me and I left.

I wandered out to the playground with this new image of sex in my head; a violent, primitive act that seemed only to gratify men. I found Emily hiding in her sanctuary, smoking. Again she started talking about the creature and research, myths and folklore, but she stopped when she realised my mind was miles away.

"What is it, Steve?"

This was it. What did I want more: to maintain the illusion that I was an experienced man of the world in front of Emily, or to admit my virginity and ask for her advice? This may seem like an obvious choice, but you have to remember that image is everything at school. Since I felt I could trust Emily and she was a social pariah anyway, I told her the truth. She didn't laugh and we talked about sex. We talked like grown-ups, without giggling or innuendo. Of course, thanks to my video, I was familiar with the basics of what-goes-where, oral technique, various positions and how to say "Harder, faster" in Dutch, but Emily told me how to treat a girl on her first time; what to do and what to avoid. By the time the bell rang I was feeling a lot more confident about the night to come. Emily twisted another cigarette butt into the ground and we began to push through the hedge.

"I hope it all goes well at the party tonight," she said. There was sadness in her voice. Maybe she was remembering the unromantic way she lost her own virginity, or maybe it was just the fact that she had been excluded from another social event.

I turned and kissed her lightly on the lips. Song lyrics and quotable movie lines ran through my head, but in the end nothing said it better than silence. She smiled thinly as if she didn't believe the kiss had been prompted by affection. Again I said nothing; in her current state of mind no words would have convinced her of her worth. We pushed out through the hedge and I began to rush to class but stopped and turned.

"You had something to tell me about the creature," I said.

"It can wait," she almost whispered.

I nodded and ran off. As I made my way to class I realised she hadn't told me because she didn't want to spoil my night.

That's when I realised just how special she was. To be selfless in solitude is something few can claim to be.

After the last class of the day I got held up talking to Porno Bill about the high quality of his merchandise. He seemed disappointed that I wasn't going to become a regular video customer. He even tried to entice me with a free Belgian Piss Vid—I didn't know what that was, but knew I didn't want to see it.

By the time I found Rachel my bus was about to leave. She still had that scared, almost puzzled, look on her face. I just had time to say I would see her later. She looked at me and eventually nodded. I ran and caught the bus just before it left. I sat down hard on the first empty seat I saw and exhaled. Tonight was going to be a historic occasion in my life, and one I would never forget.

I looked in the mirror before I left the house that night thinking: the next time I look in this mirror, I will be a different person. I was on my way to become a man and even my room seemed smaller; full of treasured possessions that didn't seem as important now. My hair was gelled to perfection, I had put on enough deodorant to accept responsibility for the hole in the ozone layer, and I was wearing a new shirt and my best jeans. This was as good as I could look, and I looked good. I could have been a drug dealer on *Miami Vice*—that's how good I looked.

My dad drove me to Boggy's house where he left with a few more of those nods and winks that told me he knew what was going on. I wonder if he did? It never even occurred to me at the time that the huge, gaping hole in my plan was how I was dressed. Why would I have dressed up like a narcotic salesman from Florida if I were just going over to Boggy's to play Poker? Maybe he did know but, as was the custom in our house, he never said anything.

With my dad gone, stage two of the plan was to get Boggy's brother to drive us over to Rachel's. The Marsh brothers did nothing without being properly motivated; his brother wanted three quid for the journey and Boggy wasn't doing this out of friendship either. He had only agreed to play along with my plan on condition that he could attend the party as well (he fancied his chances with Sharon Graham). On the hairy drive over, Boggy and I drank from a litre bottle of poteen. The stuff was like liquid fire, but went some way to calming down the nerves in my stomach.

When we got out of the car outside Rachel's house, I noticed how Boggy had really made the effort. Apart from the dirt under his fingernails he looked almost clean. His brother skidded off as soon as we were out of the car and we followed the sound of Animal by Def Leppard to the house.

The party was in full swing. Rachel had expected twenty-three people and there must have been at least forty in the living room. I turned to Boggy but he was gone, disappeared into the crowd to seek female company. He wasted no time; I'll give him that. I wandered around the room looking for Rachel, but couldn't see her anywhere. It was a real eye-opener seeing these girls outside school. They were all wearing tops that were low-cut and revealed 40% of their boobs. No one could have failed to notice (or blame me) as I stared when Double-D Tracey McCullough walked past wearing a tube-top—it looked like two bald men sharing a blindfold.

I moved into the kitchen (OK, so that's where Double-D was going, too, but it was a coincidence) and grabbed a beer from the fridge. Double-D came walking towards me, the bounce of her boobs almost hypnotic.

She smiled easily, like she had all the time in the world. "Will you give me one?"

I'd like to thank God at this point, for making me male. For making Double-D female, and not just female, but really, really female. To be desired by a girl like this was...

"Are you going to give me a beer or not?" she scowled.

I felt the blood rush to my face (or at least some of it) and I handed Double-D my unopened beer. Remembering my monogamous nature and attempting to give the illusion that I wasn't staring at Double-D's...well, double Ds, I asked if she'd seen Rachel.

"You're the boyfriend," she said. "Shame." She put her left hand to my face and ran it down my cheek. "I think she's upstairs." She leaned in, squeezing her huge breasts against my chest, kissed me on the forehead and walked off. I stood there for a while before attempting to walk.

There seemed to be as many people on the stairs and landing as there was in the living room. I made my way to a door with a small ceramic tile stuck to it saying Rachel. The final frontier. I opened the door and saw Boggy with his grubby hand inside Sharon Graham's top. Sharon looked shocked to see me, but Boggy barely glanced and continued trying to edge her top upwards and off.

"Sorry," I mumbled. "Looking for Rachel."

"Her parents bedroom, I think," Sharon said and fell back on the bed with Boggy frisking her like an over-enthusiastic policeman. I closed the door. Mental note: remind Rachel to change her sheets.

I approached her parents' bedroom door and knocked this time. After a short silence a guy with a broad accent shouted, "Yeah?"

I slowly opened the door and saw the guy was in bed with a girl under him. The sheet thankfully covered him from the waist down. "Sorry, I was looking for Rachel." The girl beneath him slid out and pulled the sheet to her breasts. She pushed her hair out of her face. It was Rachel.

"Steve. I didn't realise it was that time." She looked embarrassed. As soon as she said my name the guy looked at me as if he knew exactly who I was. He lay down on his back and lit a cigarette. I looked at Rachel again. She didn't know what to say and neither did I. I thought I would be angry, but I was more disappointed than anything else.

After letting the ridiculous silence continue for what seemed like forever, I finally said, "Well, I guess that's that. See you later." I walked down the stairs thinking I should have delivered a better line. Then I started to plan my revenge; after all, there was a house full of girls. If Rachel could get drunk and have a fling, I could, too. I grabbed a half-empty bottle of vodka from the hall table and began to drink quickly. She must be pretty drunk to do that; I had some catching up to do.

There must have been at least fifty girls in the house—and twice as many breasts—so I started trying my luck with a few that I didn't recognize. Always better in these fling situations to fling yourself at someone you aren't going to see at school every day. I had surprisingly bad luck—no, I'm not being arrogant—I admit I'm not so smooth that I can bewitch any girl I desire, but the law of averages says I should have had some positive response after trying twelve girls. Then it hit me: they all knew. That was what Double-D had meant by "Shame." Not a shame that I was taken, a shame that I was about to get shit on from a great height. I suddenly felt very conspicuous in the room. They all knew, and had watched me desperately try one girl after another. This party was bad and was only going to get worse. The vodka bottle was empty so I grabbed a fresh one and went outside.

The back garden had its share of happy couples too, but they stayed close to the door. I walked down to the back of the garden and sat on the bench. The lights from the house didn't stretch this far; I was in the dark. I broke the seal and began drinking the vodka. I wished I'd brought something to mix it with, but it didn't really fit the exit; to grab a bottle of coke, a glass and some ice in a brooding rage. And I *was* raging. I felt a real fucking idiot for loving Rachel, and I did love her. Despite my wandering eye and my overactive libido, she was the girl I wanted to be my first. It would have been tender and intimate and I knew there wouldn't be another relationship in my life where I would let that closeness and trust build for so long without having sex. I felt like a freak for even thinking like this. I'm sure if Sharon had shot down Boggy he would have moved on and found someone else willing to be molested. The girls I had tried to chat up were nothing in my eyes. Would I have had sex with them if they asked? Probably: I was a drunken teenage boy, my girlfriend was shagging persons unknown and I had five condoms in my wallet (I'd tried one on earlier). I'm sort of glad none of them did encourage my advances; I don't think it would have been a very loving union.

After a significant amount of the second bottle of vodka, a very unhealthy thing happened: I started to think. They say it's what separates us from animals, but it's also why you get so few animals ringing the Samaritans or checking into rehab. So I started to go over everything in my head; everything she'd said and done recently, and looked for duplicitous intent in it. It's the sort of activity that can only ever make you feel worse, but it's something I felt compelled to do. There's usually some little fact that I've overlooked and would be better off not knowing...and I usually think of it. Two things struck me after some thought:

      1) Rachel's school uniform had been lying in a crumpled heap on the floor. No other clothes were visible (except *his* rags; the bastard guy).

      2) The phrase "I didn't realise it was that time."

This seemed to suggest that she had never got ready for the party and that this guy had been shagging her since she got home from school. It meant this wasn't a spur-of-the-moment, drunken act against all that was pure and good in the world; she had got into bed with this guy sober and willing. She had wanted to have sex with him...with *him*! He had been pleasuring my girlfriend for (I checked my watch) nearly five and a half hours. Bastard.

In the Hollywood movie this is where Rachel would worry about my state of mind and run around the party furiously asking everyone if they had seen me. There must have been twenty people in the kitchen when I stormed through it, so her chances of finding me were high, or at least they would have been high if she *had* been looking for me. I must have sat out there for over an hour waiting for her to find me and explain her insane behaviour, but she never came. I thought of her in bed with the bastard guy, unable to enjoy the sex because of an underlying guilt in her head about what she had done to me. It was the belief in that guilt that kept me sitting there so long, but eventually I realised she probably forgot about me as soon as I closed the door. I walked across the lawn and round to the front of the house. I gave a last glance back at the happy people in the windows and the closed curtains upstairs.

4.

As I walked down the road I wondered where I was going. Mum and dad thought I was staying with Boggy—I couldn't do that. *I* thought I would be staying with Rachel—that wasn't going to happen either. So the choices were: go home and come clean with my parents or find somewhere else to sleep, maybe the old barn where Rachel and I used to go. Neither seemed that appealing so I just walked aimlessly for a while, too drunk to care.

What happened next I can't really explain. I was sitting on the grass verge at the side of the road when a compulsion seized me. I got up and started running. I was drunk and tired but I raced down that road faster than I had ever run in my life. It was like I was being pulled. I cut across fields, turned corners and negotiated obstacles as if my body knew exactly where it was going. I got close to town and realised I should be exhausted—I had come over three miles of rough terrain— but I wasn't even out of breath.

I charged through the empty streets of Portstewart with the feeling that I was getting closer to wherever I was going. The adrenaline surged through my body. The sense of expectancy was building to incredible levels. I didn't even feel drunk anymore; my mind was clear and focussed. I turned the corner into Old Coach Road and stopped dead in my tracks. I stared at the front garden of a house halfway up the street.

The creature was there. It was writhing about with its back to me, screaming in a high-pitched inhuman voice. The creature spun around and I saw Emily, hanging on around the creature's neck, punching it in the head. Her feet flung wildly in the air as the creature tried to shake her off. It was still screaming; it was in real agony. Emily was hurting it. Her punches were pathetic at best, but she was really hurting it. I ran at the fighting pair and leapt onto the creature's back. It howled louder, like a hotter flame had burnt it. I punched it with all the rage of unfaithful girlfriends and unjust worlds driving my fists harder into its shell. The shell cracked and I punched repeatedly at the crack, breaking it further apart. A dark yellow liquid began to trickle from the wound and I pounded the bleeding monster harder. My rage had a single intent, I didn't even think about how Emily was faring. I just wanted to hurt it. I needed to hurt it. I needed to kill it. I pushed my fingers into the cracked shell and pulled. The creature lost power to its legs and the three of us fell to the ground. The force of the collapsing beast threw Emily and I off to opposite sides. The creature, finally free but badly hurt, quickly jumped to its feet and ran before we could reassert our grip. I stood up; ready to give chase but noticed Emily's head was bleeding. I watched as the creature limped away as fast as it could into the darkness.

Emily had hit a rock in the garden's flowerbed. I knelt down beside her and gently parted her hair and looked at the wound.

"Its not deep, but we can go to the hospital if you want to be on the safe side," I said.

"I'll be OK." She looked down the street where the creature had fled.

I took my handkerchief out and pressed it to her wound. I looked in her eyes and there was a strange moment between us. It felt like the few seconds before you kiss someone for the first time. We didn't kiss, though. I helped her up and we started walking. My legs had lost their superhuman strength and now ached as if I'd run a marathon. Emily looked like she was feeling the same, so we were lucky that we didn't have to hobble too far until a passing taxi picked us up. I had brought a lot of money thinking that someone at the party would eventually go on a booze-run and I would get a bottle of Champagne for Rachel and me. We sat in the back of the taxi in silence. We both got out at Emily's house, I paid the driver, and he drove off.

"Daddy's on nights; you can come in," Emily said timidly. I think she was unsure if I would want to, little did she know about the disastrous night I had had and my temporary homelessness.

In Emily's hallway, I checked her head and was relieved to see the bleeding had stopped. Her hair was matted with blood and one side of her face was covered in red smudges where she had wiped the blood off. Her top, which I now realised was her nightdress tucked into her jeans, was soaked with blood on one shoulder. There was that pre-kiss feeling again as she looked at me, then she hung her head and said, "Why don't you go and have a beer while I get cleaned up." She walked down the hall to the bathroom and glanced back at me before closing the door.

I sat in the kitchen and opened my beer. I heard the shower getting turned on. I thought of Emily in the shower. I thought of that look before she had closed the bathroom door. She hadn't even closed it tight. Maybe it was one of those sexy invitations like the women in *Dynasty* make. Maybe she wanted me to come in to the shower with her. No, I wouldn't risk it. What if I was wrong? The last thing Emily needed tonight was some broken-hearted pervert trying his luck. It was hard to think of anything else, though. The house was silent apart from the noise of the shower and the sound of the soap moving slickly over her body (I swear I could hear it).

I made a real effort to think about something else. The monster, the fight tonight. Emily had been right about our ability to hurt the creature. Her hope seemed to be at a permanent low and mine, well, that night I think I had very little hope left. It seemed absurd that apathy was all it took to hurt the creature but it had howled in agony just at our touch. I wondered who lived at that house. What was the creature's plan for tonight? Who was its intended victim? Had they escaped like me, or had Emily got there before it had the chance to try?

The shower stopped. I imagined Emily towelling herself dry and listened intently to see if I could pick out the sound of individual curves. I couldn't. She walked into the kitchen a few minutes later, still rubbing her hair with a towel. She was wearing pink cotton pyjamas and looked unbelievably cute. The pyjamas clung to her hastily dried body in the most wonderful places. She dropped the towel on the table and began brushing her damp, tussled hair until it was combed neatly back from her face. She sat down and tapped lightly at her wound, checking her fingers for blood.

"I don't think it's bleeding. I thought the hot water might open it again. Will you have a look?"

I stood up and walked behind her chair and once again parted her hair. This time it was soft and damp and smelled amazing. The cut was OK; it was clean and had closed. I was about to tell her this when I looked down and saw her left breast. Her loose pyjama top had the top three buttons undone and I could see right down. Another inch and I could have seen a nipple. She turned in her chair and looked up at me with those big, brown eyes.

63

"How does it look?"

She meant the cut. Almost positive she meant the cut. "It looks good." Best to use the multi-purpose answer anyway.

She lowered her head. "Steve, I'm scared. Will you stay with me tonight?"

I put my hand under her chin and lifted her head to look at me again. "Of course I will." She stood up and hugged me. It felt so good. We held each other for a long time and then she let go and took my hand and led me out of the kitchen.

We walked into the living room. She turned me and sat me down on the sofa. She stood before me, her bellybutton peaking out at me from a gap in her pyjamas. She was going to undress before me. She leant down to me.

"I'll get you a pillow and a blanket. Thanks for doing this, Steve."

Ah, fuck.

When she came back with the pillow and blanket she said, "We'll talk tomorrow about what to do." She smiled and walked off to bed.

I lay there for over an hour thinking she was going to change her mind or get scared and come and get me. She never did and the next thing I remember is Emily shaking me awake at 6:30 in the morning. She had to get me out before her dad came home but she had made me a full cooked breakfast. I ate it slowly. Too much vodka the night before was having its effect the morning after. We didn't mention the events of last night at all. She refilled my coffee cup and asked if I wanted any more toast. I declined.

"We're just like an old, married couple," she joked.

Yeah, we don't talk and don't have sex.

She saw me to the door at a couple of minutes past seven. She was hurrying me because her dad finished work at seven and it was only a ten-minute drive home. "Will I call you later?"

I felt really groggy. "Make it tomorrow. I don't think I'll be doing much today but sleeping."

She nodded and forced a smile. It was another one of those scenes that was missing a kiss, but I was too tired to figure out if one was being offered so I just said goodbye and left. I had to walk home and my legs were killing me. The unexpected burst of energy last night had really taken it out of me. My mouth was dry and my clothes were wrinkled and sweaty. I now looked like a Miami drug-dealer's best customer.

The walk took forever and I rehashed every disastrous part of the previous night. When my house finally came into view I straightened my clothes as best as I could and put on a brave face. As I walked up our driveway, I'd thought I just like to go up to my room and lie down, maybe even sleep, without a whole inquisition from my mum. I walked into the kitchen and she was there.

"Hello there," she said with mock-surprise. "I thought your dad was picking you up later on."

"Change of plan," I said and headed for the hall.

"Good night?"

I stopped at the door with my back to her. "Not really."

"Want to tell me about it?"

"No, I just want to lie down and sleep."

"OK." I was amazed my mum was letting it go so easily. "You go and get out of those dirty clothes and I'll bring you up a nice cup of tea."

I smiled. "OK." It was nice to know there were still some things in the world that were constant.

5.

I did sleep intermittently that day. My stomach really hurt and I kept waking up and running to the toilet. "Never again"—the mantra of the remorseful drunk—was used by me for the first time (but not the last) that day. Between bouts of vomiting and sleep I thought about Rachel. Hollywood told me she would be lifting the phone repeatedly, maybe even getting the first few digits of my number dialled, before getting a faraway look in her eyes and replacing the phone in its cradle. This guilt would eventually allow her to complete dialling and explain herself to me.

On Sunday, I was excused from church with barely a raised voice. My parents were being unusually understanding, even though I hadn't told them anything about what had happened. My mum had many other sources; I think she could have found out what happened if she'd made a few phone calls. Whether she did or not remains a mystery.

They were just leaving when the phone rang. My mum answered and I listened carefully. She shouted up the stairs, "Steven, it's Rachel. Don't forget to put on the potatoes." Hollywood, how could I have doubted you? I heard the door click and the house go quiet. I got out of bed and walked out onto the landing. I didn't know what I was going to say to her. Should I be gracious and take her back? After all, she's now one of the girls that the Golf Club put on their list under the heading Lower Your Handicap. First, I want to know who that dick was, then, I want to hear he was terrible at sex, and then, maybe that he had moved to some distant corner of the world and would never be heard of again.

I lifted the receiver slowly and said, "Hello," in a tortured, brat-pack kind of way.

"Hi Steve, it's Emily. How are you feeling?"

Hollywood, you liar!

We talked for over an hour and I forgot to put the potatoes on. Mum and dad arrived home and I hung up as quickly as I could. After being chastised for delaying dinner, I went up to my room and got dressed. Emily and I had talked about everything that had happened on Friday night and had come to the following conclusions:

1) We could hurt the creature just by touching it.
2) When the creature had reached into our heads to find a trustworthy image to appear as, it had left a telepathic breadcrumb trail (my phrase, thank you). This had allowed us to sense where and when it was going to attack someone and draw on some primal strength to fight it.
3) We *had* hurt it.
4) The creature had run off in the direction of the beach. That, combined with Emily's run-in with it at the old boathouse, led us to the theory that it lived somewhere close to the sea, or maybe in it.
5) I fart in my sleep.

Emily had a great sense of humour that I didn't expect. She giggled uncontrollably as she teased me: "You know my canary's dead, don't you? Poor little guy worked the coal-mines for twenty years and never came up against anything like you."

"Yeah, yeah, yeah. Girls don't fart, I suppose."

"Of course we do, but we don't need to issue Bio-hazard suits afterward."

"You'd look good in a Bio-hazard suit."

"Is that your fantasy, Steve? Is that what you were dreaming about when I came in to wake you? Is that why there was the beginnings of a native-American settlement on your crotch?"

Silence. That may have been a step beyond innocent flirting and we both knew it. Thank God, my mum and dad had walked in at that moment. I didn't want to leave the conversation at such an awkward place, I had to let her know that I liked her and it was OK for her to say anything to me.

"That's my mum and dad home, Emily."

"Er, OK, Steve," she babbled, "I guess I'll see you at school."

Think of a line, damn it. Something to reassure her. Something clever, witty, and maybe a little flirtatious. My mind was blank. I was trying to think of something worthy of Woody Allen, but my mum shouting about potatoes and the loud gunfire from some old John Wayne western that my dad had found on TV, had me totally flummoxed. Then it came to me, and it was good, but needed a quick rewording to make it...

Click.

Emily had put down the phone. The dial-tone hummed in my ear like a booing audience...and who could blame it.

Chapter IV - Black Christmas

This year remember: A dog is for life, not just for Christmas. Unless you're Korean; then a dog really is just for Christmas…and maybe Boxing Day if there are any leftovers.

Imogen Collins, *Christmas Pet Patrol*

- December, 1989 -

1.

It didn't snow that December. It rained a lot, which seemed fitting somehow. When I was young I believed that it snowed at Christmas because it was the end of the year and the snow covered the last year so you could start clean in January. That wasn't going to happen this year.

I wasn't speaking to Rachel, which would have made me happier if she had at least tried to speak to me. I heard that the dickhead-guy she was seeing was called Tony and he was a thirty-six year-old architect. What kind of sick, sad, fucking thirty-six year-old would go out with a sixteen year-old girl? She had indeed met him when she stayed with her aunt that summer and he had been seeing her off and on, but now they were steady. Even when I passed her in the corridors, she would become fascinated by her shoes and never made eye contact. It was over. There seemed to be no guilt or regret on her part; she had what she wanted and I didn't matter. There wasn't going to be any tearful, power-ballad reunion in the last ten minutes of the movie; this was reality. Reality sucks.

It's no surprise that I was a little angry and irritable, so when Boggy Marsh started teasing me in the changing rooms before PE, I didn't take it in good humour.

"Hey, Norton, I hear Rachel and her new guy are at it like bunnies. Is it true you couldn't get it up and that's why she had to look elsewhere?" Everyone laughed.

Ten.

"Or was it the hair-trigger? I heard you had the mess made before you got your pants down." Laughter again.

Nine.

"Steve? Stevie boy? You can tell me, was she too much for you? I bet she goes like an alley cat."

Eight.

"She can suck a golf ball through a hose-pipe, is that true?"

Seven.

"But you never found out, did you? No. How many months were you with her and you never did the deed?"

Six.

"Are you sure you're not a fag, have you been tested?"

Five.

"How do you feel when you see Boy George on TV?"

FourThreeTwoOne. That was all I could take. I punched Boggy in the side of the head and he went down. The laughter was silenced. I wish I could say it was a good punch, but it was pretty pathetic. Everyone, including Boggy, was shocked more than anything. Nothing is more frightening than the rage of a pacifist. I stood above him, my fist still clenched trying to think of a Schwarzenegger-esque line when Mr. Chestnutt walked in and saw me. He dragged me out and into his office.

I could win over most teachers with a little charm and logic. As I waited for Chestnutt to speak, I thought of something to say that might get me off the hook.

Sorry, sir, but he implied I would watch a Culture Club video.

That should work. A sports enthusiast from Chestnutt's generation would be so homophobic he would probably have Boggy burned at the stake for mentioning the existence of such creatures.

"It seems you've too much energy, Norton. Maybe a cross-country run will release that aggression."

"I thought we were playing basketball in the hall today."

"The rest of them are; *you* are going for a run."

"But it's raining," I protested.

"Then you'd better run fast or you'll get wet."

He didn't want to know why I had hit Boggy; he didn't care. I knew that any protestation at this point would just make my punishment worse, so I stayed silent. Maybe he was in an especially vindictive mood, maybe he had been denied sex the previous night...or maybe he was just a bastard. I knew there was no talking to him so I slowly walked up the corridor to the door.

I stepped outside and thought of the two-mile run ahead of me. It was pouring out of the heavens and there was a cold wind blowing. Usually, cross-country running was something we did when the weather was good and the ground was firm. Even then we wore tracksuits, I had packed my kit bag for basketball today and was wearing shorts and a vest.

I was drenched before I had run two hundred yards. The rain pounded hard on the left side of my body. My head was numb by the half-mile mark and my arms and legs were a strange red/ purple colour.

I tried to think of something else to take my mind off the cold. Girls. Yes, a little sexual fantasy would make the miles fly in. I thought of Emily but couldn't imagine a scenario. My sodden feet were getting heavier to carry. Back to girls, and it was time for the big guns. Maxine. I had created dozens of fantasies involving Maxine; it was just a matter of remembering and replaying. Maxine in a bikini by a swimming pool on a beautiful summer day. She takes a drink and an errant drip slides down to her cleavage and…and…she puts on an overcoat because she's so fucking cold! It wasn't working. The numbness in my shorts wasn't going to be cured by a mere fantasy. No good thoughts could survive in my head so I turned to hate.

Tony. Bastard Tony. Rachel. Deceitful fucking Rachel. Chestnutt. Stupid, baldy old fuck, with his stupid fucking comb-over. It was working. I could feel a fire burn in my stomach making me angry and giving me a burst of energy. Billy Love. He fucked Emily around. What a bastard. Emily is the most harmless, sensitive and beautiful…yes, beautiful. She *was* beautiful. I stopped running and bent over resting my hands on my knees. Emily *was* beautiful. I stood up and caught my breath. The rain was still hammering the side of my head and my shorts and vest were stuck to me. I was over halfway there now; I could do it.

From behind me a horn sounded. A car pulled up beside me and the window rolled down. It was Chestnutt.

"Get on with it, Norton, or I'll make you do it twice."

I looked at him with renewed hate. I jogged on without speaking. His car drove past and he honked again. Good one,

Chestnutt, you really earn my respect by coming after me in a car. I thought PE teachers were supposed to be like Commanding Officers in the army: *I wouldn't ask you to do anything that I wouldn't do myself, lads.* It was how it should be. I never really enjoyed sports and Chestnutt had taken this as a sign of laziness. He didn't seem to understand that I just didn't care. All his aggressive shouting and posturing about winning was lost on me. When it came to running a hundred metres, I didn't care if I didn't win. In the grand scheme of the planet I don't think it mattered much if I passed a baton on with the right technique. Maybe I'm wrong…but I doubt it.

I hated that we had no choice in PE. Other subjects we could choose what we were interested in, but everyone was condemned to PE. It would have been great if I could have made Chestnutt act out Shakespeare for two hours every week; he would have hated that. He would have hated it because it just wasn't his scene, just like chasing a ball around a patch of grass wasn't mine.

The last two hundred yards were almost dreamlike. I began to wonder if some part of my brain had been frozen permanently. My legs felt so heavy. My feet seemed to slam the ground with each step. I wanted to go home and climb into a hot bath, but I had another three hours of school to go.

It wasn't until I got back inside the school that I started to shiver. I saw the clock in the hallway and realised I only had five minutes before the bell rang. Not even time for a decent shower. I stumbled down to the changing rooms. Everyone else was almost finished dressing when I got there. They looked at me with empathy. Boggy approached me and I steeled myself as best as I could.

"Fuck sake, Norton, you look fucked."

My teeth started to chatter.

"I'm fuckin' sorry I got you into this shit, Steve."

I nodded bravely. "Sorry I hit you."

"That's all right." Boggy gathered up his bag and walked to the door. "You hit like Boy George's hairdresser anyway." He laughed and ran out.

I wasn't going to give chase. I actually laughed. Boy George's hairdresser; that was pretty good for Boggy. I peeled off my sports gear and got into the shower just as the bell rang. I stayed there a couple of minutes trying to get my circulation going again then quickly dried myself, dressed and walked to the door. Chestnutt stood blocking the door holding a mug of steaming hot tea. He smiled and stepped aside. I pushed past him and went to my next class.

2.

The next morning I awoke feeling drained. I walked to the mirror and it was confirmed: I looked like shit. I really didn't feel right and usually this would have been enough for me to convince my mum to let me stay home, but I didn't want to stay home that day. It was the day of the annual school disco. I was definitely coming down with something, but I would fight it today and give in to it tomorrow, after the disco, after I had kissed Emily. My mum handed me a card postmarked Dublin: from Gary, with my cup of tea. He hadn't totally forgotten me, then. I had tried phoning him a few times, but he was always out with his girlfriend. I had sent him a card so he was probably just sending me one out of obligation, or because his mum forced him to. I ripped it open and looked inside.

To Steve, was crammed up in the left hand corner; he had obviously intended to write a letter like I had, but had given up after the greeting. Down at the bottom of the card written in a different pen, but the same handwriting, were the words: *Women will disappoint you.* I didn't get it. Was it a joke? Maybe a catchphrase from some TV show I should be watching. I showed it to my mum and she looked more baffled than me. I decided I would try calling him again that night and ask him what he was on about. Had he broken up with his girlfriend? Even if he had, it isn't the sort of bizarre fragment you put on a Christmas card. Shit, maybe he was telling me he was gay! I put the card on the mantle as I left the house and turned my thoughts back to Emily.

It seemed a foregone conclusion that we would kiss today. We had become close over the last few months and we would both be there alone. I would ask her to dance when one of the slow songs came on and it would just happen, like fate. The expectation was better than any pill and I was able to perk myself up so even my mum didn't notice anything was wrong that morning. I was on the bus before I let any indication of discomfort show on my face.

I've seen American TV shows and they seem to make much more of a big deal of these things than we did. They hire a limo and a hotel room; they buy Champagne and go totally over the top with tuxedos and dresses. Our school dances were a low-key affair. The main difference was that we had ours during the day and this limited the amount of fun that you could have. For ninety minutes—after dinner until the end of school—the curtains in the gym were pulled and a DJ played the hits of the day. It also meant we didn't have to wear our uniforms. Most of the guys just wore a shirt and jeans but the girls had to walk a fine line between looking good and not looking as if they tried too hard to impress.

The school was abuzz the whole day with the kind of excitement that everyone learns not to admit to as years go on. Rumours abounded of who was going to make a move on whom. Girls teased each other about who would be the worst person who could ask them for a dance. Jokers ran around with mistletoe, dangling it above any boy and girl who were close enough. Mistletoe seemed to have a strange power that nobody wanted to disobey. Instead of just saying "no" or "get lost," couples that didn't want to be forced to kiss would leap backwards; out of range of the mistletoe's influence. Four feet seemed to be a safe distance and it was funny to watch this energetic refusal happen to unsuspecting pupils walking up the corridor, almost like a snowplough cutting a track through the shy teenagers. I wouldn't jump if anyone hung mistletoe between Emily and I; in fact I intended to give them every opportunity to catch us unawares.

I was dressed casually; jeans, open shirt with a Guns n' Roses T-shirt below it and a denim jacket. I was wearing a headband that morning as well (you know, Axl Rose style) but the Physics teacher said I looked like "a bloody Comanche" and told me to take it off, so it hung round my neck now and still looked pretty cool. I looked for Emily during the breaks but couldn't find her, not even in her sanctuary. I hoped she hadn't decided not to come to school and I spent the day wondering what she might be wearing. It wouldn't be anything too sexy

73

because she would want to keep a low profile and avoid the comments of the other girls. She would be wearing something that would allow her to blend into the background. Some of the girls were wearing short skirts (in December!) and the boys had endless theories about how it was a practical decision and not an aesthetic one; it was a lot easier to hike a skirt up and go for it than it was to lumber yourself with the hassle of trying to take off trousers and shoes quickly. They also took bets on which of the girls would have scuffed knees by the end of the day.

No one could wait for dinner break to be over. Foods which left lingering odours sold poorly that day in the canteen, but the kitchen staff made up their losses with mint-flavoured chewing gum, which they had an unexpected run on. We gathered expectantly outside the gym until the teachers, our chaperones, came and unlocked the doors. Immediately we filed in, boys to the left, girls to the right and attached ourselves to the walls.

Again, the American divide was showing. On TV everyone seems to have dates for this type of thing, but there were maybe only five couples in the hundred or more pupils in the hall. Maxine and Doug sat in the corner like a royal couple in their box, watching the rest of us trying to be as perfect as them. Maxine looked stunning as ever, even though she was just wearing jeans and a lacy white blouse. If only. I couldn't see Emily, but thought she would sneak in later when everyone stopped looking at the door. We all looked at the door because there was nothing else to do. We stared at each other across no-man's land, each waiting for the other to make the first move. No one wanted to be the first to dance, what if no one else joined in? What if you went and asked a girl to dance and she said no? With so little else to look at, everyone would be watching you do it.

Finally a group of girls got up and danced with each other and we were off. Tentatively, a few guys crossed the great expanse of the dance floor. I remember watching Ken Armstrong walking over to Anne Porter. He stopped before her with his head hung. He nodded at the dance floor, shrugged his shoulders and raised his head and looked at her.

They say Christmas is a time for miracles and Ken must have believed it that day because she actually agreed and danced with him. I smirked as he strutted to the dance floor holding her hand and looked over at the rest of us smugly as if to say, "That's how it's done, lads."

I checked my watch and realised that the dance was more than half over and there was still no sign of Emily. She *hadn't* come to school today. I should have known she wouldn't. I should have called her last night and dropped a few hints. Damn it all to hell. At least Rachel wasn't there; she must have realised they wouldn't let her pensioner boyfriend in, and stayed home. Though she probably stayed home and had sex with him all day. The groggy, sick feeling I had been ignoring all day now returned and made me feel even worse.

Boggy came running over. "Hey, Norton, what's your score?"

"No score, Boggy. Pain stopped play."

"Fuck Rachel, man...oh no, you'll never get the chance now, will you?" He laughed. "No, seriously, forget her. Plenty of other wenches out there." He cast his hand over the left side of the gym. He came in close to my ear and said, "I've had two snogs and felt three tits today." He pulled away and smiled widely. As he walked away he opened his arms, spun round and shouted, "Life is fucking beautiful."

Three tits?

Last Christmas by Wham came through the speakers and I knew this was the start of the Erection Section. The next half-dozen songs would all be slow and the last opportunity to kiss a girl that year. I scanned the girls on the opposite side of the gym. A quick glance to my left and right showed that I was not the only one who understood the implications of Wham's yuletide classic. It was like a game of Battleships.

Danny Wells to B7. Miss.

Joey Turner to F9. Hit.

Porno Bill to J12. Hit.

Garth Watt to A4. Hit.

Willie McBride to D6. Miss.

Billy Love to E3. Hit.

E3 was Emily. Billy was snogging Emily. Billy's hands were on Emily's ass. Billy and Emily were together.

You have sunk my battleship.

I couldn't believe it. After all she'd said. After all he'd done to her. Last Christmas ended and the distinctive synth-bass of Berlin's Take My Breath Away began. Billy and Emily remained stuck together.

Women will disappoint you.

I looked around at everyone on the dance floor, taking full advantage of the *Top Gun* theme song. I decided to leave. Before I reached the door Doug Winters caught my eye. He was kissing Maxine's neck and she had her back to me. He grinned as he slid his hand under Maxine's blouse and caressed her luscious breasts. I showed how uninterested I was in what he was doing to Maxine's soft, supple, incredibly toned body, by walking out.

I walked outside and waited for the bus even though I was at least twenty minutes early. Twenty minutes when everyone else was enjoying themselves. Once again I trusted the old Hollywood adage that Emily would come after me because I was her true love. Once more Hollywood let me down.

3.

That night I surrendered to my illness. It actually turned out to be more serious than the flu. I had got an infection in my left lung and developed a really nasty cough and was put on many pills to counter it. The doctor said it was probably the result of being extremely cold and said I might never be able to pinpoint when it happened. I didn't say anything but I knew exactly when it had happened: Thank you, Mr Chestnutt, you vindictive bastard.

At least it meant I would be off school until the new year and maybe longer, so I didn't have to worry about all manner of stupid shit that was tying my mind in knots. I would use this time to sort my head out. It was my final year of school and I had exams to study for in the new year so I didn't need to be distracted by girls.

I didn't see much of the festive season. I spent most of my time curled up on the sofa in front of the fire with a blanket round my shoulders and a hot water bottle clutched to my chest. It got me out of doing Christmas shopping, which was a plus. I read the papers and it seemed that the creature, despite the long periods of winter darkness, hadn't tried to harm anyone else. I thought maybe I had killed it that night. I had pounded it until its shell broke and it bled. It had run off but maybe it was really hurt and had died later. Yeah, maybe in the Hollywood movie.

It was just a few days before Christmas when the creature upped the ante. I was sitting at home by myself. My mum and dad had gone to a Christmas party at the local football club and I was watching a Christmas special of Only Fools And Horses and feeling a little better. There was a knock on the front door. I got up and arranged myself in the most pathetic posture I could; bloody carollers always came when something good was on, and you had to stand there smiling like an idiot while tone-deaf eight year-olds murdered Oh, Little Town Of Bethlehem. Not this time. I was going to be too sick to stand there and listen to them; I would undoubtedly need a little lie down. I opened the door with my shaky hand and looked through my half-closed eyes and saw...the police.

"Steven Norton?"

My posture straightened and a million possibilities shot through my mind. The first, and most disturbing, was that some drunk had run my parents down. I'd be an orphan, sent to the workhouse, Mrs Wilton was *right*; Oliver Twist was relevant to my life. I tried to respond, but the most I could manage was a nod.

"Are your parents home, Steven?" the officer inquired.

Relief. It wasn't my parents; he thought they were at home. "No, they're at the football club dance in town."

The policeman turned to his female companion and said, "Get on the radio and see who's close to the football club, and tell them to go in and get Mr and Mrs Norton and bring them home."

"What's going on?" I asked.

"Why don't we go inside and wait for your parents to get home?" He edged forward and I led him into the living room. We sat there in an uneasy silence for a few minutes and then the female officer came in and closed the door behind her.

"Parents are on their way," she said.

The policeman nodded and sat back in his chair.

This was like some kind of weird dream that didn't make any sense. Maybe it was dad's shop. Maybe someone had broken in and robbed it. But why did he know my name when he came to the door? I began to get a very bad feeling. "Aren't you going to tell me what this is all about?"

"We can't question you without your parents present," he replied.

It *was* me they came to see. What could they possibly want with me? I hadn't done anything. I thought about my parents being led out of the football club dance by the police. It would have been sobering at best, humiliating at worst. I imagined them being driven here by the police getting ever more angry with me. Angry for what? I hadn't *done* anything.

After twenty minutes, my parents finally arrived home. My dad stormed in the door first and glared at me. "Right, what have you done?"

"I don't know. This guy won't tell me." I tried to sound brave but my voice was weak because of my illness. I might have been able to deny it more fervently if I'd known what I was being accused of.

The policeman said, "If we could all just sit down, we can get on with this."

My dad sat down and my mum perched on the arm of his chair. My dad looked at me again for signs of guilt. I don't know if I looked guilty or not.

The policeman cleared his throat. "This is a very delicate matter, and not a very pleasant one." He looked embarrassed. He took a deep breath. "Do you know a girl by the name of Maxine Dawson?"

My mum and dad looked at me. I shrugged, bewildered. "Yes."

The policeman began turning his hat in his hands. "Miss Dawson has made a complaint about you. Specifically, that earlier this evening she was in her bedroom when she heard a voice calling her from outside. She went to the window and says that you were standing in her garden in a state of undress...engaging in a lewd act."

I was stunned. I mean, what? How could she...? Why would she...? I couldn't speak; it was like the accusation had gone in my ears, located my vocal chords and wrapped itself around so I couldn't make a sound.

The policeman seemed relieved to have finished the story and looked around at our reactions. My mum and dad looked ashamed. They actually believed what he was saying. I had to protest.

"You don't believe that, do you?" I said to my parents. They looked at each other, totally unprepared for how to deal with a situation like this. "Come on!"

"Several other pupils said you fancied her and have been chasing her for some time," the policeman said, "Do you deny that?"

This was bad. This was turning into a stitch-up of epic proportions. "I haven't...I mean, I used to like her, but not anymore."

"That's not what her boyfriend says. I'll warn you now, he's more than a little upset."

Oh great, Doug Winters was also going to kick my head in if I ever got out of prison. Why would Maxine make up something like that? Maybe she only thought she saw me. Who else looks like me and would do something this sick? Then it came to me: the creature. That's who could look exactly like me and would do something like this just to get me off the scene. I was instantly ninety-nine percent certain that's what had happened. Cunning bastard. It had framed me perfectly and what could I do about it? I couldn't tell them the truth without proof, or I'd probably get an extended holiday in the rubber hotel. Emily might back me up, but it wouldn't be enough. I had to prove my innocence without telling them what really happened.

"She's mistaken; it wasn't me."

The policeman started twisting his hat again. "She was in no doubt about the identification, son."

Everyone was staring at me. "Look at me! I couldn't get to her house even if I wanted to."

"Do you know where she lives?" the policewoman asked.

"Yes, it's a small town; everyone knows where everyone lives. I'll bet she knows where I live."

"She doesn't actually," the policeman said. "Which is a good thing. You would have had a visit from her boyfriend tonight if either of them had known where you lived."

Think about this, there's got to be a way of proving I was in all night. "I've been watching TV since they went out; I can tell you what happened in every programme I watched." I smiled triumphantly.

"Were any of them repeats?" the policewoman asked.

Shit. Thank you, Miss fucking Marple. Of all the shitty luck, even the BBC was against me. That was my last hope. There was no way to prove that it wasn't me standing in Maxine's garden giving myself a bare-knuckle shuffle. Fall back on ignorance and denial when all else fails. "Look, it wasn't me but it seems I can't prove that to you. I don't know who it was, but it wasn't me." I sat back enraged by my inability to outwit the creature.

The policeman stared at me for a minute and when he was satisfied that I had said all I was going to, he and my dad went into the kitchen and talked privately. The police left about a half hour after that, and my dad came back into the living room.

"Well, what's going on?" I asked eagerly.

"Just go to your bed, Steven," he said, obviously annoyed.

"It wasn't me, dad, she…"

"She sees you every day at school," he yelled. "She can tell you from someone else." He hung his head and exhaled. "Just go to your bed."

Tears were in my eyes. Maybe he would have been more tactful if he hadn't been drinking, but his thoughts seemed clear on the subject. It was the most hurtful thing he ever said to me. I walked out of the room and stopped at the door. "It wasn't me," I said in little more than a whisper.

I went to bed but didn't sleep. I hadn't been doing anything about the creature for weeks, hoping it had died or moved on and all that time it had been planning its revenge on me, and it had got me. It had got me a real doozy. Imagine if the police had searched my room and found Johnny's drawings of naked Maxine, I would have been locked up for sure. They might still do that; I would have to get rid of them. Doug Winters wouldn't need a search warrant if he decided to pay me a visit and that psycho wasn't going to listen to reason. I was in deep fucking shit. I had to get better and I had to find this fucking thing and kill it.

4.

I spent most of the next couple of days in bed. I tried to think of a way of proving my innocence, but I came up with nothing. I thought Emily might have called; surely she had heard the story by now. She should have been able to put two and two together and figure out what had happened. She didn't call. The phone was far from quiet though; my mum poked her head into the bedroom at one point and told me not to be answering it. We were getting hate calls from every brainwashed idiot in town and my mum was listening to them. That upset me more. I could guess at the depths of verbal depravity to which my peers would sink, and I didn't want my mum hearing that kind of language. I was pretty sure she wouldn't know what half of it meant.

Doug Winters arrived the next morning. His brother's car skidded into the driveway and he jumped out shouting for me. I was going to go out but my mum stopped me. She had already phoned the police. I wanted to get it over with. Delaying the inevitable hammering he was going to give me wasn't my idea of safety. The longer he had to wait, the madder he'd get. He was beating and kicking the door when the police arrived. I watched through a crack in the curtains. Doug was very animated as he relayed his reasons for being there to the policeman. The most disconcerting thing was the amount of nodding the policeman was doing; he agreed with him. Doug was finally convinced to get back in the car but before he did, he looked up at my window and yelled, "This isn't over." He might have been a moron, but he was right.

I came downstairs for dinner and sipped some soup. I had no appetite. The phone calls were still coming. Some of them weren't just anonymous abuse; some of them were from friends of my parents wanting to know if it was true or 'my side of the story.' I think that day actually sickened my mother against

81

gossip for the rest of her life. When I heard her defending me on the phone I was reminded of the mothers that I had seen on the Northern Ireland news all my life; mothers of convicted terrorists who still believed that her son would never do such a thing. On rare occasions they were right, but most of the time they were just being blindly loyal.

I walked across the living room to the window. My mum had closed the curtains while Doug was outside, which made the room as dark and gloomy as my mood. I pulled one of the curtains to the side and was greeted by the excited expression of Imogen Collins, who immediately snapped her cameraman into action. I was about to pull the curtain closed again when a thought occurred to me; maybe she could be of help. All these people ringing the house would hear what I had to say without interruption. This could work. I went to the kitchen and told my mother that Imogen Collins was outside and I wanted to bring her in. My mother was wary at first but yielded when I said I was sure I could put this all to rest. I could; all I had to do was explain clearly and concisely where I was, that I was in no condition to go out and couldn't possibly have gone to Maxine's house. It *could* work.

When her cameraman was set up, Imogen Collins poised herself on the edge of a chair and leaned in close. I was quite interested to see how she was going to handle the story because you can't really talk about masturbation on the six o'clock news. She obviously wasn't prepared. She didn't expect to be invited in for an interview. She had probably just intended to shout something to provoke me to insult her, and she would be happy to have caught the venom of the monster on tape. She busied herself unnecessarily with her microphone as she tried to think of how to start.

"Steven," she finally began, "you have been accused by a fellow pupil of an unwanted sexual display. Will you tell us your side?"

I almost laughed. Maybe it was because I was on camera or maybe because she had used such a stupid phrase. "Sexual display?" It sounded as if I had parachuted into the bushes in Maxine's garden with my dick out and red smoke coming from my ankle. I tried to dispel the image from my mind and answered, "I don't know why she thinks it was me. I have been ill for the past couple of weeks and barely have the strength to climb the stairs, let alone..." The word parachute was stuck in my head. No other words existed. I was dying in dead air. I forced the word parachute from my mind but it was replaced by wank. I revised quickly. "I can't *go* outside."

"Do you deny that you have a crush on her?"

"Everyone can see she is an attractive girl, but she has a boyfriend and I respect that." Now I was on a roll. That sounded like an answer a bullshitting American lawyer would give.

"Can you explain what she believes she saw?"

"No, I can't, Imogen. All I can say is that the nights are dark and maybe she really did think it was me out there, but it wasn't. I'm sure my doctor will attest to my physical condition and assure you that there is no way I could have walked to Maxine's house." Imogen Collins was lost. She didn't know what else to ask.

"Is there anything else you'd like to say?"

"Just that I hope the police catch whoever is really responsible for this. I don't know if there was any physical evidence at the scene, but if there was it would not only exonerate me, but potentially incriminate the real perpetrator." I wondered if the police had bothered looking for forensic evidence. It seemed unlikely that they would waste resources on a phantom bush-whacker, but if the sexual display had reached its intended finale, surely they could prove it wasn't me.

Imogen Collins thanked me and got up and left. I watched from the window as she did a little bit out at the gate, probably the intro with the house in the background. I thought it had gone well, but would the public believe it? Only when the six o'clock news aired would we know.

My dad came home from work early. He said the shop was dead all day because of the holidays. His tact had returned with his sobriety. *I* was the reason for the shop's dwindling sales and we all knew it. He was excited to hear that Imogen Collins had been here and even seemed a little disappointed that he had missed her. We all waited patiently around the television and started the videotape when the six o'clock news began. It was about ten minutes in when we saw Imogen Collins outside our house. I still have the tape. This is her report:

Controversy has gripped the town of Portstewart today as a beautiful young schoolgirl was visually assaulted by one of her fellow pupils. The girl, who cannot be named for legal reasons, was too traumatised to speak to me, but I spoke to some of her friends who said she was sickened and frightened by the incident. I tried to get an interview with the accused boy, inside this very house, just a little while ago, but was blocked by the family's legal representation. No formal charges have been made at this time, but the girl's family are thought to be taking legal advice. This is Imogen Collins in Portstewart.

I should have listened to that inner voice that told me not to trust her.

My mother piped up immediately. "She's lying. She was in this house and drank my tea and ate my Custard Creams. He told her exactly what happened and she just went on TV and lied about it. The...the...vicious bitch."

I think it was as close to swearing as mum ever got. Dad just shook his head and sat back. It must be from him that I get my pessimism, he knew it was too good to be true and wasn't surprised when it all blew up in my face. The phone started ringing. No one answered it.

5.

The next few days saw the phone calls begin to lessen and by Christmas Eve things were getting back to normal. Still, I dreaded going back to school. I knew I was going to get pounded by Doug—that was a given—but it occurred to me that girls would probably be freaked out by me and guys, wanting to ingratiate themselves with girls, would most likely take turns knocking seven types of shit out of me. Six months until school ended. I guess I would just have to put my head down and work. Even the teachers might hold my alleged offence against me; what if they marked me down for it? It was a horrible situation. I wasn't getting any better either. I wanted to get out there and find that thing and kill it, but I was still weak as a kitten.

I decided to call Gary in Dublin. He was the one person in the world I could tell this whole sorry tale to and, hopefully, he would believe me. I also wanted an explanation for his odd Christmas card message: *Women will disappoint you.*

I had tried calling him a few times over the last six months, but he was always out with his girlfriend. Given his message and the fact that it was almost Christmas, I thought I had a better chance of getting him at home. His mum answered the phone.

"Hi, Mrs Richards, it's Steve Norton. Is Gary at home?"

"Oh Steve," she said sniffing, "I suppose I should have called you back but I…" The remaining words melted into a series of wails and crying. I didn't know what to do. What do you say to a crying adult? I covered the mouthpiece and called my mum.

She ran into the kitchen. "Is it another one?"

"No," I said, "I called Gary and his mum's started crying." I passed the phone to her.

She listened for a lull in the crying and said, "Hello, Jennifer, what's the matter?" She flicked her fingers at me; indicating I should leave. I was happy to leave. Adults shouldn't cry.

I sat in the living room for forty-five minutes until I heard my mum hang up the phone, then I went into the kitchen. I knew it had to be bad news, *more* bad news, but I was eager to know. "So, what's going on?"

My mum sat me down and recounted what Gary's mum had just told her. Gary had been seeing a girl in Dublin called Lisa for the past few months. She said he seemed happier than she'd seen him in a long time. He was never in the house; he was always out seeing Lisa. What she hadn't known is that Lisa had been leading Gary astray. Drugs. Mr and Mrs Richards had been oblivious in the beginning, even when Gary brought Lisa round to meet them. They thought her dress-sense was a little odd, but other than that she seemed nice. Little did they know that Lisa had already introduced Gary to her family: her sister marijuana, her brother speed, her uncle acid and aunt ecstasy (who went everywhere hand in hand),

and her mother cocaine. In fact, the only one Gary hadn't met was daddy H.

His parents noticed his lethargy and the fact that he didn't seem to eat anymore. They also noticed money going missing. But it was when Gary and Lisa broke up that he really went off the rails. He didn't even try to conceal his addictions anymore and was found crashed out in a toilet cubicle at school when he finally did meet daddy H. The school expelled him and he disappeared for a couple of weeks. He came back eventually, looking for money. His mother said the heroin had changed him completely, she said he looked like a zombie from one of those old horror movies. Somehow his mother and father restrained him and took him off to a rehab clinic. And that's how Gary was spending Christmas.

Of course his mum didn't know the details of why they broke up—just like my mum didn't know what had happened to Rachel and me—but it, coupled with the addiction and disorientation of the drugs, was enough to set Gary on self-destruct. I wandered upstairs and lay on my bed. The TV was on and some cheesy Christmas kids' movie was playing. I didn't even bother changing channel because I knew I wouldn't watch anything that was on; I just wanted background noise.

I wondered how Gary could have lost the plot so completely. I realised that the card he sent must have been written in some rare moment of lucidity.

Women will disappoint you.

It seemed like they could do more than disappoint. I couldn't believe it at first and then I thought it fitted neatly into the messy montage that my life was becoming. Gary was a half-crazed junkie; that was perfect. That was just the fucking icing on the Christmas cake.

A stray line from the TV caught my attention: "It's a Christmas meer-ickle, mommy," said a cute young girl as her family huddled around the tree and smiled inanely. I tried to think of a way out of my predicament and it appeared that a Christmas meer-ickle was the only realistic possibility. I hadn't prayed in a very long time, but that day I did. When I thought about it, I hadn't had a glimpse of a real meer-ickle since I accidentally walked into the women's changing rooms at the swimming pool and saw four naked women in the showers. That was so divine it had to have been God's will. That was two years ago and since then it seems I'd been living under a meer-ickle embargo. If the Man in charge was willing to negotiate terms, I would be willing to make some concessions. I could stop picturing the female parishioners nude when I was in church, I could try to stop swearing...so much, anyway, and I could give some money to charity. Seem fair to You? I stared at the ceiling for a sign that sanctions had been lifted and saw nothing but blank, white plaster. It *was* Christmas, so He was probably busy and would get to my proposal in time.

6.

It was a quiet Christmas. There was none of the usual nights out or people stopping in at our house for a Christmas drink. We sat, silently for the most part, and watched whatever shows were being repeated and the movies that we'd all seen a million times before. I was feeling a bit better, too, and by New Year's Eve I felt well enough to insist that my mum and dad should go and visit my grandparents. My mum was reluctant at first, but eventually gave in and said they wouldn't be late.

It wasn't until I was in the house alone that I began to get scared. It was dark about four-thirty so even if they were coming home early it would give that thing plenty of time to attack me. Maybe it watched me, my house, and had seen my parents leaving. It was a bit of a coincidence that the last time my parents had gone out and I was alone without an alibi, Maxine had been flashed. Maybe it didn't even need to physically watch the house; if I could sense when it was attacking someone, maybe it could sense when I was alone or scared. I began making preparations, now almost certain that I would be getting a visit from the creature. I locked all the doors and windows and put on all the external lights at the first sign of darkness. There was no way this thing was going to sneak up on me in a different guise.

As I fortified my home, my fear was replaced by the desire to fight it. I was expecting it and I would be ready. I could end this thing here and now. That thought alone was enough to drive me on. I had a butcher knife in my hand and sat waiting patiently for over an hour. I started to wonder if the knife would suffice, considering the reach of the creature I might not be able to get close enough to stab it. I thought of the old sickle in the garden shed; yeah, I could go to fuckin' town on its ass with that. I looked out the back door and made sure there were no trustworthy figures lurking in the shadows, and then unlocked the door and ran for the shed. The sickle was right at the back, buried behind bikes, lawnmowers, hosepipes, car-parts and all other manner of useless junk. I clambered over the top of some damp tarpaulin and reached the sickle and tried to lift it out. I pulled hard but it wouldn't come free. I remembered then that it had a smaller handle that came out at ninety degrees to the main handle; it must have been wedged under something. I scuttled back over the tarp and jumped on the ground by the door. I would have to start moving stuff at the front, just enough to create a gap big enough to release the handle.

A blanket was pulled over my head. I reacted immediately and tried to free myself. It was being held down tight. Arms locked around my torso and lifted me from the ground. I wriggled and kicked as best I could. I was going to die. I had let my guard down and it had got me. My heart was beating its way out of my chest. My lungs were trying to keep the pace, but the hands around me were holding so tight that I couldn't get a breath. I felt sick. I saw pinholes of light flashing before my eyes. I tried to speak; to cry for mercy, but I couldn't find my voice. My legs began to lose their fight and the sensation quickly travelled up my body until it reached my head and then there was only darkness.

"He's dead."

"He's not fuckin' dead; he's still breathing."

Consciousness came back to me slowly. The first thing I was aware of was how heavy my arms were. Then I noticed the smell, not a bad smell, just not the smell of my house, and I *was* inside a house, in a kitchen. Two figures came into view standing before me: it was Doug Winters and his older brother Brian. I was in their house. My arms weren't heavy; they were tied to the side of a wooden chair. I tried struggling, but I was tied tightly. I was really angry. As if a supernatural being trying to kill me and the rest of the teenagers of this town wasn't enough to worry about, I had to put up with petty jealousy crap from Doug. His gripe, which I'm sure to him, was the biggest crime in the world, just seemed so insignificant at that moment and I was pissed off that he was falsely accusing me.

"Fuckin' untie me, Doug," I shouted. "You don't know what's going on."

He stepped forward and swung a hard right hook that connected my left jaw. "Shut the fuck up, pervert," he said through gritted teeth. "If the cops aren't going to do anything, I'll sort you out myself."

"The cops aren't going to do anything because they know it wasn't me." I should have stopped there because adding, "You fucking brain-dead piece of shit," earned me another punch in the face and two to the stomach. My nose was bleeding and I could taste the blood in my mouth. Doug's brother looked worried. Good, try to work with that. I looked at Brian and said, "You two are going to be in a lot more trouble than me when the cops find out about this. Kidnapping, assault, you two are going to be bending for the soap for years to come." Doug struck me three more times in the face. My face was beginning to get numb so they didn't actually hurt that much, but I screamed in frustration. I was tied to the chair. I couldn't move. I would never have dreamed of trying to take Doug Winters in a fight under normal circumstances, but this was different. I was being punished for something I hadn't done and that made me madder than hell. I wriggled and hopped the chair about trying to get free. I wanted to hit Doug. I wanted to pound some reason into his tiny fucking brain. I didn't care if I came off worst. Just let me get a few good shots at him. Just let it be fair. Just give me a chance.

Brian was looking even more worried and finally ventured to say, "OK, I think he's had enough".

"The fuck he has," Doug shouted and hit me repeatedly again. The ringing of the phone stopped him. Doug and Brian looked at each other, terrified. Could that be mum or dad phoning home? Now you're in the shit. Doug grabbed a dishcloth and a roll of masking tape. He drove his knee into my stomach, pulled me forward and stuffed the dishcloth in my mouth. Brian stood poised to lift the phone. Doug wrapped the tape quickly around my head twice and ripped it off. He got off me and nodded to his brother.

Brian lifted the phone. "Hello…Maxine, is that you? Calm down, I can't understand you."

Doug looked concerned and walked over and took the phone from his brother. "Maxine, what's wrong?" He listened for a moment and then turned and looked at me. "When?" he asked. "But he can't be, he's sitting right here in front of me." Doug turned to his brother and said, "She says he's standing in her garden, she says she's looking at him right now."

I screamed under my gag, trying to say the words, "Tell her to shine a light on it." Over and over again I shouted it, while Doug and Brian looked at each other, bewildered by what was going on

Finally, Doug took action. "Maxine, turn out all the lights and hide. I'm on my way." Doug hung up the phone and made for the door. He turned and walked to me and ripped off the gag, tearing out some of my hair in the process. I spat the dishcloth out, but the foul taste of stale water remained.

"Let me come with you; I can help," I pleaded. "Don't ask me to explain, just untie me and get over there as quickly as possible." Doug considered me for a few seconds and then cut me loose. He stood back as I got up, maybe expecting me to hit him. I didn't have time to hit him; Maxine was in real trouble. "Come on, let's go," I said and went for the door.

We all jumped into Brian's car and he raced over to Maxine's house. I lay in the back, holding my bruises and trying to summon up my strength. I felt that feeling again, the same one I had when I had ran to the house where the creature was. The pull. There was no doubt the creature was at Maxine's house. The tingling in my gut seemed to grow stronger as we got closer. By the time we screeched to a stop, I was ready to fight. Her house was dark. Doug had told her to do the worst thing. We ran towards the house and I shouted to the others, "Turn on all the lights when you get in there." Doug and Brian nodded as if they finally realised that they were in the middle of something that they didn't understand

and if they wanted to get out alive they'd better listen to someone who did understand.

The front door was open and we ran in. I turned on the hall lights and we all shot off in different directions, calling for Maxine. Doug and Brian ran upstairs. I checked the downstairs. Lights went on in every room we searched. I heard Doug scream above and I bolted upstairs. It was a long, drawn out scream. Doug wasn't the kind of guy who screamed lightly. I heard glass break. I got to the top and looked left and right.

"In here," I heard Brian shout from one of the bedrooms. I ran towards him. When I got to the bedroom, I saw Maxine lying on the floor. Her pyjamas were soaked in blood. The floor beneath her was covered in blood. From the doorway, I could see the deep gashes in her chest. Her face was lifeless, her eyes staring off into nothingness. There was so much blood. Brian had her in his arms, holding her to his chest. He saw the look on my face and it confirmed what he thought. He started crying and said to get Doug. I stepped forward and lifted the pale blue phone on Maxine's bedside cabinet and called 999. I don't remember what I said, but I suppose I asked for an ambulance and the police. I wandered out into the hall and started looking in the rooms for Doug. Maxine was dead. Maxine Dawson was dead. It seemed so unreal, so impossible.

I heard whimpering and followed it. Doug was curled-up in the corner of Maxine's parents' bedroom. The lights were on. He was so pale. Sweat was running down his face. His eyes weren't blinking. He was staring at the broken window. I walked over to the window and looked out. I saw Emily running towards the house, racing to save the day. She looked up and saw me. She stopped running and stared at me. I shook my head letting her know she was too late, we both were. Her chest was heaving hard from the run but she looked up and down the street. The creature was nowhere to be seen. I waved at her to leave. She heard the sirens approaching and agreed. She ran to the street and off into the night. I turned to Doug and saw him still in the same state. It was what I felt like doing too; lying on the ground and curling into the foetal position until a better day, until the world made sense again. Maxine

Dawson was dead. I sat down on the bed and waited for the police.

Doug got taken away in an ambulance and Brian and I got taken to the police station. Again, my parents were picked up by the police and brought to me. I was in a daze this time. Not angry or defensive, just stunned. Brian and I told them that Maxine had called and said there was an intruder and we rushed over there and found her dead. We didn't know what had happened to Doug, who hadn't said a word, and we hadn't seen the intruder. The police were suspicious, and rightly so, what with Doug and I being sworn enemies, the past accusation by Maxine and the fact that my face and Doug's knuckles were cut and bleeding, but still they let us go after a few hours.

Outside, Brian took me to one side while our parents talked. "You know more about what's going on than you've just let on, don't you?" he asked.

I saw no point in lying. "Yeah, I do, but you're better off out of it, Brian. Don't worry, I'll find who's responsible and I'll make them pay."

"I could help you, Steve."

"I'll be OK."

"The offer's open." I nodded and expected him to walk away but he had something else to say. He paused for a few seconds and then came closer to me. "I didn't tell them this and I'm not sure I should be telling you, but Maxine said something before she died. It didn't make any sense. I mean he couldn't. I spoke to her on the phone."

"What did she say?"

He leaned closer still and whispered, "She said, 'It was Doug. Doug did this.' Be he couldn't have, could he?"

I didn't know if he'd believe me or not but I was tired and the guy really needed to hear it. "It wasn't Doug. It made itself look like Doug, the same way it made itself look like me the last time."

He walked away from me, glancing back a few times. I didn't know if he believed me or not. I wanted to go home and go to bed, but I knew there would be more questions from my mum and dad when we got back. They would get a version of

92

the night different from the police, and their version would be closer to the truth. I would tell them about my abduction and the phone call from Maxine. It would be enough to put their minds to rest about all the inconsistencies in the story I had told the police. I didn't want to press charges against Doug or Brian anymore. Doug was in bad enough shape without me adding to his woes. I wondered if anyone had told him that Maxine was dead. I wondered if he was lucid enough to understand if they had. He had seen the creature: that much I was sure of, but had the sight of it been enough to scare him catatonic or had it done something to him? I thought of that blank stare as they had carried him out. I thought about Maxine. Maxine was dead.

It was only on the car ride home that I realised I had been exonerated. I was with Doug and Brian when Maxine had said she saw me in her garden, Brian and Doug would have to concede that if she was mistaken that time she could have been mistaken before. It was small comfort. I couldn't imagine how empty the school would feel without Maxine. God works in mysterious ways, they say. If this reprieve were His idea of a Christmas meer-ickle, I would think twice about asking Him for anything ever again.

Chapter V - Mountains of Mourn

As the New Year begins, we should take a minute to remember those who didn't live to see the new decade. Not a real minute, of course; a symbolic minute.

Happy 1990! Imogen Collins

- January, 1990 -

1.

I didn't go to the funeral. I spent the first few days of the year in a daze. My mental state shuffled between intense sadness and anger, anger that would manifest itself one day soon as vengeance, and I would tear that fucking thing limb from limb.

I had to admit that the creature was not only intelligent, but also cunning. Its plan had seemed to be: impersonate me being a popping-Tom in Maxine's garden so everyone would know exactly who to point the finger at when it killed her. It would have worked, too, if it hadn't been for Doug's need to batter me. That was the one variable that it couldn't possibly have anticipated. One thing did bother me, though: why had it mutilated Maxine? The creature had used its claws to attack her until it had caused fatal damage, but Imogen Collins had said on TV that a knife that was found at the scene had caused the wounds. That smelled like a cover-up, so as to not cause panic in the town, but I never believed it. I wondered if it fed on her? It probably had; it was probably its primary motivation, but framing me was a bonus that it couldn't resist. They probably wouldn't even look for the neurological trauma they had found in Johnny. This thing had wanted to make sure that I was the prime suspect and now that its plan had failed, I knew it wouldn't be long until it tried again.

School had started again and the doc had given me the OK to go back a week after everyone else had started. School was strange. There seemed to be an element of mistrust and suspicion everywhere you looked. I probably got it worse than most because of my involvement. The people at our school weren't going to be swayed by facts proving my innocence, it was much more fun to create elaborate theories of their own. One I heard was that Doug and I were secret lovers who planned Maxine's murder between us so we could live happily ever after. The motive always escaped me on that one. Maxine was noticeable by her absence everywhere you looked. It felt like more than a person had died; it was an ideal. She had been a role model to a lot of the other girls. Maxine had never let her good looks and winning personality turn her into a bitch, like so many other girls. She always had time to speak to anyone who spoke to her, regardless of their social standing or the label on their jacket. She had been the most beautiful girl I had ever known. She was deeply missed.

Doug hadn't come back to school yet, but he was expected soon. He had 'lost the plot' according to the school rumour-mill, but had now been released from the hospital and was recuperating at home. On my first day back I saw Emily as we were changing classes and arranged to meet her at dinnertime. Her sanctuary was not looking its best. The winter cold had stripped the leaves from the trees overhead and the hedges. The sanctuary was surrounded with skinny, sharp branches and provided little protection from the elements. I arrived first and sat on the crate waiting for Emily. I wondered if she was stopping to snog Billy Love on the way. I had almost forgotten how much that had annoyed me. It seemed trivial in the light of everything else that had happened. It was the sort of thing that normal teenagers worried about. Emily arrived soon after. She looked like winter; without the myriad of colours that most of us equate with happy days, but sparse and beautiful in her own way. We talked for the whole of dinnertime, munching sandwiches and crisps in between sharing with her everything that had happened while I was off. She said she had tried calling me a few times, but the phone was either engaged or it just rang. It felt good to talk to someone who knew what was going on. I had spent most of the last month with my theories bottled up inside, lying to the police and my parents, it was a real relief not to have to run the censorship pen over everything I had to say.

When we heard the bell we walked slowly back to the main building. We had avoided the subject of Billy until now, but I couldn't let her go without asking what the hell she was thinking getting back with him. What lie had he told her?

What deception had infiltrated Emily's heart? I was really annoyed, but I had to make it sound casual.

"I saw you and Billy together at the school disco."

After a moment she said, "Yeah."

I was looking for more of an explanation than that. Stay casual; friends support friends, in even their stupidest decisions. "Are you back together?"

"God, no," she said quickly. She hung her head and looked at the ground as she talked. "It was just Christmas, you know? I was feeling a bit lonely and he said the right things at the right time. Stupid, I know."

If she was expecting me to say no, she was out of luck.

"Anyway," she continued, "It was all too fast. After the disco we went round to the smokers' corner and he asked me…"

What? To go steady? To marry him?

She sniffed. "To, ah, give him…"

To give him another chance? To give him time? To give him her phone number?

She cleared her throat. "Well, he wanted me to get my knees dirty, if you know what I mean."

Oh.

The tears were welling in her eyes and even though it seemed like a really Hollywood thing to do (and therefore wouldn't work in the real world), I took her arm, pulled her close, and hugged her. Amazingly, this outward display of support did work. She wrapped her arms tightly around me and let herself cry. I kissed the top of her head and said nothing. We just stood there, getting later and later for class, and held each other until she had got her composure back. I think it was then that she realised that I cared about her, though quite how much she couldn't have known.

2.

A few days later, Doug came back to school. He wasn't like he was before but since he was eating, sleeping and watching TV his parents decided he was on the road to recovery and that familiar surroundings and people might help. I was tense about his return; people like Doug often didn't need proof to sentence someone and I feared he might blame me for Maxine's death.

I first saw him in the computer suite as I tapped away on a BBC Micro 32k computer—cutting edge stuff at the time. He was sitting, staring at a blank screen with his arms hanging by his sides. It was like Doug had had his memory wiped and only his speech and motor skills had been re-installed. His personality was gone. He didn't joke—or for that matter laugh at jokes—and he didn't seem to know how to talk to anyone who spoke to him; he would just shuffle off. Everyone could see he was fragile, so no one dared speak to him about Maxine. As he was leaving the computer room, he looked over and saw me. He stared, like I was someone he should know, but couldn't remember exactly who. After a few seconds he walked out. It was creepy, and I wasn't sure why. He didn't seem to have any desire to beat me up, but there was something that I can only describe as a lingering intent.

At dinnertime that day I found a note in my locker. It was written in crude, shaky capitals, like it had maybe been written on a bus or under a table without the person looking. It simply said:

MEET ME IN THE ENGLISH ROOM AT 3.45

There was no signature and no explanation. My first thought was that it was Emily, but why 3.45? She would miss her bus, and so would I come to think of it. I could always walk down the street and get home with my dad, but how did Emily plan to get home? I suppose I could ask dad to drop her off. What if it wasn't Emily? Who else would want to get me on my own? Billy Love? Doug Winters? It seemed unlikely that it was Doug, so that left Billy. It wasn't Billy's style either though; if he wanted to beat me up because of my relationship with Emily, he would do it in front of an audience in the playground. Maybe it was a new player in the game. Someone else who had seen the creature and remembered the picture I put up. That would be good; another ally would help a lot. I decided I had to wait behind after school and find out who it was.

The English room was empty when I got there ten minutes early. The door was unlocked because old Taffy, the school caretaker, only locked up after he had cleaned the room at the end of the day. I wandered in and over to Mr Kawaji's desk. It was a bit of a power-trip to sit in his chair. I put my feet up on is desk and gestured to the non-existent pupils to be quiet. I lifted a copy of Oliver Twist from his desk and stood up and said, "Now, you all have to read this shite. The Board of Education is determined to put you off reading for the rest of your life." I sat down again and smiled. I'd make a good teacher. I looked at the clock: 3.41.

Another thought occurred as I sat there: what if it was Rachel who left me the note? Yes, that was definitely a possibility. Maybe her and the old pervert had broken up over Christmas. That would be sweet. Maybe things would even get physical. I looked at the little built-in store at the back of the classroom. That would be an ideal place to make up with her. The more I thought about it, the more I convinced myself that it was her who had left me the note. I opened the top drawer of Kawaji's desk and found nothing but pens, rubber bands, paper clips etc. His bottom drawer was much more interesting. It had deodorant, a little shaving kit, aftershave, a comb, breath freshener and...a packet of condoms. Kawaji, you old dog! It was a three-pack with only one left. I wondered who Kawaji was doing the old horizontal Lambada with. He wore a wedding ring, but he wouldn't be keeping this stuff here if he weren't having a little extra curricular activity. I'd have to keep my eyes open to see if I could deduce who the lady in question was. I laughed lightly and closed the drawer. It seemed like fate now that it would be Rachel or Emily. A spare condom, a private store with its own light, it just had to be all part of a grand design.

3.47.

So she—one of them—was a little late. It was a woman's prerogative to keep a man waiting. I began to worry about being discovered. I didn't know what order Taffy cleaned the classrooms in; he might be here in a minute or an hour. Maybe if we were in the store he wouldn't even notice. Some girls get off on the whole danger of getting caught, or so I had read in an adult entertainment periodical. I got up and walked to the door. The corridor was empty. The school was quiet. I still had hope that someone was coming, someone female with a thirst for sexual fulfilment. I closed the classroom door and wandered around the desks. 3.51 now. I thought I'd better check the store was unlocked and there was adequate floor space. I opened the door to the store and saw Doug standing there. He looked confused, like he didn't know what he was doing there.

"Doug, are you OK?"

He growled with his teeth gritted. He grabbed me around the throat and pulled me close to his face. For a second he stared into my eyes and then he threw me into the back of the store. My head slammed into a shelf and books fell all over me as I dropped to the ground. It took me a few seconds to register what had happened. I picked myself up from the books and noticed Doug was gone and the store door was closed. I stood up and tried the handle. It was locked.

"Doug," I shouted, "are you still out there?" I was getting a very bad feeling about this whole situation. This is the kind of shit you read about, hell, this is the kind of shit Hollywood makes movies about. It's a slasher pic about a kid who has suffered a psychological trauma and goes ape on his schoolmates. It would be a box-office smash and, as long as it doesn't say at the start Based On Actual Events, I might even go to see it.

Blood trickled down my forehead. I reached up and touched the spot where I had impacted the shelf; there was a little blood, but not enough to worry about. I was more worried about what Doug had planned for me when he finally opened this door. I put my ear to the door and listened. I could hear a kind of low whimpering, maybe crying. He was still out there. Then he screamed and I heard desks and chairs being thrown around the room. Some crashed against the door I was listening at, and I took a step back until his rage subsided. When it had been quiet for a few minutes, I tried shouting through the door, trying to reason with him, to explain that he had been with me so I couldn't have had anything to do with Maxine's death. I got no response. All I could hear was the ticking of my watch and his muffled whimpering.

Despite all his arrogant posturing, I think he actually did love her. When I was imagining Maxine being my girlfriend, I always thought she would dump Doug when she realised he treated her like a logo on his trainers. He didn't really care about her; she was just something to show off to the rest of us. He had her and the rest of us wanted her. That was what I had thought. Now I saw how wrong I was. He had loved her more than any of us, maybe including Maxine, had known. Losing her had destroyed him. Losing her had turned him into the gibbering wreck sitting on the other side of the door from me.

I was almost resigned to spending the night in the store; I didn't think he was going to let me out, maybe he didn't even remember that I was in there. I was sitting on the floor wondering which one of the terrible, compulsory novels I was going to use should nature call, when I heard a soft knock on the door. I stood up cautiously. Again came another soft knock. It was level with my face. It was Doug tapping his head on the door.

"Doug?"

He was mumbling something so I put my ear to the door again. He was saying, "I don't understand, I don't understand, I don't understand." It was so low I could barely make it out, but he kept repeating it over and over. The door slammed this time. I jumped back instinctively. It was at the same spot; he must have head-butted the door as hard as he could. Then the mumbling stopped. I heard the key unlocking the door. I stood there waiting for Doug to rip open the door and attack me, but he didn't. Had he calmed down? Had he left? Should I venture out there? I didn't relish spending the rest of the night in fear. If something was going to happen, let it happen now. I opened the door a crack and saw the tables and chairs had all been thrown to one corner of the room. I cautiously opened the door fully.

What I saw made my flesh crawl. Doug was standing at the front of the class with no clothes on. He had used the razor from Kawaji's shaving kit and attempted to shave off all of his hair. His scalp was cut and bleeding and large clumps of hair stuck out in places he had missed. His eyebrows were shaved and gashed as well; the blood was welling in his eye sockets causing his eyes to blink rapidly. His genitals were the most disturbing; there were several small cuts were he had shaved his pubic hair off, but his penis was cut deep and bleeding quite

100

badly. The inside of his legs had tracks of blood running to the ground were he stood in a small crimson pool. My stomach churned and vomit made it to my throat before sinking again. The taste of sick was in my mouth. I fought hard to stop it from coming again. This seemed scarier than seeing the creature because this was human. Doug was just a guy like me. He was fragile and his mind had crumbled and left him like this. It made me wonder what it would take to destroy my sanity.

His arm moved and my terrified gaze shifted to it. He still had the razor blade in his hand. He squeezed his lips into a pout and began making kissing sounds.

I had to say something. "Doug, put down the razor and let me call an ambulance."

He looked like he didn't even hear me. I took a step toward him and he raised the blade. I thought he was warning me to stay back so I stopped and put my hands up to show him I didn't want to hurt him. He brought the razor blade to his mouth and sliced his bottom lip in half. My body jerked as a spasm of revulsion moved through me. Blood was pouring out of his mouth and covering his chin and chest, but he didn't even move. It was like he didn't feel the pain. I had to stop him. The door opened and Taffy stood there with his broom.

"What is this?" he said, dropping his broom and stepping back.

"Call an ambulance," I shouted. He stood there looking at the red statue before him. "Now," I screamed. He ran off up the corridor.

"I don't understand," Doug mumbled. He raised the blade and stuck it into his chest. Before I could reach him he had cut a six-inch track where his heart was. I raced at him and pushed his hand to the side. The blade fell from his hand easily and he dropped to the ground, probably due to blood loss more than my overpowering skills. I dropped to my knees beside him and felt the blood on the floor seep through my trousers. I looked around for something to use as a bandage and spotted his clothes, neatly folded on Kawaji's desk. I grabbed his shirt and ripped it into pieces and held one to his chest and a bundle to his penis. They were the two wounds that were bleeding the worst.

Taffy came back shortly after and said the ambulance was coming. He stood and waited with me, but didn't offer to help. I don't suppose there was anything he could have done anyway. When we heard the sirens pulling into the playground he ran out to show them the way to the classroom. I was so relieved to see the paramedics taking over. They knew what to do. I was just applying pressure to the wound—that was the limit of my first aid knowledge. They strapped him to a gurney and actually ran him up the corridor. He had lost a lot of blood and they were concerned. My trousers were sticking to my legs and I couldn't wait to get home and get a shower. The police had come with the ambulance and a detective asked if I wanted to go and wash up. I looked down and, perhaps appropriately, I had blood on my hands.

I went to the toilets up the corridor and began washing my hands. The arms of my shirt and jumper were stained as well. I rolled up my sleeves and did the best I could. The detective knocked on the door and walked in.

"You OK?" he asked.

"I've had better days."

"Not recently you haven't," he answered.

I couldn't decide if he was being sympathetic or accusing me of something. "No, I suppose not." He stared at me silently as I dried my hands. I walked to the door and after sizing me up for a moment; he opened it and let me out.

He drove me home and spoke to my mum while I had a shower. When I came down, blissfully clean, he had left. I gave mum the bloodstained school uniform and she put them in the sink to soak. She sat down at the kitchen table and pulled out the chair opposite her. I sat down and faced her.

"I'm worried about you," she said, putting her hand on my knee.

I was worried about me, too, but I couldn't tell her everything that was going on. It was something I would have to deal with myself. "I'm OK, mum."

"But these things, horrible things, keep happening. Why is it happening to you? You're not involved with *people*."

I really didn't know what she meant and asked, "What *people?*"

She drew up her courage and said, "You don't have a problem like Gary, do you?"

Drugs. She thought I was getting muscled by drug-dealers. If only it were something so cut and dried. "No, mum, I'm not on drugs. It's just a few coincidences. I've been in the wrong place or fancied the wrong girl and things have just snowballed out of control. I think it's all over now." She smiled and hugged me. My mum hadn't hugged me since I was a kid. It felt good. I would keep my parents out of this from now on. They didn't need this hassle. I had told her it was all over so, as far as they were concerned, it would be.

"You haven't seen Gary, have you?" she asked.

I was confused. "How could I have seen Gary?"

Mum swallowed hard. "I had a call from his mum today asking if you'd seen him. I told her you hadn't. I told her you would have told me if you had. You would know if Gary asked you for help, that he needs the kind of help you can't give."

"So he's out of rehab?"

"He got out a few days ago and robbed a local shop and disappeared. Jennifer thought he might come to you for help."

I shook my head. This wasn't the Gary I knew, he was like some random baddie on TV. I never did hear from him, ever. He never came home to his parents again. I didn't grieve for him at the time because we all thought he would show up someday. He never did. He was lost forever, in more ways than one.

I couldn't help Gary, but I could help the other teenagers of Portstewart. I had to stop the creature and I had to do it soon, before someone else died. I wasn't going to wait around for it to attack someone else. I would find *it*. Let's see how it likes being on the receiving end.

3.

I was getting used to being an outcast at school. I think Emily even outranked me in the popularity stakes now, so she only spoke to me far from the gaze of others. I somehow managed to avoid Imogen Collins for the days after the incident with Doug. In the end she just made something up about me being suspected of being a drug user—she probably would have made up the same story if I had agreed to an interview. Luckily my mum and dad both knew as well as I did that she was a career liar and didn't even ask me if it was true.

I began going out at night. I told my parents I was going for walks to try to lose the weight I had put on from sitting around for almost two months eating chocolates and turkey dinners. I walked around the town, hoping I would get that feeling that it was close. Sometimes I walked down to the old boathouse where Emily had seen it. I carried my hunting knife. I had never been hunting in my life but when *Rambo: First Blood Part II* was released in 1985 everyone had bought one. I think they were called survival knives, they had the hollow handle which you screwed the compass off the top, and there was useful things like matches, string, a sharpening stone, a length of fishing line and a hook, a pencil, and two elastic bands. Quite how this stuff was supposed to save your life was always a bit of a mystery to me. I used to run around the trees close to my house with my face smudged with mud, using the knife to make arrows (that never flew) and loading them into a bow (that always broke). I had kept the knife when the fad had died and found it in my bottom drawer. I had sharpened the blade and now took it with me for protection on my nocturnal excursions. It was purely a means of defence; I took no pride in carrying it. OK, maybe a little, but I did look pretty cool with it strapped to my lower leg.

One night I was checking the old boathouse and decided to walk on up the beach. The sea looks menacing at night. I never understood people who swam at night, to me that seems like the creepiest thing ever, floating in a black void. You can't see what might be lurking under you. Maybe I just saw *Jaws* when I was too young and impressionable.

The moon was bright and the beach was surprisingly well lit. I had come a long way from the boathouse when I saw something in the distance. At first it was just a shape. Then I saw it turn and walk toward me. OK, Green Beret, this is what you trained for. I knelt down and slid the knife from its sheath. My heart was beating rapidly. The figure was getting closer, but still walking. Before I could even make out what it was, I knew it wasn't the creature. I could sense this thing's evil intent from miles away; if this were it, a couple of hundred yards away, I would know it. I bent down and returned the knife to its sheath and stood up. As I walked towards the figure, I noticed a limp. When I got close enough, I recognized immediately who it was.

"Toe-poke, is that you?" I asked.

"Yeah, who's that?" he replied suspiciously.

"It's Steve Norton. What are you doing out here?"

He reached me and stopped. He looked nervous and a little scared. "I just came out for a walk. What about you?"

"The same. Are you coming back to school soon? I think the football team's dying on its arse without you." I had no idea what the football team was doing but I had overheard that phrase earlier in the day.

He stood there considering me for a long time and then said, "There are a lot of things being said about you, Steve. There are a lot of rumours that don't make any sense."

I got the feeling a kicking was on its way. Maybe he was another admirer of Maxine's and was going to take out his frustration on me. Be diplomatic. "Things don't make sense because people don't have all the facts."

"You're out here looking for the same thing as me." He brought out his survival knife from the back of his jeans. I wondered if he was going to lunge. Could I make it to my knife in time? Keep him calm.

"And what's that, Toe-poke?"

He sized me up and replaced the knife. "It's about seven feet tall, covered in a hard black shell, and can make itself look like anyone." He looked at me for my response. My response was relief. Not only because he wasn't going to kick my ass, but also because he knew. Someone else knew. I was so relieved I didn't speak until he added, "Do you think I'm fucked in the head?"

"No," I answered quickly. "I just can't believe I found someone else who's seen it. We should compare notes."

"You've seen it, too?" He looked as relieved as me.

"Bet your ass I have. And so has Emily Matthews."

Toe-poke scrunched up his face. "I don't think I know her. Where did she see it?"

"Listen, it's too late to go into all this now. Let's meet up tomorrow and get the full story."

"OK, you could come to my house, it's close to the school, you even pass it on the cross-country run." We walked back down the beach and he explained exactly where his house was. We separated at the boathouse and I walked home feeling like I had the upper hand now. Three against one. It didn't stand a chance.

4.

Rob 'Toe-poke' Taylor was the school soccer star. He had earned his nickname by his extraordinary ability to hit the ball perfectly with the very toe of his boot and send it exactly on target into the net from half a field away. Most goalkeepers weren't expecting this and therefore our school had won the league for the past two years. I remember being bawled out by old Chestnutt for doing this very thing. Of course my shot did go off course by about a thousand miles, so maybe he had a point, but he yelled at me not to toe-poke the ball, for about ten minutes. Use the side of your foot and you will have less power but more control, that seemed to be his strategy, but when he saw what Rob could do (and how many games he won), old Chestnutt shut up and let him do his thing. I think it was even Chestnutt who gave him his nickname. I didn't really follow the football, but I had heard that Rob had been off with an injury. As I approached his house the next day, I wondered if the creature had injured him. I made sure I had my little tape recorder with me and walked up his driveway.

His dad opened the door. He looked tired and anxious and beckoned me into the hall. Their house seemed to be a shrine to all things football. I had heard that his mum and dad were divorced and she lived in the country with a milkman now. Toe-poke's trophies were on display in a large cabinet. He had a lot. On the wall was a framed letter that I wasn't close enough to read, but saw it was on official Manchester United headed paper. Toe-poke's dad lit a cigarette, as I looked at all the framed pictures, clippings and letters in the hall.

"Do you play, son?"

"They force us all to play at school, but I'm not that interested," I answered.

"Robbie's got a talent, but this injury…" He rubbed the bridge of his nose between his thumb and forefinger. He drew hard on his cig. This was obviously what had been causing him his sleepless nights. He wanted his boy to be a professional footballer and now Toe-poke's future was in doubt. "He has to rest up. You tell him that when you go up there. No more of these midnight walks; they'll do more harm than good in the long run." He ushered me up the stairs. I walked past him and gave him a reassuring nod. He walked into the living room mumbling to himself.

Toe-poke's room was what I expected. Mostly the posters on the walls were of footballers, but there were a couple of the girls from Baywatch, too. Football and sport magazines were stacked on his dresser. Various little flags, scarves and rosettes filled in the gaps. Toe-poke was lying on the bed with his right leg sitting on a couple of pillows. We tried to make small-talk to break the ice, but found that we had nothing in common. He was avoiding broaching the subject. Maybe he thought it sounded a little stupid in the cruel light of day.

"You think I'm not going to believe what you say, don't you?" I ventured.

He shrugged.

I decided to try to put him at ease and show him just how open my mind was by telling him about Justin Parke (later nicknamed Gearstick, get it?). I used to see Justin every summer when he would come to stay with his Granny Bess. Bess Parke lived further on up the same road as us, so she arranged for Justin and I to play together when he was staying with her. I never got to see inside the small cottage where Granny Bess lived, but I wish I had. According to Justin, it was an Aladdin's cave of everything a young boy could possibly want. Everything Gary or I mentioned to him, he had one at his Granny Bess's. Gary got the Star Wars AT-AT for his birthday—Justin had one stashed at his Granny Bess's. I got a Starsky and Hutch gun that you could load real caps into—Bess was packing one of those too. The year that skateboards were all the rage, Justin said his granny had got him one, too, although he never brought it out and no one ever saw it—like everything that was apparently stored at Granny Bess's.

It was one of the last summers that Justin ever came to stay with his gran, so I guess I was ten or eleven, that he took me aside one day after Gary had gone home for his tea. He said he had a secret to tell me, but he didn't know if he could trust me or not. I was intrigued and said he could trust me with anything. He said he would have to think about it and would decide whether or not to tell me when he was having his tea. He came back up to my house about six and we went out to the back garden. He was cagey at the start and jumpy. Finally, after I agreed not to laugh and not to tell anyone, he told me his secret. He leaned in close to me and told me he could fly. Suppressing a smile and remembering everything I had just promised him about having an open mind and not laughing, I said, "Cool, let's see you then." He then informed me that it wasn't as easy as that. He could only fly when it was dark. I asked if he would sneak out tonight and show me. He said he would; he felt like flying tonight anyway.

I watched TV that night as usual, but I kept glancing at the window, watching the sun creep slowly to the ground. There was a man on TV advertising bathroom fittings with great enthusiasm and I imagined him doing an advert for Granny Bess's.

So come on down to Granny Bess's, we've got everything down here! We've got every piece of Star Wars merchandise ever made, we've got The A-Team action figures and the van, we've got the Knight Rider car that really talks, we've got Action Man tanks, jeeps and helicopters. We've got video games that no one else has heard of, we've got magazines with naked women in them, we've got a video recorder and videos of films like Smokey and the Bandit. We've got BMX bikes, we've got guitars, we've got American footballs, we've got a copy of Iron Maiden's The Number of the Beast signed by the band and we've got a leather jacket with metal studs on it. In short, we've got everything that anyone ever told Justin they had. It's the bestest place on Earth. So come on down to Granny Bess's—you'll be amazed at what you see!

It made me laugh to think of the advert, but there was still doubt in my mind. Maybe he was telling the truth, implausible as it might be that an old woman kept all this stuff in her house and never let her only grandson take any of it outside, it was still possible. I went upstairs early and listened to some of *Bat out of Hell* until the pre-arranged time arrived, then I sneaked out the back door. We had arranged to meet at a field between Granny Bess's house and mine. As I walked there, I actually began to hope that he wasn't bullshitting because I really wanted to see this. I arrived first and waited for ages. I thought he wasn't going to show, then I saw him come plodding up the road. He passed me and nodded to me like I was a fan. He looked at the sky and proclaimed that it was a good night for it. He said he had a full costume and cape back at his Granny Bess's, but he hadn't bothered bringing it tonight. He turned to me and took me by the shoulders. "Are you sure you won't freak out when I fly?" he asked me solemnly.

He was going to do it. I was sure of it. I shook my head and told him I wouldn't be scared. He nodded at me and walked to the gate of the field. He climbed up the gate and perched himself on top of the large concrete gatepost. He raised his arms to the side and felt the wind direction and turned into it. "You have to wait for just the right moment," he said. I was so excited that I was going to see this amazing spectacle. Maybe it was something everyone can do but they just don't know it. Maybe Justin could teach me. Maybe I could fly in a costume and cape. He bent his legs slightly. He said it was going to be soon and that I shouldn't blink. I didn't want to blink. Suddenly he launched himself off the gatepost. He flew to the ground quickly and landed with a hard thump. I was confused. He walked back towards me with his head hung. He stopped before me and raised his head. "I hate it when I can't fly," he said and walked off.

Toe-poke laughed at the story. "You know for a minute there…"

"Yeah, you and me both," I said. He stopped laughing and nodded that he was ready to begin. I turned on the little tape recorder.

[I did rearrange this interview into chronological order because he kept forgetting things he should have told me first. All the words are Toe-poke's, I just edited it so you would understand it better.]

"Before I hit the big time with football," he began, "I was just a nobody that nobody ever noticed. The big thing happened when it was the end of school a couple of years back. It was near the end of term and there were so few of us in the last days before we broke for summer that they bundled us all together for PE—girls and all. We were going to play Basketball: shirts vs. skins. I think you were maybe there too—didn't Chestnutt throw you out for asking if Tracey McCullough could be in the skins team?"

I smiled. "That's right, I remember that day. That son of a bitch made me do laps of the tennis courts for two periods."

"Well," he continued, "I got picked for the skins team and we played the game and I didn't think too much more of it. There were girls giggling on the sidelines but girls giggle—it's what they do. I thought they were laughing because Marcus Tully was in the skins team—you know him, don't you? His mum and dad own a fish n' chip shop and I think the guy was weaned on batter. Anyway, during the game, Boggy Marsh kept running up to him and squeezing his tits and licking his nipples and shit like that and I thought that was what the girls were giggling about. I only found out afterwards that they were laughing because Mags [Margaret Towne] thought I had a great body and wanted to ask me out. It was like, totally out of the blue. I mean she was pretty high up the pecking order of the school and I was a nobody. A couple of days later one of her friends ran up to me and pressed a note in my hand and ran away giggling. The note said...I still have it, do you want to read it?"

"I don't know. Isn't it personal?" I asked.

"Oh aye, I suppose it is. Well, it was an invitation to meet her after school at the smokers' corner and talk. I didn't tell any of the guys about it because they would have come, too, and ruined it, and I thought Mags was really good-looking and wanted to see if I could get out with her.

110

"We talked that day for about fifteen minutes. It wasn't anything big, we talked about some films and music and she told me some gossip about some girls, nothing big. But it was enough. I was totally cracked on her from the start. She smoked a cigarette and I told her some stupid joke I'd heard that day. I was crapping it to be honest, but I hung in there. When she finished her cig she hung her head and asked me if I wanted to kiss. I said yes, probably too quickly to be cool, and moved close to her. There was some confusion about where to put my arms, but eventually I got them round her waist and she put hers around my neck and we kissed. I never told anyone this before, Steve, but it was my first real kiss…with the tongue, you know. I feel embarrassed telling you that, but I wanted to tell someone when it happened and I didn't. Well, I don't suppose you'll put it in a book or anything, will you, Steve? [Sorry, Toe-poke] She had a weird way of kissing, it was like, you know the way you roll your tongue, fold up the two sides? That's how she kissed. She unrolled it as she pushed it past my lips. It was nice. I wasn't quite sure what to do back, so I just waggled my tongue about a bit and hoped for the best. We walked round to the bus-stop, hand in hand, and I waited with her. Before she got on her bus she kissed me again in front of everyone. I couldn't help but smile.

"We met up every day for the next few weeks. She introduced me to Drew Dillon and we chatted about football and hung out a bit. He said I should come and try out for the team. It's more about being in with the right people than talent at school; you know that, don't you? It's like a little club and if they don't want you they'll find a way to get you out. But with Drew's "OK" I was in, and I impressed them enough to get myself on the sub bench. After getting on for a few games, I was soon on the team full time. Mags was happy about that. It was weird, but we didn't seem to do all the kind of boyfriend/girlfriend stuff that you see on TV. We never even saw each other outside school. I was dying to. I'm sure you can imagine. After weeks of ball control I wanted to go for a goal. She always had an excuse, but when we finally did go out together she was quiet and wouldn't even let me kiss her. I think the sexy temptress she played at school was all an act. She was scared stiff to be alone with me, without an audience."

"I always thought you two were the happy, golden couple," I said.

"No. I think I was in love with her, but she just wanted me so she would have a football player boyfriend. I can see that now, but I couldn't see it then. We stayed together, at school anyway, and it wasn't like I was getting *nothing*, if you know what I mean, so I stayed with her. Last year was amazing. We won the league, I was voted MVP, I had a trial for Manchester United and I had Mags. It was like I had everything. Anyway, June last year, school finishes and Mags says she's going to stay with relatives in Scotland for the summer, so I signed up for summer soccer school. It was supposed to start in mid July so I thought I'd use the month I had to get myself in shape.

"I went to stay with my mum in Portballintrae; she lives in a little housing estate in the middle of nowhere so you can run for miles around. There was a downside though, I had fallen out with this guy, Graham Norris, the summer before. I can't even remember what the fight was about, but we knocked the shit out of each other over something. I didn't mind that I wouldn't be hanging out with him because I was going to use that summer for training and didn't have time for surfing and fishing and the like. So my mum mentions to me one night at dinner that a stray dog had wandered into the estate. It's the sort of place where everyone knows everything that's going on. She said Graham had taken the stray in and was looking after it. It was a skinny Red Setter and he had named it Rusty. That was as much as I knew about it. Every day I went for a run in the morning, a bike ride in the afternoon and I did weights at night. One evening I arrived back from my bike ride and the whole street was abuzz. There were police cars and all the neighbours were out on the pavement gawping at Graham's house. I went in and asked my mum what was going on. She told me that Graham and one of his friends had gone fishing and taken the dog with them. While they were fishing the dog started eating grass and throwing up. It kept doing this for a long time. Graham and his friend decided that the dog was dying so they tied its legs together and threw it in the river. I couldn't believe what my mum was saying. They threw it in while it was still alive. It gave me the shivers just thinking about it. The dog had washed up down river and someone had called the water bailiff, who in turn had phoned the police and given them the name and address on the dog's newly purchased collar. The media were all over the story an hour later and I went to my bedroom to do weights. It was a fuckin' creepy thing to happen, though. That night I kept thinking about that dog trying to swim with its legs tied together. I gave up trying to sleep after a while and thought I would write a poem to Mags. I still have it; do you want to see it?"

"OK," I said and immediately started thinking of nice things to say about it. I doubted it was going to be on a par with Yeats. I suddenly thought of that movie with Steve Martin where he does the "Oh, pointy birds, oh, pointy, pointy, Anoint my head, anointy, nointy" poem. Toe-poke rummaged in his bedside cabinet and produced a piece of notepaper. He paused and then handed it to me.

"It's not very good. I'm sure you've written better," he warned.

"I don't write poems...and I don't know much about them." I said, hoping this would tell him that my opinion doesn't really mean shit. I read the poem aloud (for the benefit of the tape).

Look beyond my shell
See what is intangible
Holding me to you

I couldn't believe it. "Toe-poke, this is a haiku." OK, it didn't contain a reference to nature or the seasons or any of the other haiku rules, but he had the correct number of syllables in the 5-7-5 structure, and he had done it on instinct, which I think is pretty impressive.

"What's that, shite? I know it doesn't rhyme."

"No, it's a form of Japanese poetry. Did you get a book on this or something?"

"No."

"Then how did you write a haiku?"

"I don't know. It just sounded right. What do you think of it?"

"It's really good," I answered with genuine admiration. I handed the paper back to him and he smiled. "Getting back to the story, you couldn't sleep so you got up and wrote this poem. Then what happened?"

"After I wrote my high-koo, I just sat and read it a few times. It made me feel close to her. I wanted to ring her, but it was very late, or very early I should say. I went and looked out the window across the fields. Dawn wasn't far away. Then she was just there. Mags was standing in the back garden wearing red lingerie and high heels. I flung open the window and asked her what she was doing here. She said she came back for me. She said she loved me. She said she wanted to make love to me. She took off the red bra and hung it over her shoulder. Her boobs were fantastic! She nodded at the garage and turned and walked towards it. She stopped at the door and waved me to follow her inside. It wasn't that I had to decide whether or not to go, I was just dumbfounded, I couldn't believe this was really happening. I jumped out the window—it was a bungalow—and ran to the garage. I had seen a film on the TV and it said that the biggest mistake teenage boys make is being awkward and clumsy. Women prefer a strong, confident man who just grabs them and they melt in his arms—that was the theory anyway. I flung open the garage door. I could see her about ten feet in front of me in the dark. She had her back to me but she knew I was there. She took the bra off her shoulder and dangled it in her hand and then let it drop. She looked over her shoulder and gave me a little smile then turned away again. She slid her red lace knickers down her legs slowly. I couldn't stand it anymore. I raced at her and grabbed her around the waist. But I didn't feel skin. It was hard, like the shell of a crab or something. I pushed it forward and stepped back to the door. She turned, still looking like Mags in every perfect, naked detail. Its face changed. It still looked like Mags but it was full of hate or evil or something. I don't know why I flicked on the light switch at the garage door, but I did. Then I saw what it really was."

"And what was it?" I asked impatiently, hoping he knew what we were dealing with.

"It was a big, scary, armour-plated monster thing."

Of course it was.

"So I grabbed the spade and swung at it. I clipped it on the shoulder and it howled. I don't mind telling you, I was getting a little scared at this point so I ran back across the garden to my bedroom window. It came out slowly and stared at me. The dawn was coming and it flickered between the shape of Mags and its real shape until the light finally won. Its camouflage was gone and I saw its eyes. Horrible, dead eyes. And its face...I swear, man, I mean, I know it doesn't have a face that can show expressions, but at that moment all I could think of was Charles Bronson saying, "This ain't over." Then it ran off towards the sea."

"You think it meant to come back for you?"

Toe-poke nodded solemnly. "And it did come back for me, Steve."

5.

We paused for a moment as I turned the tape over. Toe-poke was shifting on his bed, trying to get into a more comfortable position. His leg did look fairly painful. I hoped he would be able to play football again. He was a nice guy. Not the sort of guy I would have been friendly with (if it hadn't been for our shared experience), but he was a decent guy. The tape started again and I asked him, "You ready to go on?"

He nodded and continued. "I rang Mags the next morning in Scotland. I knew the thing outside hadn't been her, but I wanted to hear her voice and know that she was far away from here and that thing. She told me she had met some charismatic older man, a writer called Willie, and she had fallen in love with him and wanted to stay in Edinburgh with him. I was a bit annoyed about that...and a bit upset. I stayed up that night hoping that thing would come back. At one point I even went out and sat in the middle of the garden waiting for it. It didn't show up that night. I don't know what I would have done if it had.

"Life went on. I trained a lot. I kept pretty much to myself for the next couple of weeks then my mum said there was a dance in the parish hall and I should go. I didn't want to go but my mum seemed to want me out of the house so I didn't fight her. She dropped me off at the parish centre that night about eight and I went in. It was actually pretty good craic. It was an Under 18 dance, so there was no booze at it, but there were girls, and I even danced with one. Then I started to think about Mags and nothing would do but going home and phoning her. I was sure I could talk her into taking me back because I loved her like no one else would. The problem was I had only been out for two and a half hours and my mum wasn't expecting me back for another hour and a half. I decided to walk home, that way I would get a bit of exercise and kill some time.

"I knew I was being followed as soon as I left the parish hall. The night was still fairly light and as I glanced back, I saw there were three of them. I quickened my pace—not scared, just walking quickly. The three of them broke into a sprint and were on me before I could run. They threw me to the ground and I saw who it was: Skid Millar, Mike Millar and Spud Wallace."

"Is Spud Wallace Debbie's brother?" I asked.

"Yeah. I think she got the looks and the brains in that family. So Skid Millar gets on top of me and pins my arms with his knees. I thought this was just another random beat-up— these guys usually don't need a reason but they actually *did* have a reason this time. Skid says to me, 'You killed my dog, you bastard. Now we're gonna kick the living fuck out of you.' I tried to tell him that if he's talking about the Red Setter, I never even laid eyes on it. It turned out that Skid had lost the dog, or it had ran away, while he was getting pissed at a beach party a few weeks before. He came close to my face and I could smell the beer on his breath. He said I was a fuckin' liar and that it had said in the newspaper that I was the one who did it. I told him it fuckin' didn't. It was then that he got really pissed and laid into me. I managed to wriggle free after a few digs and I got up and ran. The three of them ran after me. I had been running these country roads every day and I knew the quickest way home was cross-country. I jumped the hedge and legged it across the field. The three of them came after me but they couldn't keep up. I was leaving them for dead. I got to the edge of the field and jumped the fence without missing a beat. I looked back and saw the three of them staggering along like they were dying, but Skid was determined to catch me. I paced myself across the next field because I knew I was in no real danger of being caught. I got near to the other side and saw a stile where I could get across without slowing. I ran and put my foot on it to jump over. My foot slid on moss. My leg slipped off and caught between the rungs of the stile and I fell back hard. I felt my knee twist and pain shot up my leg. I gritted my teeth and growled as I lay there with my leg still stuck in the stile. I looked behind and didn't see Skid or the others but I wasn't sure he'd given up. I pulled my leg out and got to my feet. It was really sore.

"I sort of half ran/ half hopped home. My knee had swollen up quite a bit by the time I got there and my mum decided to take me to A&E. She got dressed—I don't know why she was undressed, she was supposed to pick me up later—and as she got ready, I rummaged through the over-stuffed magazine rack by the sofa and found the paper with the dog story in it. There was my name in black and white, right under Imogen Collins's picture—she had written the story. There was no mention of Graham Norris—he had given her my name instead of his. Bastard. My mum came back into the living room and saw me looking at the article. She said she had seen the mistake and had complained to the paper. They had corrected it the following week. My mum showed me that week's paper. The correction was about an inch square on page 38 next to the supermarket coupons. Where, obviously, the right people hadn't seen it.

"I was in hospital a couple of days while they poked and prodded, strapped and bandaged. When I got back to my mum's all I could do was lie in bed. I even needed help getting to the toilet. I was about as low as I could get.

"Then that thing came back. It was a hot night so my mum had left the window open. It came about two in the morning. Every time I shifted in bed the pain would wake me, so I wasn't getting much sleep. I hopped to the window and I saw it standing there in the garden, without a mask—as it really was. I stared it down and said, "Come on then." I wanted it to come and get me. I didn't care. I didn't care about anything. It looked at me for a moment and then it walked away. I haven't seen it since."

"You were sour," I said.

Toe-poke gave a confused look.

"My theory (he didn't have to know it was actually Emily's) is that it feeds on hope. When everything was going well for you; Mags and the football thing, you were irresistible to it—you were exploding with hope. When you lost it all the creature didn't find you desirable anymore."

"How do you think it feeds on hope, like a straw in the ear or something?"

A straw in the ear? He wasn't kidding either. "I don't know, like I said it's just a theory, but it has yet to be disproved and your story just gives it more credence. Finish up your story, or is that everything?"

Toe-poke thought for a second. "Well, that was summer soccer school fucked. My knee is still bad after seven months; I still can't walk on it for any length of time without pain. You might have seen the letter downstairs from Man U asking me to come back and try out again. My dad keeps stalling them, but its over, I know it is. I'll never be able to play at a pro level no matter what drugs, therapies or operations they do on me. I knew that almost from the moment it happened. I have had a few...feelings, I suppose you would call them. Like I should be somewhere. You can't resist these feelings. Even when I was in really bad pain, I've still crawled along the landing and down the stairs. I would've crawled down the street to who-knows-where if my dad hadn't held me back. He thinks I'm cracking up. I'm not, am I, Steve?"

I shook my head. "No, you're not. Do you remember when you had these visions?"

"The last one was late December. [That was it killing Maxine.]

"One in November. [After the party, when Emily and I had attacked it before it could hurt anyone.]

"One, early October. [Trying to get Emily, disguised as Billy.]

118

"One, late September. [Masquerading as Maxine to get me.]

"One, early September. [Where it all began, Johnny Knox.]

"And the first one in August."

A shiver went up my spine. "August? Are you sure?"

"Yeah, why?"

Who the hell did it get in August?

Chapter VI - The St. Valentine's Day Massacre

The main thing is to have hope. Everyone should have hope on St. Valentine's Day. Even if you are unbelievably ugly, someone may take pity on you.

Imogen Collins, *Ask Imogen*

- February, 1990 -

1.

There was another victim. One I had no knowledge of. I pondered for quite a while on how this could be possible. No one was missing from school without explanation. No one else had died or there would have been the same furore that surrounded Johnny and Maxine's deaths. It could have attacked someone and they repelled it like Toe-poke and I managed to do, but no one had come forward about the poster. Maybe they never saw its true face. Maybe it never stepped into the light. Maybe they thought they dreamed or hallucinated it. There were a lot of maybes, but the one that I decided was worth checking out was: Maybe the pupil it got was only transferring to our school this year. That would have meant his or her family wouldn't know anyone around here so the grapevine might have missed a runaway. Also, a tempestuous teenager would be liable to run back to his established friends if he didn't like the look of his new hometown. It was the only possibility that I thought warranted investigation. The creature's victim could just as easily have been some drifter and I might never find out who it was.

Emily and I arranged to meet at dinnertime. She would keep lookout while I let myself into the nurse's office and had a look at the transfer records for this year. All incoming pupils had to either undergo a health appraisal or submit a doctor's report on their current condition so that the school would know what to do in an emergency. The corridor outside the nurse's office was quiet when we arrived. Most pupils go outside at dinnertime, no matter what the weather is like. That day was overcast and raining lightly. I tried the door and it was open. I gave Emily the nod and went inside. There was a little waiting area with a few chairs and a door into the nurse's treatment room. I tried the door. I had decided that if the nurse were in there, I would say I had a headache and ask for a couple of paracetamol. I edged in and ventured a quiet, "Hello." It was empty. I rushed in and closed the door behind me. You may think this is highly unlikely, but they really never did lock doors at our school. The drugs were locked up in a cupboard, but apart from that it was all open. There was a padded bench covered in a drape—for pupils to lie on if they were faint I imagine, and a chair. I looked around all the posters about cutting out fried foods and brushing your teeth regularly, and found the filing cabinet. I tried the top drawer—it was locked! I pulled open the top drawer on the nurse's desk and saw the keys. These security precautions really were top-notch.

I opened the cabinet and found the Transfers 89-90 file and started flicking through it. I really didn't know what I was looking for; perhaps a big red stamp on one of the files saying HE DIDN'T SHOW UP! I perused the files as quickly as I could and found nothing. I put the file back and saw another in at the back with the word DECEASED on the cover. I took it out slowly and opened it. I saw a picture of Maxine staring back at me and remembered how beautiful she was. Her file and the details of the police report were there, too. Behind her file was Johnny's. Behind his was the file of someone called Thomas Welch. He had died in 1973 in some kind of fishing boat accident. The files were in chronological order; there were no deaths of students between Thomas Welch and Johnny Knox.

The outer door rumbled and I heard the nurse's voice. I dropped the file back where it came from and slammed the drawer closed. I locked it and threw the keys into the desk drawer and slammed it. I looked about and dived under the bench and pulled the drape down to cover me. I peeked through a crack and saw the nurse come in with Shirley Tully, brother of Marcus, and heir to Tully's Fish 'n' Chip shop. Shirley was a big girl and when she climbed onto the bench above me I feared it would give way.

"Now," said the nurse, "what's the problem, Shirley? Is it your bad week?"

Oh, Christ! I was going to be trapped here listening to all manner of things that would just humanize women. That, I didn't need. I was quite happy to think of them as these perfect curvy beings that gave out pleasure and had no bodily functions that didn't end with a pleasured scream.

"No," Shirley muttered through a Kleenex. "Oh, God," she screamed and started crying.

"Now, now, then," the nurse said in a caring but strong tone. "You have to tell me what's wrong before I can help you. And I *can* help you. Whatever it is, I can help."

Yeah, like she helped Emily by telling the whole school that she was a slut-bag. I'd forgotten that. I had a bone to pick with this nurse. I wished I'd remembered earlier and I would have broken something in her office.

Shirley got herself under control. "I think...I might...I think I'm pregnant!" she started blubbing again.

Shirley Tully, pregnant? I wonder what kind of Golf Club points you get for a mission like that.

"Now, you're not the first girl to think she's pregnant, so don't get hysterical," the nurse said. "That little Emily Matthews for one."

What the fuck ever happened to patient confidentiality?

"I knew she was up to something," Shirley said. "She's been hanging around with that Steve Norton." The nurse hummed her agreement.

Hey, hey, I've got a rep.

Shirley whispered, "He's a rare boy that Norton. God knows what he makes her do."

Hey!

The nurse got back to the situation in hand. "Now, I think the first thing we should do is make sure you *are* pregnant."

This is going to involve peeing.

"How late are you?" the nurse asked.

I looked at my watch; dinnertime wasn't even close to being over.

Shirley blubbed, "Nearly six hours."

I shook my watch and listened for the ticking.

"Six hours?"

"Yes," Shirley answered. "But I'm very regular."

Are they talking about bowel movements now?

"When was the last time you had sex?"

Shirley giggled. "I've never had sex."

The nurse (and I) took a moment to puzzle over that one before she asked, "So, how do you think you could be pregnant?"

"Well," Shirley started, "the last time we were at the swimming baths some of the other girls told me about the other way that you can get pregnant. Debbie Wallace told me that it happened to a friend of her cousin's. This girl was in the swimming pool and she was a good-looking girl and some boy saw her in her swimming suit and he...you know, did a come. And the sperm swam across the swimming pool and inside the girl's swimming costume and she got pregnant."

How I managed not to erupt with laughter is still a mystery.

"And I think it might have happened to me yesterday in the swimming pool."

The nurse (whose expression I wish I could have seen) cleared her throat and said, "Debbie has been telling you tall tales. You cannot get pregnant that way." She helped Shirley down off the bench and ushered her to the door.

As they went out the door, I heard Shirley ask, "Are you *really* sure?"

The door closed and I allowed myself a laugh. It had been so long since I had sincerely laughed at anything. It felt good.

I waited five minutes and then sneaked outside. I found Emily a little way up the corridor. "What happened to the lookout?"

"Sorry," she mumbled. "Billy wanted to talk to me about Valentine's."

"Well, I hope you told him where he could stick his card," I said in a louder tone than I intended.

"Yes," she answered quickly.

I didn't completely believe her.

2.

The atmosphere at school was playful. As the 14th drew closer, the giggling that had been gone since Maxine's death, returned. It was comforting to see things getting back to normal but it was also a little distressing that people could forget so quickly. I would never forget her. I doubted that Doug Winters would ever forget her either. Since his breakdown, when he had cut himself in front of me, they had moved him to Sycamore Acres—the local loony bin. Word had it that he had suffered a total mental collapse and was not expected to ever come back to school. I wondered if it *was* just a breakdown or had the creature done something to him when they were alone in that bedroom. Had it somehow made him hurt himself? Was it controlling his actions? Did it intend to use him to get to me?

I didn't know what to do about Valentine's Day. I was still really attracted to Emily, but I didn't know what was going on with her and Billy. The last thing I needed at this point was another knock-back. Besides, if I did ask her and she said no, what would that do to our monster-hunt? She would get weird, as girls are wont to do in these situations. I felt like the best thing was to try to ignore the whole day. The school didn't organize a dance for Valentine's, so the students had planned a party in an old abandoned house in the country. The owners had not been gone long so it hadn't had time to fall into disrepair. The members of the Golf Club were organizing the whole thing. Someone was allocated to bring candles, someone else to bring a boom-box and a lot of spare batteries. The place had a working fireplace and a huge log pile outside, so that would take care of the heating. Everyone knew to bring their own drink and some of the girls were decorating it with the kind of unnecessary streamers, posters and soft furnishings that only matter to girls. Although all the pupils knew about this, even the ostracized like me, it was a strict secret from anyone even vaguely resembling a grown-up, because the party-goers would have to break into the house, and that was just the teensiest bit illegal. It didn't take a genius to work out the Golf Club's motivations for this party, but no one seemed to care. This was going to be *the* party event of the year.

I had taken to doing my homework on my dinner-break because no one spoke to me and even Emily was suspiciously absent from the playground or her little sanctuary. Doing my homework at school also meant I had time to go out at night and look for the creature. The night before Valentine's, I checked the beach last on my little circuit of the town. I stopped, sat down and looked out at the ocean. The sea always calms me, I don't know why. I was in a contemplative mood. Well, that was the official line—the truth was, the thought of being alone on Valentine's was getting me down.

Last Valentine's had been a great day. I remember that morning before we went to school, Gary and I were standing outside the card shop laughing and daring each other to go in and get a card. Eventually we tossed a coin and I had to go in. I grabbed two cards quickly and approached the counter while it was quiet, and paid for them. I ran outside with my face red from embarrassment and Gary had teased me and laughed some more. We went to the nearest bus shelter and scribbled our heartfelt sentiments while balancing the cards on our knees. We sneaked looks at each other's card and plagiarized anything that might melt the heart of our intended Valentine. We decided to leave the inside of the cards completely anonymous—no recipient's name or sender's name—so it wasn't until we put the cards in their envelopes, licked the gum and sealed them, that we looked at each other and said, "So, who are you going to send it to?" I had thought of sending it to Maxine Dawson, but she always got zillions of cards and no one stood a chance anyway, so I opted for a girl who had caught my eye called Rachel Cole. We all know how that ended. Gary was cagey at first, but finally told me he was going to send his to Tracey McCullough—she of the huge chest. I called him a dirty dog and laughed. He waited a moment then said that wasn't why he was sending her it. He said he had seen her recently at break time, sitting in the cloakrooms crying. She had just broken up with someone. He said he was sending it to her just to brighten her mood and give her a little hope. He made me promise that I would never tell her that he had sent it. That was an unexpected thing for Gary to do. I thought I knew him so well, but that selfless gesture made me look at him in a new light. It also made me feel a bit lousy that my card wasn't intended for a higher purpose. My purpose was the old-fashioned one of getting jiggy with Rachel Cole.

I watched the sun sink into the sea and then wandered home. I felt despondent and couldn't believe it when I turned the last corner before my house, only to see Rachel sitting on the wall at the front of my house. I dropped down and slid my hunting knife out and grabbed my torch. I ran to her with the knife in one hand and the torch in the other. As I got near enough, I shone the beam on her. She was still Rachel. I stopped running and lowered the torch and knife.

"Do you need the knife? Our break-up wasn't that bad was it?" she asked.

"Yes it was. But I'll put it away anyway." I put the knife back and walked over and sat down on the wall next to her.

She was really here. The relief that she was back overcame all the hurt feelings. Hollywood had been right all along. I should have thought of it before, of course the script was going to prolong the heartache until the optimum time—the night before Valentine's—that would make it even more poignant. That would have them crying in their popcorn.

I had to be casual, though. "You lost?"

"No," she said and took a deep breath. "I needed to talk to you."

I believe there's a big Humble Pie cooling on the window ledge; shall I cut you a slice? Stay cool. Make her work for it. "Well talk, *Moonlighting* is on soon."

"It's about Tony and I…"

"Is he that old guy?" I interrupted.

"He is my boyfriend, yes."

I think you mean *was* your boyfriend, don't you?

"He's asked me to marry him."

Oh, you didn't mean *was*.

"I wanted to tell you first."

"Why did you want to tell me first?" I shouted. I couldn't believe how quickly I got angry. I was furious.

"Because when we were together we weren't just boyfriend and girlfriend, we were best friends as well. I don't know whether to accept the proposal or not. I know I love him but…"

"Rachel, I don't want to fuckin' hear this!" She looked at me as if I had just grown a second head, and who knows, maybe I had. If I had, the second head was definitely doing the talking. "You ripped my fuckin' heart out and now you come here to tell me that this pervert wants to marry you. Don't you think that it's slightly creepy that this guy is over twice your age? Doesn't it seem weird to you at all that when this guy was locked in his bathroom discovering the second function of his dick, you weren't even conceived?"

"You don't even know him. He's nothing of the sort. He's very religious, actually." She was clearly agitated by my appraisal of her fiancé.

"And what about college? Are you going to chuck that idea in to play Susie Homemaker with this pervert?"

"I thought I could talk to you. I thought you would understand. I thought you loved me once."

"Ditto." Ha! Check and mate.

Rachel stomped off down the road. I wasn't done making her feel shitty yet though. I needed one more zinger. A parting shot that would stick in her mind. I shouted, "I *do* fuckin' love you. Did! I mean did! I *did* fuckin' love you." She didn't turn around. "Shit," I whispered under my breath. I hated knowing what a Freudian slip was.

3.

St. Valentine's Day was nauseating. Stuffed animals of all shapes and sizes infested the school. They looked like rodents to me. Lemmings. I wished they would all go and jump off a cliff and die like the promises they represented.

Rachel wasn't at school. I thought the old guy had probably taken her to an afternoon tea dance or something. Fuck, I really hated him. Emily was nowhere to be found either. The teachers indulged the pupils. Very little work got done. There were various charity things going on. Miss Cocktease was selling kisses for £1 a time in aid of the African Famine. I didn't even go for one of them. On any normal day I would have jumped at the chance. Even though I doubted there would be any tongue action and the kiss would be little more

127

than a peck, just to be that close to her, maybe her breasts would even press against you as she kissed. Like I said, on a normal day it was the kind of thing I fantasized about, but today my head was in bits and I didn't want to be cheered up. I wallowed in my misery.

I was sitting in Careers class flipping through a pamphlet called Writing For A Living, when a 1st Year came in and gave a note to Mr Sloan. A few girls were up at his desk cooing around him and asking how he met his wife. He parted two of the girls and shouted back to me, "Steve, there's a phone call for you at the office."

I walked to the office wondering what else could go wrong. I really felt like I was being crushed beneath the weight of the world. I got to the office and the secretary handed me the phone.

"Hello." I said in a lacklustre voice that wasn't borrowed from the brat-pack this time.

"Steve? It's Pauline Cole. Rachel's been in an accident. She's at the hospital. She's been asking for you." Her voice was shaking, like a child trying to speak through tears.

I was numb. I sent Rachel home in the dark knowing what was out there. I had been so obsessed with making her feel bad that I didn't stop to think that she was in danger. It was my fault. I wanted to drop to the ground and never get up again. I was responsible for this.

"Steve? Are you there? Will you come to the hospital?"

The first time I tried to speak nothing came out. I cleared my throat and said, "I'll come now, Mrs Cole."

I hung up and walked out of the office. I walked to the Careers room and lifted my bag. I walked to the door. Mr Sloan stopped me. "Wait there, Steve. Where are you going?"

"I have to go," I answered. I wasn't being evasive, I just couldn't straighten my thoughts to tell him what had happened.

"Do you have permission from the principal?"

I tried to push past him. All I could think of was Rachel lying in a hospital bed.

"If you walk out of here without showing me a note from the principal, I'll have to report you to Mr Reese. Is that what you want, Steve?"

"Do what you like." I pushed him aside and walked down the corridor and out of the school.

The hospital was in Coleraine so I had to get a bus. Every second it took to get there I thought Rachel might have died. In the Hollywood movie, I would arrive just as she said her last words: "I love you" or "Remember me" or "Rosebud." Hollywood had been letting me down a lot recently and I feared I might never see her again. Might never hear her voice. Might never get to apologize.

When I got to Coleraine Hospital, I stood at the front entrance trying to decipher the map and guess which ward Rachel might be in. A porter saw my confusion and approached me asking if he could help. I said her name and burst out crying. All the emotion that had been building for months came flooding out. The porter took me to some seats and went off to find out where she was. By the time he came back, I had managed to stop crying. He told me where she was, but I think he knew that I wasn't going to be able to follow his complex directions, so he walked with me to the ward.

Coleraine Hospital was built around an old workhouse from the last century. The workhouse itself was too small a building to serve as a hospital so over the years it had been extended and built around in all directions. This may have solved a space problem for the staff, but it made negotiating the hospital fairly impossible to someone who had never been there before.

Rachel's mum was waiting outside a private room when we got there. I thanked the porter and approached Mrs Cole. "What happened?" I asked.

"We think someone attacked her while she was out walking last night. She's not making a lot of sense at the moment—the drugs I suppose, but she kept saying your name so I thought you should be here."

It suddenly occurred to me: the creature had disguised itself as me and attacked her. Her cries for me weren't for her lost love; they were to incriminate her attacker. Oh God, this was going to get me into even deeper shit. The only chance I had was to speak to Rachel first and tell her everything and hope she believed me. "Can I see her?" I asked her mum timidly.

She nodded. There were tears in her eyes. She looked tired, too; she had probably been here all night. I gave her arm a little squeeze as I passed. I'd seen this done in the movies a lot, but it felt strangely false when I did it in the real world.

Rachel was hooked up to a lot of terrifying machines. Her face was so cut and bruised, the girl I knew was barely recognizable. I began to wonder if the creature *had* done this. It hadn't done anything like this before. She had been beaten savagely, but somehow I knew the creature hadn't done it. I'm not sure if that made me feel better or worse.

I sat with her for a long time. When she finally woke up, she was weak. It was such an effort for her to do the smallest things. She turned her head to me and I saw how much it hurt. She opened her mouth to talk and I saw the splits in her lip breaking open again, the blood glistening in the light. I almost didn't want her to speak because I thought it would hurt her too much.

"Come to gloat?" She asked hoarsely.

"What? No! What do you mean?"

"He just gets jealous sometimes. When I told him I was out seeing you, he just lost his..." she coughed and I looked for water. I brought a glass and a straw to her mouth and she sipped gently. I think she saw the concern in my eyes maybe even the tears. Tears ran down her face. We just looked at each other. I didn't know what to say; I thought anything I said would start her crying and I couldn't bear to see that. We just sat there in a comfortable silence for a while and then I said I would go and get her mum. "Will you come again?" she asked in little more than a whisper.

"Of course I will; I love you, don't I?" Tears ran down her swollen cheeks again as she smiled. I saw her mum outside and told her she was awake. Mrs Cole rushed past me and into the room. I wandered around the hospital until I found an exit and then found a bench and sat down. Tony had hit her. Tony had beaten her. Tony had pounded her face over and over until she looked like that. I was raging. I think I sat down there hoping I would see him drive in to the car park. I looked in every car as it passed. My fists were aching to hit him. I wanted to hurt him. It was lucky he didn't show up because I really don't think I could have stopped hitting him if I had started. At least Rachel was awake now and would tell the police what had happened. Tony would be punished, not in the way I would have liked, but he would be punished.

I watched the orange sun disappear into the horizon and I knew where my fury could get an outlet. I had been planning to crash the Valentine's party. Not because of amorous intentions, but because all those teenagers hoping to get laid would attract the creature. It should be impossible for it to resist. It would almost certainly show up and I would be waiting to release my wrath on it.

4.

The party was just starting to get lively when I got there. There were a lot of cars parked inside the driveway. They had taken the precaution of putting cardboard over all the windows so that the lights couldn't be seen from the road. I got some strange looks walking into the house still wearing my school uniform. Everyone was dressed to impress. There were very few people downstairs and I realised from the bass thumping the ceiling that the main party was happening on the first floor. The house was huge; a mansion, and there was a large ballroom on the first floor. I looked in and saw the candles all around the walls and couples slow dancing and kissing, even though Bon Jovi's Born To Be My Baby was blasting from the speakers. Everyone looked happy and safe. I left and walked downstairs. I found an abandoned bottle of beer and took it to the outside steps, where I sat down. I felt like a security guard on the front gate and I suppose that's what I was.

I saw everyone who came in and they all looked at me as if to say "What the hell are *you* doing here?" I ignored the looks, the sneers and even the occasional kick and remained at my post—until Emily walked up the steps. She was dressed in a very short skirt, black stockings and a tight top. She was wearing too much make-up as well. She looked like someone else had dressed her for the night. She saw my disapproval but didn't comment on it.

She sat next to me. "You on duty?"

I nodded. "What are you doing here?"

"I'm on duty, too, but I'm with the plain clothes branch," she said smiling.

"I don't think there's anything plain about *those* clothes." That was actually supposed to come out as a flirty little joke but it didn't, and we both knew it.

"Well," she said, standing up. "I'll go inside and I'll check back with you later."

It was a real drag to be there. I was in no mood to be around happy people. I felt miserable and I selfishly wanted everyone else to feel miserable, too. Of course, it could save their lives if they were miserable, but I never thought of that at the time.

I had just found another orphan beer and returned to the steps, when I was picked up from behind by Spud Wallace and Danny Wells. They took a shoulder each and dragged me off to the side of the house. At first I was apologizing, thinking it was their beer that I had been drinking, but then they threw me against the wall and said that Billy Love wanted me to stay away from his woman.

"Emily and I are just friends. If Billy..." Spud punched me hard on the cheek and my head flew back and bounced off the wall. I dropped to the ground. The whole world was spinning. I felt sick. Danny ran in and kicked me in the stomach. Spud rushed to his side and started throwing punches at me wherever he saw a space. I was getting punched and kicked from every direction. I couldn't muster the energy to hit back. I don't know how long they kept hitting after I lost consciousness.

I woke up face down in the grass with the coppery taste of blood in my mouth. I hurt all over, but there was something else as well. A pull. *The* pull. The creature was close. I dragged myself to my feet and staggered round to the front of the house. Blood was running into my eyes and I rubbed it away. The steps were blurry, but I climbed them and ran into the house. I could smell it at once. Fire. Something was on fire. I ran through to the kitchen and saw the creature. It was holding Joey Turner off the ground. Its claws were wrapped around his throat and there were tentacles coming out of the top of its wrists. The tentacles were going into his ears and they were pulsing. Feeding. Feeding on Joey. A straw in the ear.

I glanced around quickly and saw a knife. I grabbed it and charged the beast. With my first lunge I cut the tentacle going to Joey's left ear. It howled and dropped Joey. He looked dead. The creature ran at me and slammed me back out to the hall. The hall was now filled with smoke. It was coming down the stairs. The fire was upstairs. The creature swiped at me with its huge claw and I leapt back. I needed something with a longer reach. I grabbed an umbrella from the stand at the bottom of the stairs and swung at it. I got scared. I had no weapons and I was still very shaky on my feet. The creature seemed like it was prepared to tolerate the discomfort of touching me, if it meant I would die. I swung and got it a good whack on the side of the head. It pounced forward and grabbed me around the throat and lifted me off the ground. The umbrella fell from my hand. I grabbed its hands and tried to release their grip. I tried to kick at it but the reach of its arms was greater than the reach of my legs. I looked up and saw the orange light behind the smoke. Doesn't anyone see that fire? Get out, and notice this fucking thing as you go! I struggled and looked down for something I could use. I saw the tentacle emerging from its left wrist. The right one was bleeding that horrible yellow blood. The left tentacle crept towards my ear like a snake. I kicked and swung wildly. It had no effect. I looked into its black eyes for a sign of emotion; it had none. It was going to kill me.

I heard a noise from above. Finally someone had noticed the fire. I looked up. Emily climbed over the banister and leapt from the first floor onto the creature. She caught its head on the way down and tried to break its neck with the force, but just bent it backwards. It dropped me and I fell to the floor and tried to get some air back into my lungs. I only allowed myself a few seconds. I got up and stood before it. My courage and rage were back. Emily had made me strong. I lifted the

133

umbrella again and stabbed it in the stomach. The shell didn't break and I charged it again. Emily was hanging on trying to snap its neck. It was having trouble dealing with both of us. I stabbed it again and again until the shell cracked slightly. It flailed wildly at me, trying to keep me from hitting the wound again.

"Keep at it, Emily! Kill this fucking thing once and for all," I screamed.

The creature reached behind and grabbed Emily and pulled at her little thin arms until her grip gave way. The creature swung her round to the front and threw her at me. Emily hit me and we both went skidding across the polished wooden floor. We hit the far wall hard. I was winded and exhausted. I hoped the creature would use this chance to escape, but it came towards us. It growled like a rabid dog.

Emily was lying on top of me. "Come on, Emily. We have to get up." She didn't move. "Emily?" She may have looked like a little waif, but I was finding it hard to get her off me. I wriggled with my remaining strength, trying to shake her off gently. She moved a little. The creature stopped and looked down at us. I looked around for anything within arm's reach. There was nothing. The creature bent down, then dropped to the ground on its side, revealing Toe-poke standing behind it. He was balancing on his good leg and holding the crutch he had just cold-copped the beast with. I saw the fire behind him. The creature got up groggily. Toe-poke helped get Emily off me. We both kept our eyes on the beast. It wasn't waiting around for the three of us to take it on. It ran for the front door and disappeared.

"Get Emily outside," I shouted. She was starting to come round and leaned on Toe-poke as he leaned on her. I ran to the stairs and flew up, them despite my fatigue. The fire was getting out of control. I kicked open the doors to the ballroom and looked inside.

They were all dead.

I ran in and checked the one closest to the door. It was Ken Armstrong—the biggest Golf Club loser of all time. He was lying next to a girl I didn't know. Neither of them had a mark on them but they were both dead. I looked around at everyone. There were no signs of life anywhere. At least twenty, maybe thirty, dead bodies lay on the dance floor. My heart sank into my stomach.

In the distance I heard sirens. Someone had seen the smoke and called the fire brigade. I came out of the ballroom and saw the flames burning out of control in the rooms beyond. There was no one I could save. I ran down the stairs and found Emily and Toe-poke outside.

"Come on, across the fields," I said, coughing up the smoke I had inhaled.

"Aren't we going to wait for the police?" asked Toe-poke.

"No. I can't explain being at yet another crime scene. Besides, there's nothing we can do to help…they're all dead in there." Emily walked to me and threw her arms around me. She was crying on my chest. The sirens were getting closer. We all hobbled quickly over to the back fence. We crossed two fields and then stopped; content we were far enough away not to be seen.

We rested under a tree in the corner of the field. The sky was glowing as the flames consumed the house in the distance. We listened to the sounds of the firemen screaming at each other. Maybe we should have stayed behind and told them that there was no one left alive in there. I worried about the firemen risking their lives to try to rescue the people inside. There was no one to rescue. The world had changed. I knew school would never be the same after this. Considering how subdued it had been after Maxine's death, I couldn't imagine how this many deaths would affect everyone.

I sat down and Emily sat on my knee and wrapped her arms around me. We were silent for a long time. None of us spoke because none of us knew what to say. It was a noise from the bushes that finally drew our attention from the fire. We all stood, poised for action, and tried to ascertain where the noise had come from.

"It's probably just an animal," Toe-poke said.

Emily and I remained quiet, still trying to get a fix on its location.

"You don't think it came after us, do you?" Toe-poke added nervously.

135

"No," I said quietly, "we would all feel it. This is something else."

The noise took off quickly and, without thinking, I ran in the same direction. I could see something ahead of me in the darkness and it was human. I fought through the trees and hedges slowly. I was beaten and tired, so, he/ she/ it, evaded me easily. As I walked back to Emily and Toe-poke, I could have sworn I saw someone at the other end of the field, ducking through a hole in the hedge. It was so dark and it happened so fast, I couldn't be sure who or what it was. I made it back to my pensive companions and told them that I had lost whoever it was. They didn't seem to mind. I think we had all had enough excitement and fighting for one night. The glow in the distance was shrinking—the firefighters were getting it under control.

"Let's get out of here," I said wearily. Emily put her arm around me and we walked off together, with Toe-poke beside me.

Just before we separated from Toe-poke, he asked me, "Who do you think that was?"

I had been thinking about it and I offered my theory. "I think that was 'August'."

5.

Emily and I walked on together. Neither of us had discussed it, but I assumed I was walking her home. She was quiet. She was more shaken than I had expected. Maybe the reality of all those dead bodies had sunk in a little quicker with her. I hadn't accepted it yet. I hadn't allowed myself to until she was home and safe. That was my only concern. I would mourn the others later.

We walked up the path to Emily's house and she said, "I hope you know you're staying with me tonight." It was such a direct statement and yet it seemed full of fragility and fear. She kept her head down, as she had done on most of the walk home, and I answered that I wouldn't leave her alone.

When we got inside, the domesticity suddenly jolted me into realising that my parents had no idea where I was. They had last seen me when I got on the bus this morning. No doubt they would have heard about the fire by now and my mum would be in the panic to end all panics. I used the phone in the hall after I had thought up a plausible story. I told my mum about Rachel and that I gone to see her after school and lost track of time, and then on the way home, I had run into Emily who had been there when the fire had broken out at the party. So I had now come back with her and was going to stay here with her until her dad came home in the morning. She was angry but also relieved that I had called. She arranged that my dad would come and pick me up in the morning and, after a lot of reassuring that I was OK and that Emily didn't need to go to the hospital, she hung up.

While I was on the phone Emily had showered and changed into her pyjamas. She looked at me and suggested I have a shower, too. I said I was OK.

"Have you seen yourself?" She asked. She led me to a full-length mirror in her bedroom and I saw how bad I looked. My hair was matted with dried blood. My face was covered in cuts and bruises. Blood, mud and soot practically covered me from head to toe. "You're not going to convince your mum looking like that. Give me your clothes and you go and have a shower."

Amazingly, a sexual scenario didn't appear in my head. She gave me one of her dad's bathrobes and I gave her my school uniform. I kept my socks and boxer shorts—she didn't need to see or smell them. I had a long, hot shower and felt much better for it. When I looked in the bathroom mirror, I was more like the guy I remembered. I put my boxers back on under the bathrobe and went out to the kitchen where Emily had made tea. Emily smoked one cigarette after another. Her nerves were still frayed, but being home had calmed her down a lot.

After the tea we went into her bedroom. We sat on the bed and listened to the banal whining of New Kids On The Block, a band that, she informed me, was going to be bigger than The Beatles. We were both exhausted and eventually got comfortable lying next to each other on the bed. She was curled in close to me with her hand across my chest. I hoped her eyes were closed because my bathrobe was beginning to stir. Her hair smelt so good. I had to get my mind off my rising problem. I tried to remember the names of the Seven Dwarfs to distract my thoughts. There was Sleepy, Grumpy, Bashful, Dopey, Happy…it was seven wasn't it? Who the hell were the other two? Horny? Lustful? No, Snow White wouldn't have put up with that shit. I wondered if I had ever actually read the story and seriously began to doubt that there were seven. Maybe the two I'm forgetting had small parts in the story and weren't that important. Snoozy? Was that one? Or was that just Sleepy on a good day? No, it was Sneezy, not Snoozy. I fell asleep still trying to figure out the last dwarf.

When I woke the next morning Emily was gone and I could smell a cooked breakfast. I smiled. I had just spent the night in a girl's bed. It made me feel like a bit of a grown-up. I was quite proud of myself, until I sat up and saw a baseball cap sitting on my crotch. Oh shit. There had been an 'up periscope' without the captain's order. She must have woken up and saw it and put a cap over it. Oh God! I lifted the cap and looked at it. It was one of those cheeky caps you get in holiday resorts that say things like Kiss Me Quick and Hug Me, I'm Irish. This one had a picture of Ireland and said Come On, Enjoy The Craic. Oh, the irony.

My clothes had been dried, ironed and left on a chair by the door. I got dressed and reluctantly made my way to the kitchen. Emily was dressed in her school uniform and ran around officiously making the breakfast. I was surprised that she planned to go to school; I didn't intend to. The radio was reporting on the fire when I sat down at the table. We said very little as we listened to the radio. We ate breakfast and my embarrassment was forgotten as I heard the newscaster say that twenty-six bodies had been recovered from the house.

"Twenty-six," Emily whispered. "That's why it was so strong. That's why it could bear us touching it." The radio moved to an interview conducted late last night. We both knew the voice at once.

Billy Love said: "I was here with my girlfriend, but we had a fight and I left. I don't know if she's still in there or not. God, I hope she got out. This is unbelievable. Everyone was having a good time and then this. I can't believe it."

Emily was breathing hard and got up from the table. She ran to the phone and I heard her ask for Billy when it was answered. I walked to the other end of the kitchen and put my plate in the sink. I looked out the window at the sunrise and tried to tune out the sound of her phone conversation. I saw my dad's car coming up the road and was thankful I could leave. I didn't wish that Billy had been killed; I just didn't think he would ever change and would no doubt use this as an excuse to treat her like shit yet again.

I walked past Emily in the hall and nodded that I was going. She told Billy to hang on and covered the mouth-piece. "Are you going to school?" she asked.

"Not if I can get out of it," I answered.

"I might not go either. I'll call you later." She returned to her call with Billy and I let myself out.

My dad drove home slowly, probably hoping I would tell him what had happened to my face. When we were getting close to home and he asked me directly the most I managed was, "I was just trying to…" A lump rose in my throat and I feared I was going to start crying. He didn't press. He pulled up outside the house and left the car running. I realised he was going to go on to work when he left me off. I felt I needed to finish my sentence and tried again. "I was just trying to…" I choked again. He nodded that it didn't matter. I got out of the car and walked in through the kitchen door.

My mum looked at me and immediately asked, "What happened to your face?"

Then I did cry.

6.

It was Sunday and I decided to go and see Rachel before church. My dad took me to the hospital and said he would go and get a cup of tea while I visited her. I had bought a bunch of flowers from a petrol station on the way there—don't ask me what kind. I approached her room and got very nervous. I didn't know what she had told the police or her parents. She had come to see me that night and I had sent her away. It wouldn't be unimaginable that I would be blamed in some way or another.

Luckily she was alone when I got there. She was awake and seemed in brighter spirits. "I was pretending to sleep because I thought you were that creepy old doc," she said.

Doc! That was the last dwarf.

We exchanged pleasantries and then I sat down and looked at her like I used to look at her; like a boyfriend. I asked her what had happened with the police.

She was uncomfortable. She answered slowly. "We decided not to involve the police. Everyone thought it would be best."

It was then I noticed the ring on the third finger of her left hand. I couldn't believe it. It made no sense. "What? Are you still going to marry him after what he did to you?"

"He promised me it would never happen again. He just got angry. I do love him so I think I should give him another chance."

If someone had put my brain in a blender and then put it back in my head the world would probably be making as much sense as it was now. For the next half hour I argued with her. I pleaded with her. I begged her. She still wanted to wear that ring. She thought she was such a grown-up, by looking at the situation rationally and objectively. He had done a number on her head. She was totally brainwashed into thinking that beating the living daylights out of her was excusable. Our debate gradually grew angrier and became quite nasty. I just wanted her to be safe. I left in a very overly dramatic manner saying, "This room is nice. You should book it now, no doubt you'll need it again."

Outside in the corridor, I ran into Rachel's mum and, still fuming, barked my objections again at her. "How can you let this go on after what he did to her?"

"It was just a little squabble that got out of hand. They're in love. These things happen." Mrs Cole was a nice-enough woman but she wasn't the sharpest tool in the box. She liked soppy romance novels and weepy films, and undoubtedly believed that this little obstacle made their love even more special. Still, I couldn't believe that when it came to her daughter's safety she was being so flippant. She was a very religious woman and Rachel had said that Tony was religious, that was obviously his way in, and so he probably had to do no more than say an insincere prayer before Rachel's mum to get her back on side. There was no point in talking to Mrs Cole anymore. She just thought I was jealous and she seemed proud that her little girl had found a man and left behind boys like me. Her head was filled with dream wedding scenarios and no amount of blood on the wedding dress would distract her. I walked away without saying anything more to her.

I didn't feel like I was ready to see my dad right away, so I sat on the steps in one of the stairwells and composed myself. I always thought I had a fairly good handle on how the world worked, but now I realised that I knew nothing for sure. Well, I did know one thing: *Women will disappoint you.* I looked at my watch and thought I should go and find my dad if we were going to make it to church. Just before I got up I thought I would say a prayer. I was going to ask to keep Rachel safe and ask for Tony to get what he deserved, but I thought that if God was omniscient and had a masterplan, there seemed to be little point. But He had given mankind free will so how did that fit into the equation? I decided there would be no harm in restating what mattered to me, so I rhymed off the names of everyone close to me and asked to keep them safe. I said He could do what He liked with Tony.

I found my dad and we drove to church without speaking. The silences between us were becoming more common. It was just because he wouldn't understand and I wanted to keep him and my mum as uninvolved as possible. We got to church and took our seat. I was always bored in church. Sometimes I looked around at the other members of the congregation and I reckoned, on a good day, maybe ten of them weren't just as fed up as I was. The difference was they tried to hide it and I didn't. My usual way of killing time was to drop a sweet wrapper on the floor at the start of the service and spend the rest of the time trying to move it using the Jedi mind trick. I really thought I could nail it, given enough time and thought. Every so often we had to get up and sing, and I would open my mouth in time to the words. That Sunday the minister said he had a change to the service. It was great when this happened— a change to the routine. I raised my head and left my thoughts of pulling a lightsabre out of the ice with only my mind aside for a moment. I looked at the pulpit and saw the minister welcome Tony, our guest speaker.

Every word Tony said burned me up inside. From his great Christian work setting up a children's youth club in Belfast, to his generous contribution to the church's stained-glass window appeal, to his recent engagement to one of our local girls. The faces in the congregation were grinning inanely. Another brainwash complete. I wished I was in a football stand and could bounce a bottle off his head anonymously. At the end, the minister gave a touching tribute to the teenagers killed in the fire and announced the funeral times for those who belonged to our church.

When the service ended, Tony was shaking hands with everyone at he door. I stood on the stairs and watched him for a while. I already had a pretty good idea of who he was and as I watched him, I knew my initial estimation of him wasn't wrong. The way he was Jack-the-lad with the men, quiet and polite with the women, and the way his eyes lingered just a little too long on some of the teenage girls. My dad shook his hand and welcomed him to the parish, then it was my turn. He didn't recognize me as the guy who had walked in on him shagging Rachel at her party. He extended his hand and I let it hang in the air and looked him in the eyes.

"What's the matter, young fella?" he asked, more for the benefit of those around him than me. "Maybe you don't do handshakes. Maybe you want to lay on five, eh?" He smiled at everyone around him and they smiled at how in touch he was with the young generation.

"I've just been to see Rachel," I said coldly.

His face dropped and he was instantly panicked about anyone discovering his true identity. He quickly reapplied his smile and put his hand on my back and pushed me forward as he stretched to shake the hand of the man behind me.

We sat at the dinner table that day and my dad recounted to my mum the highlights of the church service. I picked through my food as I thought about everything. I thought about the twenty-six funerals this week. I thought about how unbearable school was going to be. I thought of Emily setting herself up for another fall with Billy. I thought of Rachel being pummelled by Tony in the future. I thought about Tony and his cleaner than clean image. I thought of approaching the minister and telling him the truth about Tony, but I didn't think he would listen to me. I didn't tell my parents either, even though they would have listened to me. Nothing was going right. Nothing made sense. I stood up from the dinner table after my dessert and said, "I'm never going to church again." My mum and dad were gob-smacked and wondered where this had come from. I told them I didn't think anyone was listening.

Chapter VII - Sanity's Edge

Everyone always says Hitchcock was the master of suspense, but I don't really like his films. Why does he always keep you waiting so long before something happens?

At The Movies, Imogen Collins

- March, 1990 -

1.

School was a functional place now. In the weeks following the fire, classes had become sombre and restrained. It was partly because all the most popular and charismatic people weren't there to brighten our days, and partly because the remaining pupils didn't want to be disrespectful to their memory. Even practical jokes and teasing seemed to be gone. No one was in the mood to have frivolous fun. Everyone had grown up quickly and saw just how cruel life could be. Some people weren't coping well. When faced with their own mortality and the fragility of life some pupils had crumbled under the stress.

Emily and Billy's reconciliation lasted almost a fortnight. Long enough for them to hold hands at gravesides and for Billy to have his wicked way a few more times, then he broke up with her. He told her it was because he was in the running to win the Golf Club's prize and having a steady girlfriend would mean forfeiting his stake. Emily saw where his priorities lay.

Rachel and I hadn't spoken since the hospital, but I was told that wedding preparations were well underway. I saw her occasionally at school but she never made eye contact with me. She looked ashamed. On some level she must have known that her relationship wasn't the healthiest. The other girls made a fuss of her ring and clucked endlessly about what flowers, colour-schemes and music would be used in the ceremony. I think they were all excited about a wedding, but few thought about the marriage. To be grounded so early in life was never going to make Rachel happy. I was surprised she didn't see that.

It was just after a period in the library listening to this ignorant chatter that Taffy shouted at me from down the corridor. He was always ragging on us for dropping litter or marking the walls or floor—I think he took the mantle of caretaker a little too seriously. He hollered my name again and waved me to come to him. I was in no mood to be led out to the football field to lift a stray crisp packet that his forensics team had somehow linked to me. I made eye contact with him and smiled, then I raised my middle finger and mouthed the words "Fuck off." His face dropped but he kept staring at me. I turned and walked away.

I had started spending all my break-times in the cloakrooms, making sure all my homework was done so that I would have my evening free to search for the creature. Sometimes Emily joined me. We were both sitting there trying to get through our Physics homework when Spud Wallace and Danny Wells came in and kicked the books from our hands. Since they had beaten me up outside the party they had been giving me dirty looks that implied worse was to come. Not that I wished them dead but there did seem to be something very unfair that they had left after our altercation that night. They hadn't gone back into the house where the fire or the creature would have got them, but other, more innocent people, *had* died that night. There was something really wrong if these two losers, who were destined for jail anyway, were allowed to live and people like Anne Porter or Ken Armstrong, who might have grown up to be something useful, were in the ground. There was something wrong with the masterplan. They hassled us for a while, trying to provoke a fight, but Emily and I weren't biting. Petty high school insults just didn't carry the same weight anymore. Even Emily, who was so fragile and self-conscious of what everyone said, ignored them as they called her "two-timing slut" and other highly original and accurate slurs. Eventually they left, happy that they had fulfilled their daily quota of moronic aggravation.

"Am I ever going to hear the end of my fling with Billy Love?" she asked as she picked up her books.

"Not if you keep going back to him," I answered. I knew she probably wanted to hear something more positive and supportive, but Billy and her really bugged me. I didn't understand why she kept going back to him.

"He's the only guy that ever lov…said he loved me. Except Colin next door, remember him?" I nodded. "I think it was one day when I was about eight or nine, Colin came running to the door and started knocking very impatiently. I was having dinner with my dad. It was summer and I was trying to eat it fast so I could go outside again. My dad answered the door and brought Colin in to wait for me. I asked him what he had to tell me. He said it was a surprise. He stood there like he was on hot coals as I threw my dinner in me. My dad tried to embarrass him and said, 'Are you Emily's boyfriend?' and Colin came back straight away and said 'Yes, I love her. Two other boys at school said they loved her, too, but I pushed them down on the grass.' He said it so seriously, but my dad roared with laughter.

"When I finished my dinner we went outside and he dragged me round to the back of my house saying I was never going to believe it. He pointed across the back field at a rainbow and said, 'Look how close it is!' It really did look close; like it was only a field or two away. Colin said we had to go before anyone else realised how close it was, so we could get the pot of gold at the end of it. He said it was very close to the Campbell farm and if they saw it, they would take the gold for themselves. I told him we had to hurry, then. The two of us set off walking across the fields. We didn't seem to be getting any closer, so we started running until we couldn't run anymore, then we walked again. We walked all afternoon. Dear knows how many miles. Things were a lot simpler in those days. Colin eventually had to convince me to turn around and go back. I might have walked forever. I guess that's who I am." The bell rang and she lifted her bag.

I didn't know what to say to her. It was a story that was obviously very close to her heart and I didn't want to blurt out, "Billy just calls you when he's desperate for a shag." I said nothing. She smiled and walked off to her next class.

That night I was preparing to go out on my usual circuit of the town when a car pulled into the driveway. It was Brian Winters, Doug's brother. He got out of the car and sat on the bonnet. He lit a cigarette while he waited. I didn't know what this was about, it seemed like some kind of John Wayne posture and I half-expected him to yell, "I'm calling you out." I walked out cautiously. He didn't move from the car. I walked over to him and leaned against the car. I waited until he was ready to speak.

"Doug's not getting any better," he finally said.

I didn't know what to say to that so I stayed silent.

"Doesn't even recognize my mum or dad. Only recognizes me sometimes. It's driving my parents nuts." He took a long draw on his cigarette. I could see tears in his eyes. He took a deep breath and continued. "But he does remember you. How do you figure that? The doctors say you're what he talks about most. Half the time he's saying he wants to kill you and the other half he's saying he has to talk to you—that it's very important that he talks to you. What do you think he means by that?"

"I don't know, Brian."

"I'm on my way to see him. I wondered if you might come with me and see if he talks to you." I nodded to Brian and he flicked away his cigarette immediately.

Sycamore Acres was on the far side of Ballymoney. It had been built in 1903 to house the worst of the criminally insane. The institute had been full to capacity in its opening years, when people were considered crazy if they held a different religious belief other than Christianity or had homosexual inclinations. Our history teacher had even told us—off the record—that parents who caught their kids masturbating had sent them to these places because they thought there was something wrong with them. In these more enlightened times it didn't have quite as many inmates—someone must have decided long ago that instead of imprisoning wankers they could train them as PE teachers. It had received its nickname a few years ago when a trend emerged among convicted terrorists to claim Temporary Insanity to get a lighter sentence. After the first of these cases was successful, everyone thought it was the soft option. It was packed to capacity again and the locals, who all knew the scam, renamed it Sick-of-more Fakers. The inmates had got more than they bargained for in 1987 when there were a lot of deaths and some scandal about the doctors conducting illegal experiments on the patients. I can't remember the details of it, but I'm sure someone will write a book about it someday.

There were two huge iron gates at the entrance and trees lined the driveway on both sides for the half-mile stretch to the building. The building was typical horror-movie fare; dark, gothic architecture, gargoyles, bars on the windows, etc. All it needed to complete the illusion would be thunder and lightning crashing through a rainstorm. This night was calm, but the building was still daunting. It towered high above and looked down on us like we were insignificant.

The inside was no better. I expected a place like this to be impeccably clean and gleaming white. The paint on the walls was flaking off and the bile-green colour suggested that the paint was at least thirty years old. Brian signed us in as I looked around the corridors for an impending attack from some serial killer who was out for a stroll. There were none—must have been nap-time. Brian led me down the corridor to Doug's room.

There was a man sitting on a chair outside the room. I don't know if he was a nurse or a guard, but he was dressed in white and had the keys that unlocked Doug's door. It was a padded cell. Doug sat against the back wall on the floor facing the door. He had his knees drawn up to his chest. I could see he was wearing a straightjacket. His hair had grown back a little. His face was scarred and had new cuts as well—I supposed that was why he was in the straightjacket; he looked like he had been clawing at his face. One of his eyes was badly bloodshot, probably from a poke or scratch.

Luckily I had my little tape-recorder on me and I started recording. He stayed where he was and started talking. This was what I could make out from the tape.

"So, so, so. He sees. Not what *you* see. Inside. Hurting now, naughty of you. Going to have to pay for that. Don't know the price, but maybe you can barter. Barter. Make a deal. A deal with the devil? A deal with the devil. There's too much and she didn't know. It was me, you see, me but not me. And I never told anyone that. No, but I wouldn't, couldn't and that's what happened, you see? It only makes sense when you know. You only see when you look. It wasn't supposed to…Steve Norton.

Seeking me and seeking it. Hide and seek. Run, hide, little one. Nowhere to hide. Not anymore. Inside. In here, Steve Norton. Steve Norton is nice. Harmless. Just a crush. Just a harmless crush. Nice really. But will Steve Norton see it through?"

He screamed and got to his feet. He charged me and pinned me to the wall. Brian was trying to calm him down and pull him back. Doug's face was only an inch from mine and he screamed in my face. He was in pain. It looked like he was hurting inside his head.

Doug whispered slowly, as if it was an effort to release each word, "You have to find it. Stop it. Go to The Source...all of..." He screamed again.

"Where?" I asked impatiently. "Where is the source? Where does it come from? Where does it sleep?"

He screamed and his knees folded below him. "The Source," he screamed. Brian had even stepped back at this stage, scared of what his brother might do next. The guard outside heard the commotion and unlocked the door. Doug jumped up and charged at him. The guard held his ground and Doug's attack was deflected and his head slammed into the doorframe. Doug fell backwards and started blinking rapidly as fresh blood trickled down his forehead. A doctor was called and Brian and I were ushered out of the room.

When we walked back down to the reception desk, Imogen Collins was standing waiting for us. Brian was angry and shouted, "What the fuck are you doing here?"

"I wanted to talk to Steven after he had seen your brother," she replied, placidly.

"How did you know I was here?" I asked. When the woman at reception quickly got up and busied herself elsewhere, we knew how Imogen Collins had found out. "What do you want, Imogen?" I was pissed off, too. I had had enough of this bitch for one lifetime.

"I want to talk to you about what it feels like to see Douglas. I think it would help the family and other people who have been through similar..."

"Aw, shut the fuck up," I shouted. "I don't believe that for a minute. Besides, what's the point of interviewing me when you just make it up anyway?"

149

She considered me for a moment. She looked furious and that she was swallowing the fury slowly. She quickly stepped forward, grabbed my arm and led me into an office opposite. She pushed me inside and slammed the door behind us. The office was empty. I don't know if she had arranged it that way, more likely she had just stormed into the nearest office without asking anyone. "OK, let's cut the fuckin' shit, you little bastard. I know I've fucked you over in the past but when you grow up a little bit you'll realise that's how the world works. People want a happy ending and if they don't get a happy ending, they want someone to blame. This time it was you. Well boo-fuckin'-hoo. You'll get over it." Her face was burning red. "I'm writing this book about survivor guilt and all you have to do is give me a couple of fuckin' quotes and I'll fill in the blanks. This book is my nest egg. That fuckin' weather girl, Tracey-Ann, talentless fuck, is after my job and it's only a matter of time before she gets it. I can't last much longer on TV. What age would you say I am? Go on, what age?"

She looked in her mid-forties. "I don't know, fifty-six?"

"I'm not fuckin' fifty-six, you cheeky wee shite. Look, are you going to give me a few quotes for this book or not? There might be a few quid in it for you."

"No thanks," I said and walked to the door and opened it.

She slammed her hand on the door and closed it again. "You've been getting in trouble a lot recently, haven't you? You think about my offer some more, because if you decline and I have to do another report on you, I'll fuckin' crucify you. The stupid bastards that watch my report will drive you out of town. You think about *that.*" She pulled the door open and stomped off down the corridor.

I told Brian what she had asked me to do and told him to warn the family in case she approached other people. By the time we got to the car park, the wicked witch had flown. I tried to put Imogen Collins out of my mind; she was the least of my worries. I was totally freaked-out by what Doug had become. Brian was quiet, the sadness evident in his demeanour. We hardly spoke as he drove me home. As we got close to Portstewart I asked him to drop me at the beach instead of my house. He didn't ask why. He didn't say OK. He just dropped me where I asked and drove away. It was one thing that seeing me hadn't helped Doug, but it was another that I had made him worse. I don't know if he blamed me for that or himself.

2.

Little did I know that the night still held a few surprises. I walked around to the old boathouse and saw someone standing outside on the beach, looking out to sea. I thought it might be Toe-poke at first, but as I got closer I saw he wasn't tall enough. Closer still and I realised it was Taffy, the school caretaker. I was tempted to turn around, not wanting a lecture from the old duffer about disrespecting him earlier that day, but then he turned and saw me. He watched as I walked towards him. I kept my head down and tried to walk past him as quickly as I could. When he realised I wasn't going to stop he spoke.

"I wanted to talk to you today."

I stopped walking and reluctantly turned to him. "Yeah, sorry. I've got a lot of things on my mind. I didn't need to be chastised about litter."

"I don't give a shit about litter. I know you've got things on your mind. Big, black scary monsters killing your schoolfriends." I was shocked and it obviously showed on my face. "Yes, that's right, I know what's going on. An old git like me can know things. Damn kids think they know everything. Do you even know what it is that you're up against?" I shook my head. "See? Fuckin' clueless. If you hadn't been such an ignorant wee shite, I would have told you today." He looked me up and down. "If you think you can bear to listen to someone as old as me, I'll tell you now." He walked up to the boathouse and opened the front door with a key.

"Is this yours?" I had never thought about who owned the old boathouse. I thought it had been abandoned years ago.

"Sure is. And don't think I don't know that you kids come in here and get up to no good. Little bastards." He settled himself in an old rocking chair that was thick with dust and beckoned me inside. I closed the door and sat on a pile of tarpaulin. Taffy took a silver flask from his pocket and took a swig. His skin was lightly tanned and weather-beaten. His eyes

151

were so small there was only a tiny difference when they were open and when they were closed. His hair was grey and slicked back to cover a bald spot. Still, he looked strong and I'm sure if we got onto the subject he would have told me that back in his day they had to *work* for a living. I took my tape recorder out and started recording.

"It attacked you in August, didn't it?" I asked, confident I had found my missing link.

"No," he said irritably. "You gonna let me tell this or not?"

"Sorry. Go ahead."

Taffy rummaged in his pockets and produced a pouch of tobacco. He rolled a cigarette almost without looking and lit it. When he had got a few puffs into his lungs he began.

"Back in seventy-three, I was working as a fisherman, after I got turned down by the civil service, which was just because I didn't know anyone who could put a word in for me. My brother and I had sunk all our money into buying a boat, The Argo, in seventy-one and she was just starting to turn a profit. But seventy-three was a bad year: storms, bad weather and the like. We were finding it hard to get the boat out on the water, let alone catch any fish. So when we got a spell of good weather in June we hired all the hands we could to help. The good weather lasted for the guts of a month. We knew it was going to break soon and we knew it would be bad when it did. It was a Friday. We both looked at the sky that morning and didn't know what to do. Matt—that's my brother—said he didn't think we should risk it. The stretch we were fishing was way out at sea and he was scared about us getting caught in a storm. I convinced him to go. I told him that another day fishing that stretch would leave us OK for the rest of the year. We wouldn't make a profit, but we might break even with one more good day. Matt had given the hired hands their final cheque the day before so when we decided to go out one last time we couldn't get anyone."

Taffy's eyes were starting to glass over. I never thought a tough old seadog like him would cry. He took a few quick drags and finished his cig and stubbed it out. I think he was trying to distract me from looking at him until he had composed himself. He must have succeeded because he didn't let the tears escape.

Taffy cleared his throat and continued. "So that's when I came up with the idea that Matt should get his son, Tommy, to help, and the three of us could manage."

"Wait a minute," I interrupted. "What was his full name?"

"Tommy...I mean Thomas Welch." Tears welled again in the old man's eyes. Thomas Welch—the other deceased kid from the school files—was Taffy's nephew. Killed in some kind of fishing accident. Now I understood the tears.

Taffy started rolling another cig as he went on. "He'd helped us a few times over the summer, but he didn't want to come that day. I think he had arranged to spend the day with his sweetheart. But Matt and I guilted him into coming. The sky was uncertain as we launched. The day could have gone either way at that point. We got to our usual spot after a couple of hours, but the fish weren't biting. Maybe they knew the storm was coming. After a few hours we only had half a dozen fish between us. Matt and I were determined not to come home empty handed so we moved on. The sky was starting to darken even though it was only about four in the afternoon. The clouds looked meaner than a rabid guard dog. We should have turned around then, but Matt said he knew somewhere we could definitely score a huge catch. He gave the boat full throttle. Tommy and I sat in the back. Tommy was sketching the sky. He was always drawing. He was real good, too. It's a damn shame. He packed up his drawing things when the rain started. It wasn't too bad to start with. We put on our slickers and thought we could ride it out. Then the wind picked up. Matt kept going for another half-hour or so, then he realised that this little fishing boat was never going to be able to stand up to the storm that was coming. He turned around and tried to head back, but the boat was getting thrown off course. Waves were crashing on our port side, almost tipping the boat. It was all we could do to hang on. Then the engine flooded and we were adrift. Matt and I tried to fix it, but there was no hope. The waves were hitting constantly and the boat was being spun like a bug down a sinkhole. All we could do was weigh anchor, batten down the hatches, and try to ride it out.

"It was a long night. The boy talked. He was scared and I think it helped to take his mind off things. He told us about this girl of his. She was one of the Harper twins. They were the bad family in the town back in seventy-three, that was before the bad families outnumbered the good ones. Fuckin' civil servants relocating the scum of the Earth to my town. Anyway, I believe the twins were called Daisy and Sarah. Everyone knew their names because they had been in the papers when they sneaked into the kitchen of the school canteen and put dog shit in all the food. It was a protest over them not getting free dinners as I recall. Their dad was a real waste of space. They lived on Cretan Dicte Drive and I swear I think their old man was allergic to work. Matt and I offered him a job on the boat at a time and he said he had a sure winner in a horse race and wouldn't need to work anymore. Asshole. Needless to say, his horse didn't come in—I think he was on the dole his whole life. Tommy saw something in that girl, Daisy, though. The two of them hit it off and...well, who knows what might have happened had things been different. He talked about her all night as the storm raged outside. None of us got much sleep but in the morning the sea had calmed a little. The storm wasn't over, in fact the worst was yet to come, but we needed to use the lull to try to get the boat operational again, and at least get part way back to shore. We couldn't raise the coastgaurd on the radio—I would later discover it was because the storm had brought down the aerial at the coastguard station, and most of the phone lines for thirty miles.

"We worked quickly on the engine and eventually got it running. The second it kicked to life Tommy ran to bring the anchor up, but he couldn't. The anchor was caught on something on the bottom. The anchor line was steel chain so there was no way to cut it. The three of us crowded round the winch and tried to turn the handles but it was useless. Matt hooked the mechanical winch—the one we used to lift the nets—up to the anchor line and turned it on. It was damn heavy. We thought we were going to capsize the boat at one

154

point, but Matt kept going because he knew it was our only chance to get free. When the anchor came up none of us knew what to think. It was caught on what I can only describe as a big, black pod, about six feet end-to-end. The outside of it wasn't smooth though, it was more like, like a woven basket. Big strands of God-knows-what were interlaced, leaving gaps between them. The very tip of the anchor had slid into one of these gaps and lodged itself there.

"I'll admit that Matt and I could not claim a lifetime at sea, but we'd never seen anything like it. We hadn't a lot of time to decide what to do. Matt said we should bring it aboard. He said there was bound to be some scientists or professors who would pay big money for this thing. He even joked that there might be one big motherfucker of a pearl in there."

Taffy laughed slightly and took another swig from his hip-flask. Even when he was smiling I could see the hurt in his eyes. I think he had been carrying around this story for too long. I knew there wasn't going to be a happy ending, but I couldn't wait to hear the rest.

Taffy's face had lost all traces of the laughter when I looked back. His look was sombre as he spoke. "We dumped the pod on the deck and started back. We got maybe twenty minutes of good sailing before the storm got its breath back and decided to hit us again. The little engine sputtered and tried to keep a forward motion as best as it could, but it was fighting a losing battle. God alone knows how many hours we fought the waves. Then we saw the old Dempsey Lighthouse. Matt said he thought he could get the boat ashore. Said he knew a narrow channel and with the increased water level he thought we could make it. We got close and waited for the storm to calm a little. Just a little lull was all we needed. Just enough to manoeuvre through the rocks and get ashore. We all watched the waves. We looked at the sky. We prayed to God, and then we got our chance. It wasn't calm but Matt reckoned it was as good as it was going to get. He gave The Argo all she had and made for the little island.

"It was a slow procedure. We had to wrestle the boat every minute. The boy was scared. He suggested going back to the open sea where at least there was nothing to crash into.

Matt kept going, confident he could make it. We almost did make it through, but only a matter of yards from the shore we were thrown to starboard and the hull scraped along some rocks and split. It wasn't too bad a leak, but now going back to the open sea wasn't an option. We *had* to get ashore. Every time we thought we were getting closer, we drifted back out again. In the end I think it took almost two hours for us to travel five hundred yards. We ran aground hard on the rocks with the bow pointing skyward like an accusing finger. We moved carefully across the rocks. Matt or me always had hold of the boy. When we reached the shore Matt and I looked back at The Argo. Waves were crashing it from all sides and it was rocking slightly but it looked like it might be well enough wedged on the rocks to hold its ground. We walked to the lighthouse.

"Dempsey's Island is only about a quarter of a mile square and there is nothing on it but the lighthouse, so why the fuckin' door was locked is beyond me. The lighthouse was activated by a radio signal in those days and someone came over every once in a while to do maintenance. Why you need to lock your door on an unpopulated island is something only a civil servant could answer. We were in no mood to fuck around and Matt and I started kicking the padlock. Then Tommy reaches up and finds a spare key on the ledge above the door. I mean, do you see any fuckin' sense to that at all? Lock the door and leave the key. *Had* to be a civil servant." Taffy shrugged his shoulders and said, "Getting a bit chilly in here. I'll build a fire.

As Taffy busied himself with the fire I fiddled with my tape-recorder. There was nothing to do with it, but I thought it would look very technical and professional to him. I found it hard to believe that the old man I had seen lifting litter and sweeping floors every day at school had had such an adventure, and it wasn't over yet. He snapped pieces of branch over his knee and threw them into the fire for kindling. He wasn't the figure of ridicule everyone thought he was. You never can tell from looking at people what they are capable of.

3.

The fire was soon roaring. Taffy rolled another cig and dropped back into his rocking chair. He looked like he was trying to remember where he had left the story so I prompted him. "You were on Dempsey's Island and just got the lighthouse open."

He nodded. "The lighthouse had a generator from back in the day when there was a full time lighthouse-keeper. Matt got the generator going while I built a fire. The boy was soaked to his skin. When we got the lights on, we looked in the living quarters and found a bed and some dry clothes—they stank of mildew but we were past caring. Tommy lay down and went to sleep on the bed when he had got into some dry clothes. Matt and I went down and sat in the armchairs by the fire. When we looked in the little kitchen we even found a bottle of whiskey and helped ourselves. It was blowing a goddamn gale outside, but we were snug. They really built those old lighthouses to be able to take anything. That was the worst storm I've ever seen. Matt and I sat up talking for a long time, until exhaustion and whiskey put us to sleep.

"Next day when we woke we searched the kitchen for something to eat. We found a few cans of peaches and some beans. So we had a third of a can of beans each that morning and a third of a can of peaches for dessert. Then we set about trying to get a message to the coastguard. The lighthouse had a radio but it wasn't working. I found a screwdriver and decided to unscrew the radio from The Argo, thinking we might be able to make one working radio out of the two broken ones. The storm had calmed, but it was still really windy as I walked down to the rocks. The Argo was still perched where we had left her. I made my way over the slippery rocks and got on board. What I saw first was the pod, split in half. I walked over to it. There was a dark yellow…I don't know how you would describe it—mucus maybe, all around the inside of the pod. Stank to high heaven as well. I knew something had been in there and it wasn't a pearl. I looked around but didn't see anything. I got the radio and spied the few fish we had caught still in the bucket. I brought

157

the fish and the radio back to the lighthouse. I was uneasy. I had that feeling that I was being watched.

"Matt and I worked on the radio while the boy cleaned the fish for dinner. We stopped in the early afternoon to eat. Both the radios were pretty beat, but we were making headway. A few hours later we got the lighthouse's radio working and called the coastguard. We were all so relieved. Tommy even got to speak to his girlfriend, who had been waiting at the coastguard station for word of him. The coastguard said the whole coastline was in chaos. There were boats lost and even a few of the boats that were docked in the harbour had sunk. People were missing; they had had to jury-rig another antenna just to keep up communications. All the volunteers were out on calls. He asked if we were in immediate danger. We had to say no—If there were other people they had to rescue first, we would be all right to wait. He knew we were on Dempsey's Island and said he would send a boat as soon as he could. Matt asked them if they could bring something to patch the hole in The Argo—just so it could be towed home without sinking. The guy said he would do his best and we signed off.

"We all relaxed after that. The uncertainty that had been hanging over us all day was gone and we were excited about going home. The boy spent most of the evening staring out a window in the direction of home. We had the last of the fish in the evening and then Matt and I celebrated by helping ourselves to the rest of the whiskey. Since the worst of the storm had passed and things were calming down, Tommy went outside to look for the lights that would signify our rescuers approach. I hadn't told them about the pod being split. I didn't think there was any danger. I just thought it was some sea creature in its larval state and when the pod had split it had probably been swept out to sea. It probably hadn't even been mature and was dead when the pod split. That's what I thought. It got late and Matt and I decided they would probably wait 'til the morning to send help. Matt went outside and called Tommy. We couldn't see him anywhere. We went down to The Argo. Matt thought he might have gone to get his sketch-pad. He wasn't there. I saw the pod again and something inside me knew, I just knew. Matt didn't even notice the pod, he was too worried about Tommy. Like I said, the island was only a quarter-mile square so Matt went one way and I went the other. I walked around the coast looking for anywhere that he might have fallen. Then I heard Matt scream. I climbed off the rocks and ran towards the sound of his cries. When I saw him he had the boy in his arms. Tommy looked so white. I wanted to ask if he was alive but when Matt broke down and started weeping I knew he wasn't. We took Tommy back to the lighthouse and laid him on the bed. I looked him over and couldn't find any signs of blood or bruising. Matt slid to the floor against a wall and put his head in his hands. Then the lights cut out. Matt said the generator must be out of fuel, but I told him I thought there was something out there. Something we had brought up from the depths of the Atlantic. The thing from the pod. Matt picked up his head. There was a cold vengeance in his eyes that I had never seen in my brother before. He had a purpose now. He had something to blame. He had something to hurt. He went to the kitchen and armed himself with the biggest knife he could find. I walked outside with him.

"There was still a stiff breeze and a thin drizzle was falling. The generator hadn't run out of fuel, it had been ripped apart. We both knew the strength it would take to do that kind of damage. Matt wasn't being dissuaded so easily. We followed the coast round. We circled the island three times and stopped at The Argo on the fourth. Matt wasn't giving up—he said he knew it was here and he *was* going to find it and kill it. Matt examined the pod while I went below decks to find the flare gun. With the lights being out in the lighthouse the rescue boat would need something to guide them if they did come at night. I was rummaging in the emergency box when I heard a voice up on deck. 'You talkin' to me, Matt?' I shouted. He was still talking and I crawled back a bit to hear what he was saying. I heard him say one thing: 'Tommy, you're alive. You're all right. Tommy's all right!' I was filled with relief. I crawled out and saw this huge black monster with a hard shell holding Matt's head between its hands. I screamed and shot the flare gun at it. The flare hit it in the back and it wailed. Matt dropped to the ground. The monster dived into the ocean. I ran to Matt and checked his pulse. He was dead. I'll never forget the look on his face because, well, it was weird. He looked almost happy. I carried him back to the lighthouse and laid him on the bed beside his son.

"I barricaded the door and windows and armed myself with a knife. I sat beside the bed where the corpses of my brother and my nephew lay, all night. I must have fallen asleep at some point because the next thing I remember is a member of the coastguard rescue team shaking me awake. There was a helicopter outside that took the three of us back to the mainland. I told them what I've told you. I don't think they believed me at first, but when the bodies were autopsied they had more questions than answers and my story was looking as plausible as anything they could come up with."

Something didn't make sense to me. "If you barricaded the door and windows how did the rescue guy get in to wake you in the morning?"

Taffy grinned like he admired me. "You know, the police never picked up on that little inconsistency. You're a hell of a smart kid." He lit yet another cig and rocked for a moment on his chair before answering, "What I'm going to tell you now I never told the police. I never told this to anyone, matter of fact. That night while I was sitting on the floor by the bed I heard something outside and I went to the window. I saw someone out there and I went down to open the door. It was like being in a dream or some kind of daze. I took the barricade off the door. I had been sitting up there with two dead bodies that used to be my kin, for hours. I had done a lot of thinking and I had started to think that maybe I was to blame in some way. I had left the flare gun upstairs because I think I had lost hope that anyone would come for me before this thing killed me. I didn't care. I wanted it to kill me. I knew who I saw standing outside *couldn't* be there, and I was probably being lured to my death, but like I said, I didn't care. I removed the last of the barricade and opened the door and faced her. She came close to me and I closed my eyes. I felt she was going to kill me and I felt I deserved it. When I opened my eyes again she was gone. I went back upstairs and sat down on the floor next to the bed. I guess I fell asleep some time after that."

"And why didn't you tell the cops that?" I asked.

"My story already sounded far-fetched. In the beginning I'm sure they suspected me of the murders. If I had told them who I saw that night they would probably have stuck me in Sycamore Acres."

"Who *did* you see that night?"

Taffy took another long drink from his hip flask before answering. "You might think I was drunk or dreaming or hallucinating, but with God as my witness, I swear, it was Dolly Parton."

4.

I told him at once that I believed him and that similar things had been happening recently. He said he had seen Johnny's drawing that I had put up in the school and that's how he knew that it was back. I wondered if it was the same one that he and his brother had dragged up from the bottom of the sea, or was it maybe its offspring? It had been almost seventeen years since all this had happened. Could it have survived that long without coming ashore before? Maybe it had come ashore before. There were a lot of unexplained deaths around our town. There were even rumours that there were vampires living in the area, but no one really believed those stories. Maybe this thing had been feeding discreetly on the population for the last seventeen years.

Taffy broke the silence saying, "Well, you figured out what it is yet?"

I shook my head. I didn't think it was anything that anyone had ever seen before. It was a totally new predatory lifeform. New to us anyway. It could have been lying at the bottom of the sea for thousands, maybe millions of years. It could be some animal in some stage of evolution, long since forgotten. I wanted to share this theory with Taffy but I didn't think he'd understand.

"Maybe you ain't as smart as I thought. It's a Siren. You know what that is?"

They didn't teach Greek mythology at our school, so again I shook my head.

Taffy strode around the floor like he was a teacher giving a lecture. "The myths tell of Sirens as beautiful women who lured sailors onto the rocks with their songs. I don't think they were women at all. You've probably worked out that they can appear as anything to their intended victim, well what else would they appear as to a boat-load of horny sailors who haven't seen a woman in months. Of course they appear as beautiful naked women, or in my case the heavenly Ms. Parton. As for the Siren's song, I'm not sure if that's literal or not. I have a feeling the Siren's song is something like I experienced when I was going out to Dolly: that dreamlike intoxication drawing me to her. These things have been around a hell of a long time so they know how to push our buttons."

It was amazing to me that Taffy had researched this all and had a theory that sounded very plausible. There was only one thing he hadn't told me. "How do you kill them?"

"Much the same as anything else I suppose. Stab it, shoot it, get it hooked on cigarettes. Records for ancient Greece aren't the most coherent. I only found one reference to one being killed." He cleared his throat like he was going to give a speech. "And I quote: *'And she beguiled Butes and he leapt into the sea to be with her. All thought him lost, but Butes was strong of mind and fought the temptation with steel and grace, and the serpent was loosed.'* Make of that what you can."

It all made sense—not that quote, it made no sense—but that it was a Siren. I somehow felt better knowing that. I knew my enemy; didn't someone once say that was the first step to victory? I asked Taffy if he had any idea where it was, or if he knew where the source was. He didn't. I asked him if he had felt any urges around the times of the murders. He hadn't. I guessed that this was either a different Siren than he had encountered, or it had happened so long ago that he wasn't still psychically connected to it.

I thanked Taffy for telling me about the story, but as I was about to leave he stopped me and said, "I think there's someone else at school who knows." I told him Emily knew, too, but he was convinced there was someone else. He said when he saw my poster he had taken a copy of it and put it up in his tearoom. He knew that one of these things was on the loose again and he had gone to the school library and borrowed a few books of Greek mythology and kept them in his tearoom, too. A few days ago he had come in to find the poster ripped up and the books in his bin burning. He got the small fire out quickly, but the books were ruined. As I walked out the door he warned me in a low whisper, "Someone else knows. You be careful who you tell."

I walked along the beach trying to figure out who the other player might be and why they would destroy the books. Could it have been the Siren? Taffy works quite late some nights and I had neglected to ask him whether it was dark when this happened. The Siren could have waltzed into the school in the guise of anyone, but it didn't seem like its style. It was cunning, but I doubted it had the intelligence to destroy evidence. That left only one other alternative: someone was helping it.

Chapter VIII - Final Straw

Certainly, play a joke and have a laugh, but be responsible. I
had a boyfriend once whose nickname was Rocketpants and I
played a very literal April Fool on him that got out of control.
Now he has to pee through a tube.

Imogen Collins, *Educational Safety video*

- April, 1990 -

1.

I was suspicious of everyone. In the Hollywood movie, of
course, it would have been Billy Love who was the Siren's
accomplice; that would set everything up for a happy ending.
Well, even though Hollywood had been batting a big, fat zero
of late, I still kept an eye on Billy. He seemed to have lost
interest in Emily completely and after a while he even spoke to
me, if only to ask something about homework. It was as much
as anyone was speaking to me these days. Even though I
hadn't been accused of anything outright, there were enough
loose ends that ended with me to make everyone a little wary
about approaching me. Girls, especially, gave me a wide berth.
So, I threw myself into study. School was nearly back to
normal. Laughter could even be heard occasionally, like the
song of a migrated bird that had returned. I rarely laughed; I
rarely had anything to laugh about. I studied. I decided if by
some miracle I made it to the end of the school year, I would
have at least a good grade in English.

In Career Guidance class, Mr Sloan was calling us in one
at a time. It was time for the big decision: what are you going
to do when you leave school? There was no supervision in the
classroom, as we each had to go into Sloan's office one by one
and have our little chat. The pupils sat on tables and laughed
at the preposterous careers that some of them were planning to
suggest to Sloan just to see him squirm. Gynaecologists and
porn stars were two hot favourites with the guys. Teachers
that were fresh from teacher training college were just too
easy to fluster. Debbie Wallace had apparently told him she
wanted to be a topless model—and she wasn't kidding! I would
have loved to be a fly on the wall for that one. There would be

no way you could avoid looking at her boobs after she said that. I wonder if he did. She did have more than adequate sweater stretchers. Others knew what they were going to do and took it very seriously, like Alana Quigg who was certain she was going to be a detective and Anna Hughes who was going to join her father's undertaking business—good luck, rather her than me.

When it was my turn, I sat down opposite him and he lifted his head with that bright enthusiasm that teachers have in the beginning. He asked if I had any thoughts as to my career path. I told him I wanted to be a writer.

"Journalism? Marvellous! I can certainly suggest a lot of good further education courses that will put you on the way to Fleet Street," he said, smiling.

"No, not journalism," I interrupted. "I want to be a novelist like J.D. Salinger." I had just read The Catcher in the Rye and was blown away by how such a short book could speak to me so personally, and huge telephone-directory-sized classics, such as my friend Dickens had written, bored me rigid. Like I said to Mrs Wilton, the wrong books are on the syllabus. The education board seems to believe that teenagers have never heard a swear word and don't know what sex is, beyond a gender description. I had a plan to write a novel to speak to my generation. It would avoid any obvious references to those things we weren't supposed to know about, but the subtext would speak volumes. It was a brilliant plan and I was going to write this book. I told Sloan this and he looked at me. I imagine he looked at me the same way he looked at the pupils who came in and said they were going to be rock stars or Hollywood actors. It was a patronising little grin that said: *I admire your moxie, kid, but it's never going to happen.*

We eventually compromised with him giving me the leaflets for the journalism courses. He said they would give me the confidence and experience to be able to write a novel. I know he was right now, but back then I thought I was going to go off and live in a cabin in the woods and write my novel on an old beat-up typewriter. Now I understand the grin.

I exited Sloan's office to silence. Everyone else was being whoop-whooped on exit and immediately asked a dozen questions. No one spoke to me. I told Billy Love that he was next. He walked past me and pretended to punch me in the stomach, then laughed and patted me on the back as he went into the office. Billy was on good form that day.

That morning we had been 1st Year bowling and this was the reason for his jocular camaraderie. 1st Year bowling is another fun game but, like Three Hole Golf, is not on the syllabus. 1st Year students at our school (probably every school), are so terrified of any of their books or sports gear being lost/ stolen/ left at home, that they carry everything with them all the time. They are prepared for any eventuality—if at the last moment Religious Education is replaced by a cross-country run, they're ready. You would wonder how they got so much stuff into their bags, until you saw the size of them. It's the fear of doing something wrong and being punished for it that leaves these weedy little eleven-year-olds walking around with huge, heavy bags on their backs. Most of them are crouched forward with the weight—it does look sort of ridiculous, but I did it when I was that age and so did you. After a few years you don't really care what happens to your books; losing them is a good excuse if you want out of some class. But the 1st Year students had yet to learn this, and someone had figured out that when they waddled with these huge TARDIS-like schoolbags, they were very easy to topple. The trick was, one person would put his bag behind the 1st Year's feet and the other would throw his bag at the 1st Year's head. And they fell. And we laughed. Sometimes it didn't even take an impact; they saw the bag coming towards them and they reflexively stepped back. It was funny. It was done to me when I was a 1st Year and that morning I had done it with Billy.

The kid in question was Joshua Wright. I didn't know many of the 1st Year students, but everyone knew him because he was different. You see, schools in Northern Ireland are segregated into Protestant and Catholic. Someone must have decided long ago that the best way to heal our country's troubles was to instil a 'them and us' mentality into children as soon as possible. The problem (or one of the problems) with this brilliant idea was: what school do you go to if you are

166

neither of those religions? I really don't know how parents decided; maybe they flipped a coin. There were no Buddhist kids at our school but there were some Hindu pupils. I don't think they got any special consideration when it came to saying prayers in the morning assembly or going to Religious Education classes. This was before Political Correctness went mad so it may be different now. Joshua Wright, our skittle that morning, was not Hindu; he was a Jehovah's Witness. He got a hard time, but everyone did as far as I can remember. When you said something, or did something, or wore something, you got the piss taken for a few weeks—it's the law of the schoolyard: you take your licks and keep your mouth shut. This law was apparently not part of his dogma.

When I had put my bag at his feet and Billy had toppled him, he had lay there for a few seconds like a turtle on its back; unable to get up. Everyone in the corridor had roared with laughter until he finally got himself flipped onto his side and wriggled his arms out of the straps of his bag. Billy was running on the spot and playing to crowd shouting, "Steeeeee-rike!" Joshua got up and stared at me with real hate and fury in his eyes. When I had been bowled in 1st year, I had stood up with a resigned "you got me" smile on my face and had taken a bow. That was how it should be done. Joshua was so serious and angry that I knew he was just setting himself up to be targeted again. It's strange that he took it completely differently than I did. I saw it as a hazing; a kind of initiation that meant I was one of the guys now. I actually felt a little swell of pride that despite Joshua's religion, he was being treated no different than any other 1st Year. No better, but no worse—as it should be. Joshua looked at us all with contempt, lifted his bag like a wounded comrade, and stomped off down the hall, with the cries of "Ooooooh!" following him all the way.

Even though Joshua had played the situation all wrong, I couldn't help but be a little happy. For the first time in a long time, I had been on the same side as everyone else. The suspicion left the other students briefly and we all had a laugh together. I felt like one of them again and I cherished it.

The effects of that morning had worn off again and I sat in Sloan's class at a table by myself, reading. A girl I didn't know came into the room, I think she was a 2nd Year, and went into Sloan's office with a note. She came out first and left, then Sloan popped his head out the door and said that Mr Kawaji wanted to see me. I quickly bundled my stuff into my bag and left.

I knew what this was about. I had written the greatest short story in history for my English Language essay. The brief was to write a story set in World War Two from a soldier's point of view. Everyone else, and I mean *everyone*, had written themselves in as a hero that somehow saved the day by blowing up a tank, or capturing the Enigma machine, or shooting off one of Hitler's testicles (Copyright 1990, Boggy Marsh). I had taken a different approach and written myself as a soldier who was drafted. He didn't want to be there and when he couldn't stand it anymore, he shot and wounded himself just badly enough to be sent home. He blamed the injury on a German he had found who looked as if he hadn't been dead very long. He had made up a story of the bloody one-to-one fight they had had. The soldier had returned home to a hero's welcome in his hometown. I knew Kawaji would like the story's originality, but I thought I knew why he had called me, too. I would have bet anything that Kawaji was going to tell me to change the ending to one where the soldier's guilt gets the better of him and he is either exposed or confesses. Teachers always wanted a moral ending. I liked my ending better and was prepared to defend it. In my ending the soldier had not been plagued by guilt, but had used his heroic persona to enter politics and was very successful. His whole life was based on a lie and he could live with that just fine. I knew what Kawaji's arguments were going to be, but I had an answer for all of them.

I entered his classroom smiling. It was empty except for Kawaji himself, sitting behind his desk. He continued writing and asked me to take a seat. His skin was dark and leathery. I don't know where he was from originally; he wasn't black but he wasn't white either, he looked like he might be from the middle-east somewhere. I didn't think he was handsome—as girls my age defined handsome anyway—and wondered who he was having an affair with. I was brimming to debate the finer points of my story. Kawaji finished writing and got up and closed the door. He didn't look at me at all. He walked back to his desk and lifted a coloured cardboard folder. As he got closer, I realised it was one of the autobiographies from the wall. In 1st year everyone has to write an autobiography for English class. You're supposed to write about key moments in your life and stick photos or pictures in that relate to them. It always struck me as a very girlie thing to do, maybe because they went to more trouble decorating the cover with glitter and sequins and stuff like that. Mine was a sparse document from what I remember: no photos and I made up the anecdotes; I didn't want everyone knowing who I was. Some people were excruciatingly candid about operations, illnesses and phobias, which to me just seemed like painting a bullseye on your face, because they were all destined to be tacked up on the English room wall for all to see.

Kawaji dropped the folder in front of me. I read the cover: My Autobiography by Joshua Wright.

Oh, fuck.

I knew immediately where this was going now. I had watched from the other side of the room two days before as Billy Love had defaced this very memoir. Kawaji wanted me to squeal on Billy.

"Look at it," he commanded.

I opened it up and flipped through pages. Billy had altered several of the photo captions: 'My first girlfriend' had become 'My first whore'; 'In the hospital getting my appendix out' had become 'In the VD clinic.' It went on in that vein for most of the time, but there was one picture of Joshua in camouflage clothes holding a Rambo knife, the original caption had been scored-out and Billy had written: 'Training to be a hova.' I almost laughed but caught it just in time. I closed the folder and looked up at Kawaji.

"What have you got to say for yourself?" he said, his voice cracking with rage.

"What do you want me to say?" I asked.

"Well, an apology would be a start," he screamed.

"An apology for what? I didn't do this."

He grabbed me around the neck and lifted me to my feet. "Don't you lie to me, boy! I know what class it happened in, and I compared the handwriting to everyone in the class, and it matched yours!" He took his hand from around my neck and poked me hard in the breastplate with his forefinger.

Oh great. Kawaji thinks he's fuckin' Lieutenant Columbo. Billy's writing and mine were similar, but had he stopped when he reached mine? I knew all it would take would be to say that out loud, and if I wasn't exonerated at least there would be another suspect. The law of the schoolyard was ingrained in me: take your licks and keep your mouth shut. I followed the law.

Kawaji poked my chest hard again. "You're a racist, Norton. The lowest form of life. I've had to deal with people like you all [poke] my [poke] life [poke]. You're a bully. A pathetic little shit who gets his pleasure from tormenting younger students. Just because you've been brought up to hate other religions doesn't [poke] mean [poke] you can do it in my [poke] classroom."

I was swallowing hard. I could even feel tears welling in my eyes. Not from the pain of the poking, but from the totally wrong opinion that Kawaji now held about me. He thought I was one of those brainless morons who filled their time hating everyone who didn't think just like they did. And I couldn't tell him the truth.

"You're lucky I don't have you suspended," he said with a harder poke. "The only upside is that in a few months you and your stupid bigoted ideas will be gone from this school."

Where are you Mrs Wilton? Mrs Wilton would *know* I wasn't capable of this. I wanted her to waltz into the room and bawl Kawaji out for making such a stupid mistake. She didn't.

"I hate people like you, Norton," Kawaji said closing in on me. He stopped half an inch from my face. "I can just imagine the kind of small-minded piece of shit you're going to grow up to be. You'll never amount to anything because you're too fuckin' stupid. You're worthless. You're shit, Norton!"

My eyes had definitely glassed over, but I refused to let tears escape. Kawaji grabbed me by my tie and dragged me to the front of the room and pushed me against the blackboard. He let go and walked to the door. He opened the door and brought in Joshua. How much worse could this get?

Kawaji brought Joshua to face me. "Is this the boy that's been bullying you, Joshua?"

Joshua sniffed and nodded. He looked at me triumphantly and with a sinister pleasure. Joshua thought he had won; he had beaten me. I got very angry and was even more annoyed that my eyes were glassed over. Kawaji started poking me again, as if he was now justified to do so.

"Apologize," Kawaji commanded.

The schoolyard law may have convicted me but I was damned if I was going to bend over for the soap. "Apologize for what?"

Kawaji slammed me against the blackboard. "Do you not even have the decency to apologize for destroying Joshua's photos?"

I gritted my teeth. "I didn't do that. I think I already mentioned that."

"You're a goddamned liar, Norton," Kawaji screamed, his face almost touching mine. "Are you going to lie about assaulting him in the corridor too?"

Assaulting? Was he joking? Joshua Wright, whom previously I had no feelings about one way or the other, now appeared to be a snivelling little shite, and would have been no matter where he went on a Sunday. "No, I did that," I answered. "And I'm sorry. Sorry he doesn't have a fuckin' sense of humour."

Kawaji caught me round the throat and pulled me close to him. "You insolent little bastard!" He threw me at the door. "Get out of here. Get out of my sight. I'm sick looking at you," he screamed.

I stepped outside the door and looked up the corridor. Every teacher was standing at their door wondering what the commotion was. I stepped out and heard Kawaji say, "Good luck passing English, Norton."

I went to the nearest toilets and locked myself in a cubicle and cried the tears I wouldn't release earlier. It was the middle of a period so there was little chance of anyone walking in.

171

That was it. I might as well give up on getting any passing grades this year. The soldier had wounded himself for nothing. In the Hollywood movie, Kawaji would discover the truth and seek me out to apologize.

Hollywood, why can't you be right just once?

2.

My story about the soldier came back a couple of days later with a mark of 37% on it. Even Boggy's highly implausible story about de-balling Hitler gained him a mark of 49%. I know nowadays—in American teen shows, anyway—high school students seem to have a law degree and know all their rights inside out. They stand up to any teacher who may have graded them one point lower than they deserve. They call their parents, their lawyers, the PTA and anyone else who will listen. We never dared challenge a teacher. I had to live with what Kawaji did. I never told anyone. But I did vow not to waste any more good writing on him. If we were assigned anything else I would scribble something out in twenty minutes and he could do what he wanted with it. I was past trying to impress him.

Poor little put-upon Joshua, suddenly found his voice and wasted no time in telling the whole school that I had cried my eyes out when Kawaji had shouted at me. Another thing to tease me about. Another reason to avoid me. It's ironic that in the classic definition of the word, he actually brought more bullying on me than I ever brought on him.

It was such a relief when Toe-poke came back to school. We had been seeing each other fairly often, but having a popular jock speaking to me in full view of everyone did a little to ease the constant heckling. He was walking without crutches now, though he still had a significant limp.

A couple of days after Kawaji had bawled me out, Billy approached me and said he had heard what had happened. For a single, shining moment I thought he was going to go to Kawaji and confess. My grade would be reappraised and I might at least pass English. Billy said, "Cheers for doing that." Then nodded and left.

I was tempted to go to Kawaji and squeal. I knew if the situations were reversed, Billy would have done it to me. As I

172

sat in Emily's sanctuary at dinnertime, I tried to convince myself to do it. I tried to rationalize it by thinking: how much worse can school get? OK, if I squeal I get branded a grass for the rest of the year. So what? One more thing shouted at me isn't going to make a difference. Besides, this wasn't just bullshit schoolyard politics, this would affect the rest of my life. The soldier story counted towards my final grade. It would be worth the stick for a couple of months if I ended up getting into journalism. I couldn't think of a single logical reason not to squeal. But I didn't.

I know now that I was different than most of the other pupils. I value that kind of moral fortitude even though it almost always goes unnoticed. I guess I'm a bit of a martyr at heart. I used to watch old war movies when I was young and maybe that's where I got the idea that staying tight-lipped under interrogation was the mark of a man.

"Vere are ze secret plans? Tell me now, or I vill hurt you."

"Do your worst; you'll see the boys from Nu Yawk don't crack."

"Soona or later, you vill talk, mein friend."

"Nothin' doin', Fritz. You can torture me all you like; I'll never talk."

I used to think that's how it was done, but two years ago I was captured behind enemy lines and saw how things really worked. The woodwork teacher had just stained and varnished his classroom door, so a guy called Gunk (he wore too much gel in his hair), and I, being members of the species Teenagus Horriblus, decided to kick the hell out of it. We waited until we could see him on the other side of the room and kicked his door until it was sufficiently scuffed, then we ran. I thought we got away with it, but someone must have squealed. Gunk and I were brought to his classroom at dinnertime and taken into his office one at a time. Gunk was leaving as I entered and I gave him a nod that said "Don't worry, I'll never talk."

The teacher tried every trick in the book to make me confess, but I was as cool as a long green vegetable.

"You were seen."

"I don't think so."

"It's your footprint on the door."

"Shall we go and check?"

173

"I don't want to have to get the headmaster involved. Do you want me to phone for him?"

"If you have to, go ahead."

"The other boy said it was you."

"No, he must be mistaken." (Imagine using that old chestnut.)

"He said he saw you doing it from up the corridor."

"I'll say it again: Gunk must be mistaken."

He lifted the phone to reinforce his headmaster threat. He looked at me to see if I'd crack. "Last chance. The other boy will tell Mr Reese it was you."

"I don't think he will, sir."

He put the phone down and told me I could go. I saw Gunk in the playground and walked over to him.

Gunk hung his head in shame and mumbled, "Yeah, so? I told him it was you. I didn't want to get in trouble."

That's what people are really like.

I never heard any more about that incident. I wasn't punished for it so I guess the woodwork teacher let it go. I did, as the law allows, spread the word that Gunk was an untrustworthy, squealing bastard. He had that title for only two months, and then his family moved to Australia.

Now I felt I could sense whether someone could be trusted or not. It's a very intuitive feeling that's rarely wrong. Toepoke, I felt, was a stand-up guy. He spoke to me at school without a care for what it might do to his place in the popularity hierarchy. On his first day back we walked back to his house where he changed and loaned me an old shell-suit to wear. We patrolled the town and talked. He was excited to be back at school and seeing hundreds of girls on a daily basis. He still felt the loss of the pupils the Siren had killed in February, like we all did. I explained my theory that we hadn't seen it in so long because it had fed so greedily. It might be months before it needs to feed again. That was why we had to find it now. If it were in some sort of semi-hibernation, it would be vulnerable. We circled the town twice and were going to pack it in for the evening when we were accosted by Skid and Mike Millar.

"We've been waiting for you to come back to school, Toe-poke," Skid said.

"You've got a fuckin' kickin' comin'," Mike chimed in.

"Come on guys," I said, "Toe-poke told me about your dog. If you'll just let him tell you what happened…"

"Shut the fuck up, freak," Skid shouted. "You fuck off before you get a kickin' too."

I looked at Toe-poke and answered Skid, "I'm afraid I can't do that."

The words, "Your choice," had barely left Skid's lips as he lunged at Toe-poke and me. We fought like teenagers fight. Quite pathetic to watch, I'm sure, but when you're in the thick of it, it feels like a fight to the death. It was mostly a lot of head-locks, kicking and the occasional punch that landed on target. I will say that Mike and Skid came off worst, and they were the ones that ended it by running away. Toe-poke and I hobbled home. Compared to fighting the Siren, it was fairly tame, but we were both bruised and bleeding a little. Toe-poke's bad leg had taken a hit or two during the fight and was really smarting on the way home. I walked with him to make sure he got home all right. By the time we reached his door he didn't want to put any weight on it at all. We went in and his dad fussed and worried about Toe-poke's knee. He made me a cup of tea and went upstairs to help Toe-poke into bed. I finished my tea and Toe-poke's dad drove me home. He was silent on the way. I don't know if he blamed me for the fight or whether he was just panicking about his son's future.

I had to listen to a similar barrage of worry when I got home. The cuts and bruises had my mum wanting to phone the police and ambulance. Eventually, I calmed her down and told her it was just a misunderstanding. She made the point that there had been a lot of those recently. I shrugged as I went upstairs to get changed and cleaned up. When I came down again, my mum and dad were both sitting at the kitchen table waiting for me. They asked me to sit down and I did.

"Your dad and I have been talking. We think there's something going on and you don't want to tell us. You can tell us. Whatever it is; if it's a girl or…a boy." My mum and dad's faces froze as if someone had pushed pause on the VCR that was playing my crazy life. They wanted a reaction to that before they went on.

"I'm not gay. If it was something that simple I would know how to deal with it," I answered. They looked relieved, my dad more than my mum, I think.

"And you're sure it's not drugs?" mum said.

I shook my head. "Drugs are a lot rarer than you think at school. I could count on one hand the pupils who smoke dope, and none of them bring it to school."

"Are you being bullied?" My dad's voice made me jump.

I wanted to say yes: a mythical creature from ancient Greece is bullying me, but I didn't. "No. I'm not being bullied, but with eight-hundred pupils in the same school there are bound to be disagreements. It's nothing, really. I can handle it."

"You shouldn't have to handle it," my mum said. "You should be concentrating on your exams."

Right then, I imagined another one of these little sit down chats when my exam results came in. I was under no illusions: I was not going to pass anything now, thanks to Kawaji. I thought of telling them about Kawaji's botched investigation and how he had sentenced me to fail. I think I kept quiet because I just didn't want the extra hassle. "I'll do fine in my exams," I lied.

My mum looked at my dad and then turned to me and said, "If you are having problems around here it might be possible for us to move. Your dad and I have been looking at some nice houses far from here where no one knows you [Note: not, where no one knows *us*] and we could start again, fresh."

I appreciated the lengths they were willing to go to, but I wasn't going to let the Siren drive me from my home. "I don't want to move," I said. "Look, I know there have been a lot of weird things that have happened this year and I look like the prime suspect in most cases—hell, I would probably think I was guilty, too, if I was on the outside—but I'm really not responsible for any of them. I know how it looks, but that's the whole point—things are not always how they appear."

176

The conversation wasn't really resolved, it just seemed to peter out and I eventually got up and went to bed. I lay on my bed and thought of telling them everything, but the odds of ending up in Sycamore Acres far outweighed the odds of them believing me. It would be so easy to explain everything if they did know, but I would just be taking myself out of the game and ringing the dinner bell for the Siren. I couldn't do that. I would see this thing through without telling them, no matter how tempting it might be. The Siren wouldn't beat me.

"Go ahead, do your worst. I ain't talkin'."

3.

Next day Toe-poke wasn't at school. I didn't really expect him. His leg had been in agony the night before. I called at morning break and his dad said he would be off for a few weeks at least. His conversation was short and again I got the feeling he blamed me for Toe-poke's relapse. I saw Emily in the playground and she spoke to me in full view of everyone. She thought it was stupid to meet in secret and she was right. Why should we care about the opinions of a bunch of people we would probably never see again when we left school? We were friends and, finally, we didn't care who knew it. Emily apologized for not patrolling with me recently. I said it was OK. She had been studying really hard and looked like she was going to do very well in her end of year exams. She added that she hadn't seen Billy. That seemed weird. Why did she just say that out of the blue? Maybe she realized how stupid she had been. Maybe she was even flirting with me.

I killed the mood by saying the wrong thing of course. "You'll probably be seeing him soon. I hear he's dropped to second place in the Golf Club." That came out all wrong. I was trying to warn her that he would probably show up sometime soon giving her some phoney line and I wanted to prepare her. Unfortunately, it sounded more like she would shag him as soon as he asked. She looked hurt when I said it. Our talk turned to the Siren. I asked if she wanted to patrol with me tonight but she said she had to revise Physics because she was struggling badly with it. She said she would patrol with me at the weekend.

Now, you'll remember Justin Parke—the boy who couldn't fly. Since becoming a teenager he had put thoughts of flight aside and concentrated on becoming a dickhead. He worked hard at it and was now possibly one of the biggest dickheads in the country. Though he still had a weedy, skeletal frame, he now considered himself a bit of a tough guy, but only to people younger and smaller than himself. He had once threatened me not to tell anyone about his flying days or any of the other lies he had been caught out on. I had no intention of telling anyone and told him so. He thought he had scared me into this decision and walked away with a kind of John Wayne swagger. He still eyed me with suspicion and felt compelled to show me his fist and nod menacingly on occasion, ensuring I didn't forget his threat. I found him a bit of a joke to be honest. I knew that if push ever came to shove I could beat the shit out of him without breaking a sweat. Still, he enjoyed being a paper tiger and I wasn't on safari so I let him run free. I much preferred the boy who thought he could fly to the boy who wanted to live in the gutter.

I was queuing for dinner in the canteen and Justin was a couple of people behind me. I ordered my usual: chips and curry sauce with strawberry milk. I got to the till and lifted the last straw from the box and put it in my mouth while I counted out the change in my hand and gave it to the canteen assistant.

"Where's all the straws?" Justin shouted.

"I got the last one," I said, chewing my straw. "You want it?" I thought this would get a laugh, but Justin had an audience of his cronies.

"I don't want your fuckin' AIDS," he spat. He dipped two fingers in my milk and flicked it in my face. "Wipe the come off your chin, you fag." The cronies laughed. I tipped my tray and threw chips, curry sauce and milk all over his chest. He stood there, dumbfounded. I looked at him, covered with my dinner, and all I wanted to do was hit him. I drew my fist back and it was seized. I turned and saw Kawaji holding my arm. He told Justin to go and get cleaned up and dragged me out of the canteen and to the headmaster's office.

The downward spiral my life had been taking of late concerned Mr Reese. My grades had been slipping consistently

178

all year and my anti-social attitude towards fellow students was getting out of control. He said this behaviour wasn't like me and he was right. This wasn't me. I didn't have a short fuse. I would never have let Justin away with what he did, but I wouldn't have tipped my dinner over him, I would have done something equal to what he did to me. I suppose I was different without Rachel, without friends and without a chance of passing English. Reese said I had been one of the best essayists the school had ever produced, but Mr Kawaji said my marks had slipped to well below average. I was tempted to ask Reese to read my last story and tell me if he thought the standard had slipped. I should have said that. I really should have. I said very little. I let Reese talk and I sat there, not really listening. I thought about the last time I was in this office and Maxine was sitting beside me. It almost made me cry.

More good news that afternoon: Rachel and Tony were having an engagement party. She was still going to marry that asshole. The world made no sense! When I got home that afternoon I even found an invitation to it. Was she joking? Did she really think I was going to show up to this thing and stand there, smiling, as she flushed her life down the crapper? Reese had phoned my mum. I got another sit-down, though dad was still at work so it was only half-strength. At least this latest incident didn't have any paranormal overtones so I just told her exactly what happened. After hearing the whole story (and asking what a fag was), she said I shouldn't have done it but she understood that I had just lost my temper.

I must have walked double the distance that night. I was so frustrated and annoyed. I wished I had a punch bag at home. I would have loved to just punch and punch and punch until I was exhausted. The last place I patrolled was the beach. It was starting to get dark by this point and I had pretty much walked off my aggression. I saw a light in the old boathouse and went to investigate. I thought it might have been old Taffy but as I got closer I heard the unmistakable grunts that only passion produces. Either old Taffy had got lucky for the first time since the American civil war or it was a member of the

Golf Club playing a few holes. I couldn't resist sneaking up and taking a peek.

I went to the first window and could only make out movement; I couldn't see who it was, so I moved on round. The expectancy was giving me a real stiffy at this point. The second window gave a clear view and I saw Drew Dillon, football captain and all round alpha-male, French-kissing Mr Kawaji. I dropped to the ground and almost threw up—not politically correct, I know, but that's what happened. My erection had retreated in shame at being duped. I sneaked away from the cabin and hid behind a sand dune, out of sight and thankfully out of audio range, too. It was one of the most shocking things I had ever seen. You have to remember this is before soap-operas used gay kisses to improve ratings and pop stars had gay kissing in their videos to make them controversial. And, I suppose I was quite naïve. Someone actually had to tell me that Boy George was gay! I knew he had a funny haircut and wore make-up, but I thought he was just having a laugh. Here was Drew: no funny haircut, no make-up, no sandwich board around his neck, but quite clearly being gay and enjoying it. Next to seeing the Siren, it was the weirdest thing I had ever witnessed.

This could be my chance, I thought. This is how to get my grade restored: blackmail. I sat and thought it over for a long time. On one hand I wasn't homophobic and didn't want to give the impression that I was as bigoted as Kawaji had accused me of being. Hey, each to his own. It wasn't my scene, but if it made Drew happy then fair play to him. Drew was gay. It was unbelievable. The amount of girls that fancied him; what a waste. I didn't want to 'out' Drew so going public wasn't an option, therefore any threat I made to Kawaji was going to be a bluff. I didn't want to lay down some overly dramatic speech to him and demand an A, I just wanted him to mark me fairly. Drew left the boathouse first and ran off smiling. I ran down the sand dune to the boathouse and sat myself on the ground. My heart was going like a machine gun. I still had no idea what I was going to say to Kawaji. I was hoping my presence would be enough to scare him into doing all the talking. He waited ten minutes exactly and then came out.

I could see the blind terror in Kawaji's face as soon as he saw me. He took a while to gather his thoughts. It's times like this I wished I smoked; it would have looked so cool as he panicked. His first hope was that I had just arrived.

"How long have you been here, Norton?" he said in a non-committal tone.

"Long enough. I waited until Drew left before I came out." I actually think I missed the main event and just witnessed a goodbye kiss, but he didn't need to know that.

I could almost see him checking his bank balance in his head. "You want money, don't you? People like you…"

"Let's cut the 'people like me' crap, Kawaji. I don't want your money and I won't tell anyone about you and Drew."

"In exchange for what?" he asked nervously.

"In exchange for you marking my essays fairly. I don't really give a fuck what you think of me, but I did not deface Joshua Wright's autobiography. I could tell you who it was, because I *do* know, but the law of the schoolyard…you know. I hope you believe me because we're out of school now and you have no power over me, so I have no reason to lie. You were fuckin' wrong, Kawaji. You played detective and you thought you got your man but you didn't. You were wrong and what you said to me, what you called me, made me sick."

"But your handwriting…" he said quietly.

"It wasn't my handwriting, you moron. You're not the detective you think you are. Didn't you form any opinion about me during the months you've been teaching me?"

"You were a very gifted student," he said.

"I still am. And do you really think that someone with my passion for English would have spelled whore, H-O-A-R?"

He hung his head and sat down on the sand beside me. He was quiet for a long time and then finally said, "Maybe I did get it wrong. Who was it then?"

"I can't tell you that."

"Just for my peace of mind, it won't go any further."

I considered him and believed what he said. "You won't take any action? You promise?"

"What can I do, really? School will soon be over. Mrs Wilton will be back in September and, I assume, the culprit will have left by then. I just want to know. It won't go any further, I promise."

"OK," I said. "But I really shouldn't even have to tell you. Can't you guess who it was? Isn't it obvious?" I wanted him to work it out for himself. Even if it wasn't going to go any further, I still didn't like the idea of breaking the law of the schoolyard.

Kawaji shrugged, honestly bewildered. He had never considered anyone else after matching my handwriting.

"It was Billy Love."

"Hmmm," he said, nodding. "I suppose that does make more sense."

"So, can I assume my 37% will be reassessed?" I asked.

"I'm really sorry, but I can't do that."

"Why the hell not?" I said angrily. "That mark isn't fair."

"I know it isn't, but since that essay counts towards your final result, when they're graded we have to send the marks off to the examinations board. I've already posted the form to them."

"But you can tell them you made a mistake. Tell them the three is supposed to be an eight; it should be 87%." I pleaded.

"That essay is worth more than 87%. The form is typed so I can't say they read it wrong."

"Say it's a typo then." I could see this brilliant plan was falling apart.

"I can't. I have to think about my career. If I was to admit to such a mistake, I would never get another job again."

That's what people are really like.

I was speechless. Kawaji was happy enough to send my life down the crapper to save his own reputation. News had spread quickly around the school of our confrontation and now he was feared by the pupils and respected by the other teachers, who commended his no-nonsense attitude. He wasn't going to destroy the image he had created for some pupil who would be gone in a couple of months. He could have changed my result easily, of course he could, I'm sure he's not the first teacher to make a mistake. He just didn't want to. This was what we had to learn from. When we were talking in class about possible themes for the wartime essay he extolled the virtues of truth, honour, bravery, personal sacrifice and a sense of duty. He may as well have been an actor reading lines at the front of the classroom. He didn't believe any of what he said and he knew any respect I had for him was gone.

"If it helps," he mumbled, "I know I was wrong and I won't be so quick to accuse in future. I was pretty sore on you and you didn't deserve it."

Sarcasm was my parting shot. "I'm sure your regret will get me into any journalism course I choose." I stood up and walked away from him. In the Hollywood movie he would have come after me and said he was going to confess everything and get me the grade I deserved. When I had walked a few hundred yards up the beach, I turned and looked back at the boathouse. Kawaji had left.

"I thought he'd never fuckin' leave."

I turned and saw Justin Parke standing at the crest of a sand dune. I was in no mood for him. "Fly away, Justin. I can't be bothered with you tonight."

"You and me have unfinished business." That's how he talked—like he was in a gangster movie.

I was so pissed off about the outcome of the Kawaji gambit that I would gladly have fought with him. After fighting a Siren, this little shrimp wouldn't be a problem. "Well, fuckin' do something if you're going to," I shouted.

Now any After School Special will tell you that if you stand up to a bully he will leave you alone because a) he is scared of you now; or b) he respects you for standing up to him. This is, unfortunately, absolute bollocks. The truth is: if you stand up to a bully he will come after you again and again with more and more reinforcements until he has beaten you to a fine pâté.

Skid Millar appeared behind him. Then four of Justin's portable audience came up behind him. I should have known the little fucker wouldn't have the balls to take me one on one. I bolted down the beach towards the road. Behind me I heard the cackles and screams as the posse closed in on me. One of the unknowns brought me down with a rugby tackle. When the rest caught up they kicked and punched me a bit. It wasn't as bad as I imagined and when they relented I thought it was over. Then Justin ordered me taped. One of his lackeys wrapped tape around my wrists and ankles while the others restrained me. They carried me to the boathouse and threw me on the tarp. Tied up and kidnapped twice in the one story? Hollywood would not have approved, but in the real world the baddies are as unoriginal as they are stupid.

Skid Millar commented, "Smell this fuckin' place. Were you and Kawaji at it in here, Norton?"

Justin came close and slapped my face lightly, like he was Brando. "No, Norton just comes in here to give himself a hand solo, don't you, Norton?"

"Yeah, very funny, Justin," I nodded. "Now fuckin' untie me. This is beyond a joke."

"I think there's more laughs to be had," Justin replied.

"Well, see how funny it is when my mum calls the cops when I don't come home. You know her, Justin. You know how she panics. You know she will."

Justin's face remained blank but my threat unnerved some of the underlings. There were mumblings and a few of them said I had had enough. Skid and Justin were the only two who disagreed. After some heated words everyone but them left. Skid and Justin sat down and lit a cigarette each.

"I thought this was a hit, Justin. Is it actually a kidnapping?" I asked, knowing his language.

"No, it is a hit," Justin said, trying to blow smoke rings. "We're just waiting on a couple of others. Skid and I might get tired hitting you while you're still alive—then what would we do?"

Skid laughed sycophantically. We waited and Skid and Justin talked about music. They listened to those bands where the music sounded like a car trying to start and the singing sounded like someone trying to clear their throat. "You like metal don't you, Norton?" Skid asked.

"Yeah, tell him who you like, Stevie-boy," Justin said excitedly.

Justin knew who I liked and because it was at odds to what he and Skid liked, he knew it would give them a laugh and cause for ridicule. I didn't care. I answered, "I like Def Leppard, Bon Jovi and stuff like that."

They wailed with laughter. "He likes that kind of wimpy, girlie shit," Justin said.

"Why did you steal my Slippery When Wet album then, Justin?"

I swear his face reddened. I think it occurred to Justin at that moment that I could say a lot more embarrassing things about him. "I stole it and burned it," he said to Skid. "We should gag this mouthy fuck."

"Def Leppard," Skid said, shaking his head. "They don't even head-bang."

"And everyone knows you can't play guitar with a steady head, right Skid?" He didn't answer. He stuck duct tape across my mouth. We waited for ages and all I could do was sit and listen to their wildly uninformed opinions about music. Then I felt something, something beyond the nerves in my stomach. It was the Siren. It was attacking someone. I felt the urge to run to it. I felt the pull. Billy Love walked into the boathouse and was greeted by Skid and Justin. I got up and fell down immediately. I tried to wriggle towards the door, all the time trying to shout through my gag for them to release me. They just laughed and said the fear had got the best of me. I thrashed around wildly trying to get free. It took the three of them to hold me down. Now I knew how Toe-poke must have felt not being able to act on the impulse when the Siren attacked someone. I was filled with energy and didn't stop kicking. I thought at one point I was going to be able to break my bindings. After about twenty minutes the urge quieted. It was done. Someone else was probably dead.

If I hadn't been gagged I would have given them an earful. I didn't have time for this petty teenage bullshit. People were being killed out there and they had let it happen. I was so angry I would have blurted out everything in that moment, even if it had meant a luxury suite at Sycamore Acres. I thought we had been waiting for Billy, but when they had calmed me, the three of them sat down and we waited again. Justin reported my meeting with Kawaji to Billy. Billy was immediately suspicious and worried.

"Did you squeal on me, Norton?" Billy shouted.

I shook my head.

"If you did I'll fuckin' kill you," he added.

"And if you're lying, I'll kill you, too," Skid said.

Killed twice? Good threat, Skid.

"When Mike gets here," Skid continued, "you're going to tell us where that bastard that killed our dog lives. And he better be there."

So, we were waiting for Mike Millar. We sat again for a long time. They smoked and talked shit. Only the three orange dots at the end of their cigarettes gave away their position after a while. In the dark, I tried to work on breaking the tape around my wrists but had no luck.

"Where the fuck is he?" Skid asked. "I'm going outside to see if there's any sign of him."

Skid had been outside only a couple of minutes when I felt it again. The pull. The Siren was going to attack someone. I heard voices outside. The urge got stronger. It crawled like maggots around my chest. It was becoming unbearable. The door opened and Skid walked in with Mike.

"I found him," Skid said.

Mike looked at me and at once I knew that it wasn't Mike. The Siren had taken his form. It glared at me, incapacitated and powerless, and smiled.

Justin said, "OK, if we're going to do this, I'll light one of the lamps."

"Don't bother," Mike said. "I work better in the dark."

4.

The power was within me. I had the power to fight it. I had to break the tape and get free. I writhed around like crazy. Skid, Justin and Billy laughed at my attempts. They were gratified that their presence was causing such an extreme reaction in me. They didn't realise that I couldn't give a shit about them and was actually trying to get free so I could save their stupid, worthless lives.

Mike came close to me and I could see the Siren behind his eyes. They were dead eyes behind the illusion it had created. It used Mike's mouth to grin at my efforts to escape. It turned to my three jailers and approached. I was trying to shout through my gag, but nothing was coming out. I wished that one of them would light a cigarette. The flame from a match would be enough to expose it. It walked along and examined them; probably sizing up who had the most hope.

"What's up with you, man," Billy asked. "You're acting weird." Mike didn't answer Billy. "Hey, Mike, what's up?" he asked again.

Just then the Siren grabbed Skid around the throat and lifted him off the ground with one hand. Skid's legs swung and kicked. Confusion gripped the other boys in the darkness. Billy stepped forward and grabbed for Mike. The Siren used its free arm and pushed him, sending Billy flying backwards and slamming into the back wall of the boathouse. Justin ran out the door and into the night. I looked to Billy, he wasn't moving. I tried again to loosen the tape. The moonlight from the open door was illuminating the Siren now. I could see the tentacle coming out of its wrist. It slid over Skid's jaw and across his cheek. I saw it enter his ear and then he screamed. A horrible choked scream. Skid kicked harder and swung his fists at the Siren's body. His punches had no effect.

Emily raced into the boathouse with a large kitchen knife and jammed it deep into the Siren's arm-pit. It dropped Skid, he fell to the floor and didn't move. Emily pulled the knife out and lunged again. The Siren parried this time and hit her on the back of the head. Emily went head-first into the floor. I saw the dark yellow liquid running down the Siren's side. It went for the door but stopped. It looked at me. I looked for Emily. It stepped towards me. Emily was groggily getting to her feet. The Siren's hand reached for me with the tentacle still extended. I pushed myself back against the wall. Emily threw the knife at the Siren, but it bounced off its shell and landed at my side. The Siren turned and saw Emily running at it. It ran outside and Emily ran after it. I jumped for the knife and started cutting the tape on my wrists.

It was achingly slow work. Every second I thought Emily could be dying. She needed my help. Finally, I cut through the tape on my wrists. I slit the tape on my ankles easily and ripped the gag from my mouth. I ran outside with the knife.

I could see the Siren a few hundred yards down the beach. Emily had jumped on its back and was hanging round its neck, punching wildly at the side of its head. I ran as fast as I could. My legs were numb from being restrained in the same position for so long. I saw the Siren reach round and try to grab Emily. Emily used the opportunity to punch the wound she had made under its arm. It shrieked in pain. That's my girl! I was closing on the pair when the Siren saw me. It turned and ran towards the sea. Emily hung on, trying to pull its head back and break its neck. I ran faster, but I wasn't going to beat it to the shoreline. It ran through the wash and dived into the black water. Emily was still hanging on when it disappeared under the waves.

I ran into the sea and called for Emily. I couldn't see her anywhere. I waded in up to my waist and kept calling for her. I was getting really scared. The waters on the beach could be treacherous even if you weren't exhausted from fighting. My calls to her became more panicked. I moved further up the beach. I wasn't even sure anymore where she had gone in. I scanned the surface of the sea, desperately looking for a sign of life. Don't let it take her, I thought. Not Emily. I had no concept of time, but I thought she had been down there too long. I needed help. I would have to call the RNLI and get the Lifeboat to look for her. But while I was away she could surface and need my help. She might not last until I got back. Billy, I thought. He's still in the boathouse. He could go for help and I could keep on looking. I walked backwards, out of the sea, still watching the surface. I edged slowly out of the water onto the sand, and then something caught my eye. I couldn't see clearly. It could just be a piece of driftwood or…no, it was Emily! I ran into the sea and swam towards her. She seemed to be conscious, but just treading water. She was too tired to swim. I thrashed the water on either side of me, the waves fighting me all the way.

When I got close I shouted, "Emily, are you all right?"

"I've been better," came the reply.

I was so relieved. She was still kicking and still smiling. I reached her in the water and hugged her tightly. We both hovered there for a moment, treading water. I released my embrace and looked her in the face. "Where the hell were *you*?" she asked. I was about to launch into a summary of the night's events when she smiled and added, "Only joking."

It was one of those times that I couldn't help but love her.

I helped her to the shore and we walked back to the boathouse. Skid was lying motionless where the Siren had dropped him. Billy was gone.

"Billy must have came to and run off," I said.

"Billy was here?" said Emily, suddenly interested.

"Yes, he and the other two were going to beat the shit out of me."

She hung her head, somehow embarrassed by Billy's actions. She knelt down and put her hand on Skid's chest. "He's dead. I thought I might have got to him in time. Strike two for tonight. Their poor mother."

"What do you mean strike two?"

"The Siren attacked Mike earlier; that's what got me into town to start with. When I got there he was already dead. In the car park at the end of the promenade."

It's hard to know how to feel when two people you hate die. It's terrible when anyone dies so young, and when I thought of what their mother would go through when she heard, it made me shiver. I didn't want to think about it anymore. One answer would make me a hypocrite and the other would make me a ghoul.

"I suppose we should phone the police," Emily said, standing up.

"No," I mumbled. Emily looked startled. I was tired and we were both soaking wet. I put my arm around her waist and guided her to the door. "Let someone else try to explain it this time." We walked to the end of the beach, through the small grouping of trees and onto the road. We hadn't been walking long when an empty taxi picked us up. We both got in the back so the driver wouldn't notice we were going to soak his upholstery. When we got to Emily's, she ran inside and came back with the fare. I didn't want to presume that I was staying, so I left the back door open and stood beside the taxi until she came back. She quickly handed the driver the money, slammed the back door and waved him away. We exchanged a glance that for once I didn't see as a sexual question-mark, but as genuine admiration and friendship. She put her arm around me and we walked into the house.

I was getting used to the procedure: I went to the bathroom and got undressed, threw my clothes out to Emily, had a shower and put on a bathrobe. She had a big mug of hot chocolate waiting when I entered the kitchen. She suggested I phone my mum and went to take a shower herself.

My mum was in understandably frantic form when I called. I didn't realise it was so late. I was running out of plausible lies so I just told her I got in a fight and it turned into a whole 'thing.' I was relieved that she didn't ask me to elaborate. I told her that Emily had been involved, too, and I was at her place now. I played up that angle because I thought a disagreement over a girl was something believable that my mum would understand. She asked if I was staying the night. I could hear the shower had been turned off. I shouted to Emily if she wanted me to stay. She said she did. I left it with my mum that we would work it the same as before; dad would pick me up in the morning before work. I hung up, went back to the kitchen and boiled the kettle so Emily could have hot chocolate when she was done.

We both went into the living room and snuggled up on the sofa before the fire. We didn't speak for a long time. We were comfortable together and I began to think that this is the closeness that girls talk about. When they give you that old line 'I can't go out with you because you're my friend' this is what they mean. That's not to say they don't abuse and overuse that excuse, but on rare occasions it's true. I felt more intimate sitting here in silence with Emily than I had ever felt with my hand inside Rachel's blouse.

I spied a familiar object on the mantelpiece. "What's that?"

Emily followed my gaze and said, "An invitation to Rachel's engagement party."

"I didn't think you two were friendly."

Emily got up and grabbed the card and brought it back to the sofa. "We're not. Read it."

It said: You are cordially invited to a party to celebrate the engagement of Rachel Cole and Anthony McMaster.

Then below the time and date details Rachel had written:

Emily,
I see you and Steve together a lot at school and rumour suggests that you are at least good friends. I hope you will come to our engagement party with Steve. Steve and I were together a long time and I really do love him and want him to be happy. He was one of the best friends I ever had and I hate to lose him like this. I'm sure he will really like Tony if he just gives him a chance. I hope I see you both there.
Rachel

I was thinking how to tell Emily diplomatically that there was no way in hell that I was going to Rachel's party when she spoke.

"She really hurt you, didn't she?"

Emily's eyes were unbelievably inviting in the firelight. Maybe it was the suggestion of a relationship between us in the card that had got me thinking about her again, but I swear she never looked so beautiful. "Yeah, I guess she did."

"I didn't think for a moment that you'd want to go. You don't, do you?"

"God, no."

"Do you think Rachel sounds a little jealous in that note?"

"She's upset that I'm not mooning after her like a little lost puppy dog. She doesn't want me, she wants the attention."

Emily shifted closer. Sometimes a girl looks at you and you can't be sure what her eyes are saying and other times, like this, you just know she is asking you to kiss her. You can see the excitement, longing and vulnerability that need to be shared. We were close. I moved closer and smelled the shampoo in her damp hair. I breathed her in. Our lips touched and I saw her eyes close just as mine did. Her kiss was extremely gentle and tender. We lay there just kissing. I don't remember falling asleep. I don't remember stopping kissing her. Maybe my dreams of kissing her took over without missing a beat. I like to think that's what happened. I hope it happened to her too.

We overslept the next morning. My dad honking the horn outside at ten to seven woke us. I quickly got my clothes from the drier and pulled them on.

Emily shook her head at my wrinkled attire. "I never got a chance to iron them. And you never even got any breakfast."

"Yeah, the service is really slipping at this place." She smiled and we stood there in an uncomfortable pause. Neither of us knew if this was a kiss goodbye situation or just a goodbye. The thinking time seemed to go on too long. In the end I just smiled, nodded and left. My dad may have spoken on the way home, but I was on another plane and didn't hear anything he said. I was actually happy.

When I got home my mum was in a serious panic about me fighting all the time and getting hurt. She said Toe-poke had phoned last night and said it was urgent that I phone him as soon as I got home. I had forgotten about Toe-poke. He would have felt the pull, too, but was probably laid up and unable to act on it. After I had calmed my mum down, I rang Toe-poke and told him what had happened. He apologized for his incapacity and I told him about Emily kicking its ass. He said he should be back at school in a couple of weeks and ready to fight. I told him if anything happened I would let him know. I changed and caught the bus to school.

I looked for Emily at break time and couldn't find her. At dinnertime I did see her. She was on the other side of the playground having a heated discussion with Billy Love. I strolled towards them, but Billy left before I got there.

"He's a bit freaked out about last night," she said.

That made me feel a bit better: just business. Emily and I walked slowly round the football pitches talking about the Siren's latest victims. The police had found Mike and Skid and their deaths were all over the news. Billy and Justin had kept tight-lipped about being there and that suited us just fine. There was still suspicion about us, but we were used to it by now.

"Do you think him and Justin will feel the pull now too?" she asked.

"I don't know. Maybe. Though maybe they got a diluted dose of the Siren's mojo because it was making four of us see it at once." I wanted to add that maybe there isn't heroism inside everybody to activate, but I didn't. As far as I know neither of them ever did feel the pull.

As the bell rang to signal the end of dinnertime, Emily said, "Listen, about us kissing last night…"

This wasn't good. I felt like she was going to explain how a magic trick was done. I always hated those guys—give me the magic every time. Revealing the mechanics of the unexplainable was like ripping the beard from Santa's face and seeing your dad.

It wasn't magic. It was just an illusion, see? Let me show you. Here's the smoke. Here's the mirrors.

"…it probably wasn't a good idea," she continued. "Both of us have too much stuff screwing up our heads at the minute to know what's going on."

And here's the trap door.

"I don't think we should do it again. I need you too much as a friend."

I gave her an insincere hug and she ran off to class.

I was late for English, but Kawaji seemed unusually tolerant. He was doing his best to act naturally, but I could tell he was nervous that I was going to reveal his secret. The whole class was uneasy and I was relieved when the bell sounded. As I shuffled towards the door my day got a whole lot worse.

"Billy Love, please wait behind," Kawaji said.

I turned and saw he had taken Joshua's Autobiography from his drawer and left it on his desk. Billy saw it two seconds after I did and his head twisted and glared at me. I wanted to stop and say something, but there was nothing I could say. Kawaji, who would probably say he was tipped from an anonymous source, had just got me in a whole heap more trouble.

I saw Emily at the end of school and asked her if she wanted to patrol with me. She told me she had invited Billy over to explain to him what he had seen. "He really needs to talk to someone, Steve. We're just going to talk."

I got off the bus hoping that my day couldn't get any worse and saw Imogen Collins standing in my driveway. She looked naked without a cameraman and soundman flanking her.

"Steven, we need to talk."

"I wish you would just fuck off. I'm in no mood for you today." She followed me to the door. It was locked: mum's shopping day. I rummaged in my pocket and found my key. I got the door open and went inside.

I was about to slam it in her face when she pushed her way inside. "Listen, I know you know what's going on around here. All these unexplained deaths; you're linked to them all. I'm not saying you're doing them or that you're even involved, but you know a hell of a lot more than the local flat-foots. There's a book in this! Let me be the one to write it. Tracey-Ann is going to have my job—her tits are fake by the way—and I'm going to end up as a host on Radio Alaska or something. This could earn us a fortune. You and I: partners, what do you say?"

"You wouldn't believe me if I told you what's going on, so just leave," I said.

"I would, I would, honestly."

"No, you wouldn't."

She considered me like she was counting her chips at a poker game. She raised the stakes. "Do you want to have sex with me?"

I couldn't disguise the surprise on my face. Added to which, I had forgotten how to speak, temporarily.

"I know what kids your age want. You've got one thing on your mind: losing the V. Well listen, kid, I'm willing to make that happen right now if you'll work with me on the book."

I was a shocked statue, with a very fast heartbeat.

She came closer and continued, "Anything you want to do to me. Anything you want me to do to you, I will do it right now if you want. Just give me the exclusive." She started rubbing the crotch of my trousers and seemed gratified to find that it was not only my face that resembled a statue. She took my right hand and pressed it to her left breast. "You like that, don't you?" she whispered hoarsely. She slid down to the ground and rested on her knees. "Just relax and enjoy," she said.

Her hand had almost reached my trouser zipper when I heard the driveway stones crunch under the weight of my mum's car. "My mum," I said. I stepped back as Imogen Collins got to her feet and slipped her high heels back on. She took a business card from her pocket and pressed it into my hand.

"The offer's still open. Call me. We can go to a hotel if you like, I'll pay for it. You think about it." She turned and let herself out. I stood in a kind of stunned awe for a few minutes, then my mum asked me to help her bring the shopping in. I did it in record time and then decided that I really should go to my bedroom and see if that lock was still working.

After testing the lock thoroughly and repeatedly, I thought about Imogen Collins's offer. I think I was scared of her experience more than anything. I mean, a girl my own age would be on a par, more or less, with me as far as sexual experience goes, but Imogen Collins? She'd been round the block more times than a retiring postman. I decided that I wouldn't take her up on her offer, but I made sure I kept her card in a very safe place.

Chapter IX - The Grate Escape

We still haven't had any calls so I'll play some more music. Remember today's topic is: This secret could ruin my life. Call now to share it with the audience. Here's someone with no secrets; gorgeous George Michael, singing his hit, I want your sex.

Talk Radio, Imogen Collins

- May, 1990 -

1.

Billy Love looked at me like a lion looks at a zebra, but he didn't do anything. Something was keeping him from taking out the vengeance he so obviously desired. Maybe Kawaji had spilled everything and told him if he hit me that he would be failed, or expelled, or something. Or maybe Emily was keeping him at bay. Since their last meeting I had the distinct feeling that more had happened than a frank discussion on the Siren and it's motives. He had wormed his way back into her affections somehow. Whatever was holding him back, I knew one thing for sure: it was not permanent. One day soon his leash was going to snap and I would be on the receiving end when it did.

Emily hadn't been patrolling with me. She was studying hard and wanted to do well in her final exams. I had given up hope of passing anything. Occasionally I flipped through a book to make it look to my parents that I was trying, but I really wasn't. This year had been a total mess and I wanted to write it off. I would repeat whatever GCSEs I thought I needed next year, when things were calmer and when the Siren was dead.

I was returning from patrolling the beach on the first Friday of the month when I saw a lone vehicle parked on the sand. As I got closer, I saw it was Brian Winters's car and he was sitting on the bonnet. He was smoking and staring out to sea. I walked over and sat beside him. The smoke didn't smell like a cigarette and from its crude construction I guessed that it was a joint. He took a drag and held it in as he passed it to me. I took the joint and sucked timidly on the end. I coughed out whatever I had inhaled and Brian smiled, taking it back.

"Not one for the dope, are you?"

"No, I suppose not," I said. "I didn't think you were, either."

"When I realised that Doug was getting an extended stay in Sycamore Acres, I started to wonder if there was an answer somewhere. Maybe I'd overlooked something. Maybe we all had. Maybe he was going through something that none of us knew about. So I went through all his stuff and you know what I found?"

I shook my head.

"Nothing. Sure, he had love letters from Maxine, some porn and a stash of weed hidden, but nothing that explains him being…like he is now."

There was very little emotion in Brian's voice; it was like he was going through the machinations of life without any real interest in them. I knew how he felt because I had been there, too. "I guess you want to be alone, so I'll go."

"I'm actually waiting on Dave Drake and Dave Watt. They said they wanted to try some weed to see what it's like. I told them I'd meet them here. Maybe you should go, they might think you're a cop and run for it."

I smiled. "Yeah, those two are wound a little tight. Maybe a bit of smoke will chill them out a bit." I left Brian and walked home. I thought about Doug, stuck in Sycamore Acres, trying desperately to make someone understand what he had to say.

The weekend passed without incident and Monday morning brought the same tired faces going through the same routine. I was edgy. I think it was a combination of anger (about failing school, Emily and Billy, etc.) and frustration that I was actually risking my own life to save these people who were treating me like shit. I think that's why that day, for the first time in my life, I actually initiated a fight.

His name was Scone. They called him Scone because his head looked like a scone: hairless, lumpy, fat and round. Scone would usually be the kind of kid that would be picked on because he was overweight and had roughly the same IQ as the baked-good he was named after. But Scone had been smart enough to ally himself with Bull Brennan. Bull Brennan wasn't going to be winning any academic achievements in the near future, either, but he was short and well built, and there were few who would take their chances against him. His stupidity was an asset when it came to being Scone's monkey-boy. Bull never had the sense to quit. There was a story that five guys had put him down and knocked the living hell out of him, but, as soon as he was able to stand, he charged at them and won the fight. Like a lot of stories similar to that, no one had witnessed it first hand, but they all knew someone who had. It was good to see that Bull had found his niche so early in life. He would never be qualified for any work other than hired muscle, so he may as well start serving his apprenticeship.

Scone and Bull were both a year younger than me. Frankly, anyone could have taken Scone in a fair fight; he was badly overweight and smoked like a chimney. It was just the obstacle of Bull that stopped people from hitting him. But that day I didn't even think about the danger, I just reacted.

We were in the dining hall. Julia Parkhill had a new ski-jacket (remember, they were all the rage at the time?). It was a mustard colour and looked very good on her. She sat down, to the admiration of her friends, and slipped the jacket over the back of the chair. I saw Scone clock the jacket and when he walked toward it with a jug of water in his hand, I knew he was up to something. He 'accidentally' spilled the water over Julia's new jacket and she jumped up immediately. Scone was apologizing. Definitely something amiss. He said if she gave him the jacket he would dry it off. Julia was suspicious, too, but eventually nodded and released her hold on the jacket. Scone snapped the jacket into his grasp and said, "Cheers. My sister needs a new coat." He laughed and then added, "You say you lost it or I'll fuckin' fell you, bitch." Scone walked away. Julia started crying. Where was a teacher when you actually needed one? Bull joined Scone and the two of them laughed and left the dining room. My blood was boiling. I didn't know why it was so maddening, but it was. I stood up and followed them out of the dining room.

I found Scone and Bull outside. The jacket was hanging on a tree, drying. Scone and Bull sat below it. Bull had rolled up his sleeve and was showing Scone a tattoo of a dragon on his arm. I walked towards them. They looked up, dismissed me as no threat, and returned to their conversation. I continued towards them. They looked up again and seemed confused by my presence. Bull leapt to his feet and Scone rolled around on the ground until he found his feet.

Bull walked to me and faced me. His bottom lip protruded as it always did and his eyes seemed to convey that he was more-or-less permanently baffled. "Got a problem?" he said, his head bobbing and twitching.

"I'm taking that jacket back to Julia."

If someone had explained to him the meaning of astonished, Bull would have said that was what he felt. "Wanna fight aboot it?"

Before I could answer he had thrown an arm around my neck and put me in a headlock. I could hear a crowd swarming over and the chant beginning: Fight, Fight, Fight, Fight! I grabbed Bull's arm and gave it a sharp twist. I was free. Bull was furious and charged at me. I just reacted. I don't even remember hitting him. It was like reading frames of a comic with one missing.

1. Bull charges at me, speech bubble says "Grrrrr!"

2. Steely eyed, I grit my teeth and draw back my fist.

4. Bull is lying on the ground with blood spurting from his nose.

There should have been a frame 3. where I hit him, but I never saw it. The crowd was silenced by this unexpected defeat. I turned and looked at Scone. He was obviously scared. I walked towards the jacket. My legs disappeared from under me. It was Bull. He had got up and tackled me. I fell to the ground and turned instantly. Bull sat on my stomach. His eyes were watering. I must have hit him square on the nose. He drove his fist into my jaw. This time the frame wasn't missing. It didn't hurt as much as I thought it would. I got mad all over again. I sat up and threw him backwards. He fell on the grass and I was on top of him. It seemed almost too easy and I hesitated for a moment before punching. His fist swung at me and I dodged it. I punched him four times in the face.

199

"Do you give in?" I screamed at him. I punched him again. He brought his arms up and covered his face. "Do you give in?" I repeated and hit him on the unprotected side of his head.

"Aye!" he said through his tears. "Now fuck aff." He was crying. Bull Brennan was crying. Crazy. I stood up and released him. He quickly got to his feet and ran off with his head buried in his chest. I turned to Scone again. Scone plucked the jacket from the branch of the tree and handed it back to Julia Parkhill, who was standing in the crowd. I walked over to Scone. I wanted to hit him as well, for no other reason than I didn't like him. I didn't like people like him. And I was on a bit of an adrenalin buzz from the fight. I squared up to Scone and looked him right in the eye.

I don't know where this line came from—probably too many Schwarzenegger movies—but I said to Scone, "You see what I did to Bull, I *want* to do that to you. You just give me a reason." I left a dramatic pause and then walked away.

Instead of that incident ingratiating me with my fellow pupils, it just alienated me more. Now I was not only weird, but also unpredictably violent. Julia Parkhill never even thanked me.

2.

Later that day I found a note in my locker from Taffy saying that he thought he had a lead on who was helping the Siren and to meet him at the boathouse at seven. When I got home and changed I found out that my parents had other ideas. They had arranged for me to go and talk to 'someone.' No matter how many times they denied it, I was still left with the distinct impression that this 'someone' was a psychiatrist. I had a full-blown argument with both of them that I eventually lost. Any other evening I would have gone without a fight just to please them and put their minds at rest, but Taffy would be waiting for me and I had no way of contacting him. I was bundled into the car and just hoped that whatever Taffy had found out, he could handle.

We drove to Ballymoney. At first I had the dread suspicion that they were taking me to Sycamore Acres, but we ended up in a large townhouse with spacious grounds. I was quickly escorted to he door and introduced to Dr Roberts. He was in his mid-fifties and bald apart from tufts of grey hair above each ear. He was about my height, but with a big belly and a neck that was MIA. He wore a dark, well-tailored, three-piece suit and looked like he wasn't short of a pound.

He led me into his study and my parents waited outside. He started making smalltalk with me (to gain my trust) as he fussed with papers on his desk. I wasn't giving anything away. Ever since I had reconciled myself to the fact that my parents weren't going to take no for an answer, I had been thinking about what to say to him. I had prepared a normal teenage persona based on an approximation of what your average sixteen year-old thinks about: girls, sex, music, sex, exams, girls, fashion, popularity, sex, career, girls and sex. I had to respond to everything he asked me with an answer that related to one of those things. He didn't even make it difficult. He started me off with the old Rorschach Ink Blot Tests. Now, if you know what old Herman Rorschach was getting at, these things are easy to beat. The thing to remember is that those blots aren't supposed to look like anything. Everyone sees what is predominantly on his or her mind. So it was easy to prepare something to say.

Card 1 looked like a murdered body. "That's a girl lying on a bed in her underwear."

Card 2 looked like a mouth full of razor-sharp teeth. "That's a woman bending over."

Card 3 looked uncannily like Maxine. "That looks like that pop singer. She's in a bikini in her video. I forget her name."

Card 4 looked like the faces of Skid and Mike Millar lying dead beside each other. "Breasts. That looks like breasts. Nice ones, too."

Card 5 looked like Emily in a rabbit costume. What the hell. "That looks like my friend Emily in a rabbit costume."

Next he tried me with the old word association, which I was prepared for as well. It's basically the same deal as the ink blots—just don't say what comes to your mind first. He talked to me about school and getting into fights and I told him that there was some kind of soap-opera love triangle going on with Emily, me and Billy. He seemed satisfied. He took me out to the waiting room and took my parents in for a private chat.

On the way home in the car I joked, "So are you taking me to Sycamore Acres? What did the doc say?" I was brimming with confidence.

My mum spoke first. "He says you should probably see him every week for a while. Just until things get better."

"What?"

My dad chimed in. "He says you lied to him the whole time you were in there. He says you're hiding something and you're noticeably under a great deal of pressure."

Shit.

We stayed silent until we got home and then I got the third degree again. It would have been so easy to just tell them the truth, but they would never have believed it. They wanted me to go back and see Doctor Roberts again, but I fought them. I told them it was just exam pressure combined with a girl problem. I made them a deal that if I wasn't back to normal when all my exams were over and school was finished, I would go back and see him. I would even sign myself into Sycamore Acres if they wanted. I assured them that I would be OK. They begrudgingly accepted my offer and I went upstairs to bed. It was gone eleven. I thought I might have been able to get out for a quick patrol and try to find Taffy, but it was too late and I was too annoyed at the night's disastrous outcome. I had to double my efforts. The clock was now ticking. If I didn't kill the Siren and sort myself out by the time school ended, there was a very real possibility of me ending up in Sycamore Acres.

Little did I know that as I was having a shouting match with my parents in my kitchen, one of Sycamore Acres' current residents had knocked out a guard and was running towards my house.

3.

It was the cold air that woke me. I sat up groggily and noticed my window was wide open. I didn't even feel threatened, just annoyed. I got up and closed it without ever thinking who might have opened it. It wasn't until I got back to my bed that I saw him. Doug Winters was sitting in a darkened corner of my bedroom, shivering. I looked down and saw his feet were bleeding. He must have run from Sycamore Acres without anything on his feet and wearing nothing but hospital whites. He didn't look like he was here to kill me. He could have done it while I was asleep if that was his intention. His face was contorted in concentration. I took a blanket from my cupboard and wrapped it round him. He came out of his daze and recognized me. "Steve Norton. Just a crush, Steve Norton. Maxine says it's just a crush, Steve Norton. Steve Norton. Steve Norton. Something to tell just a crush, Steve Norton. Something inside…" He slapped the side of his head a few times.

I knelt down in front of him and stopped him hitting himself. I turned his head and looked him in the eyes. "The source. Do you have to tell me something about the source?"

His eyes widened. He was trying so hard to remember. "The source? Just a crush, Steve Norton. No, not the source; The Source. Just a crush, Steve Norton. The Source!" He jumped to his feet and dragged me to the window.

I stopped him and convinced him to stand still while I put some clothes on him and a pair of trainers on his feet. I got dressed, too. I thought about calling Emily, but it was almost 2.30am. If Doug were going to lead me to this thing's hiding place I would need help; I couldn't take the Siren alone. Still, what if he wasn't taking me anywhere? The poor guy was confused, make no mistake. I decided I would go with him on a reconnaissance mission. If he led me to the Siren's lair, I would come back tomorrow with Emily and Toe-poke.

Doug was ahead of me all the way to town. I had trouble keeping up with him. He did seem to know where he was going, or so I thought. In the middle of town he stopped dead. He looked around like he could hear something that I couldn't. He waited a few minutes and then ran off in a different direction.

"Doug? Are we still going to the source?"

He didn't answer, but was running even faster now. He led me to Wrenfield; a little estate of eighteenth century houses that had been renovated and were now fitted with every mod-con. People who lived here had money. People who lived here had security systems. Doug seemed to know exactly where he was going. He ran to a specific house and stopped when he reached the door.

"What are you doing, Doug? Who lives here?" I looked around, expecting to see curtains twitching and silhouettes of phones being lifted. "Doug, we have to get out of here!"

Doug lay against the door gently. He ran his hand down the grain of the wood and closed his eyes. He slid down to his knees, still rubbing his hand up and down the varnish on the door. He looked so passive that I thought he might fall asleep. I put my arm around him, lifted him to his feet, and turned him from the door. His eyes opened, blinking. He looked at me as if he was surprised to see me. "Just a crush, Steve Norton."

I nodded and led him away from the door. We had only got a few steps when his body stiffened and he stopped. He spun back to the door, inadvertently pushing me across the lawn. He turned his shoulder to the door and charged. I couldn't intercept him in time. He crashed through the door and fell on the hall carpet. I ran to him and tried to help him up, but he was staring into the darkness of the house. A low growl caught my attention. Then a loud barking and the patter of paws running at us. Doug got to his knees and launched himself forward. I stood up and hit the light-switch. It was a mean looking German Shepherd and it had its teeth locked around Doug's forearm. Doug was punching it with his free hand. Blood was squirting from his arm in small jets. Doug launched himself forward and pinned the dog with his weight. It yelped under the crushing weight, but still bit and clawed at him. I looked around for something that I could separate them with. The dog swiped a paw at Doug's face and cut him from his forehead, through his eye, down to his cheek. His eye filled with blood, making him look inhuman with rage. I heard movement above. We had woken the owner. I heard the footsteps run across the ceiling and descend the stairs. When he came into the light I saw it was Mr Sloan.

"Aeetes, heel!" he screamed. He started towards the fighting pair, but stopped, realising they were both as wild and unpredictable as each other. "Aeetes, release! Release, boy! Aeetes!" Just then, Doug bit the dog's throat; it let out a high-pitched howl and tried to struggle free. The dog's blood sprayed in Doug's face. Its front paws clawed at the floor, trying to drag itself to safety. Doug used the opportunity to get behind the dog. He put one arm under its neck and used the other to twist its head sharply. There was a loud crack and the dog stopped moving. Doug released his grip and it fell, limp and lifeless, to the ground. Doug stood up and spat the dog's blood from his mouth. Then he turned to Sloan.

Sloan turned and ran. Doug raced after him. I followed them. I heard them struggling in the kitchen. When I reached them, Sloan was lying on the floor. Doug sat on top of him punching him repeatedly in the face. Sloan was fighting back at first, but Doug's rage had made him powerful. The punches that did hit Doug were ignored. Doug hit him again and again. I felt sure he was going to kill him. I didn't know whether to stop him or not. Everyone thought Doug was crazy, but there was something about his ramblings that made me believe that in some distorted way he was doing the right thing. The right thing in his mind, anyway. Sloan couldn't keep up with the punches that were being thrown and he stopped fighting back. Doug stopped punching him, put his hands around Sloan's throat, and began to squeeze. Sloan's face began to redden and he used the little strength he had left to try to pry Doug's fingers from his neck. I couldn't let Doug do it, not without being sure.

"Doug, stop," I shouted. Incredibly, he did. He loosened his grip and slowly raised his head and looked me in the eyes. He looked like The Phantom of the Opera, with one side of his face masked in the dog's blood. Sloan took a deep breath as soon as he was able and then coughed as the air rushed down his bruised windpipe. Doug grabbed Sloan by the wrists and dragged him out of the kitchen. I followed nervously.

Doug deposited Sloan on the rug in his living room. I walked in and Doug closed the door behind me. I walked over to Sloan and offered him my hand. He slapped it away and weakly pulled himself up and into an armchair.

"You're going away for this, too, Norton," he croaked hoarsely. "That fuckwit is going back to the loony bin, but you're going to a detention centre."

He might be wrong; I might end up in Sycamore Acres, too. Doug kicked the handle on the door until it broke off. Doug looked at me and then pointed to Sloan. I didn't understand what he meant and shrugged. Doug ran closer and pointed to Sloan again, more vehemently this time.

"I don't understand, Doug. What are you trying to tell me?" It was like one of those old Lassie movies.

"He's fuckin' crazy, Norton. He's not trying to tell you anything."

Doug punched at the wall in frustration. He made attempts to speak, which only angered him more. Finally he slid to the floor and put his head in his hands. I had to bide time. I hoped Doug would tell me eventually. I was putting a lot of faith in him, but it felt right. I wandered around the room and looked at the photos on the fireplace. I lifted Sloan's wedding photo. His wife was well tasty.

"Where's your wife, Mr Sloan?" It seemed bizarre that I still called him mister, but I didn't even think about it. Besides, after it came out, I thought I sounded like a cop.

"At her mother's."

"She's not upstairs phoning the police?"

"No, but I'm sure someone on the street has. I have very conscientious neighbours."

"You're very composed for a man who was almost killed." Sloan remained silent. "Maybe they train you for this type of thing. Not specifically two students—one a mental patient— breaking into your house and terrorizing you, but I'm sure they tell all teachers, even Careers Advisors, how to deal with this kind of Lord of the Flies rebellion."

He stayed silent. He looked smug. He knew something that I didn't. Doug was staring off into space. I needed to keep Sloan occupied until Doug got instructions from the mothership, or whatever he was looking at. I couldn't see how I was going to get out of this without the police charging me with something. Was it still technically kidnapping if we were in his house? I thought I remembered the term unlawful imprisonment, from a cop show on TV. That sounded like what we were doing. Or was it what *I* was doing, since Doug wasn't mentally competent? I would be blamed for all of this. I had to try to convince Sloan that I didn't initiate this little visit. I had to be friendly and not accuse him of anything.

"It's a nice house, Mr Sloan," I ventured.

"It was," he answered dryly.

"Lived here long?"

"Since August."

August. Now that was interesting. Sloan saw my face brighten; he suddenly looked guilty and scared. I ran my finger along the fireplace and cut a track along the thick layer of dust. "Your wife isn't much of a housekeeper."

"We both work." His tone wasn't smug anymore. He was choosing every word very carefully. Doug turned his head to us, suddenly interested.

I looked at the telephone and the little book beside it. "I think I should call your in-laws and check on your wife."

Sloan tensed. "It's the middle of the goddamn night!"

He was scared and I knew it. "Your wife isn't there is she? I'll bet my freedom on it. If I call your in-laws and your wife is there, I'll tell her we've broken into your house and she should call the police. That OK with you?"

Sloan leapt from the chair and made for the window. Doug pounced on him before he got there and they started fighting again. Doug was not as vicious this time and seemed to just want to subdue Sloan. Sloan got free and ran to the far corner of the room. Doug lifted the poker from the fireside and advanced on him.

"You can't win, Norton," Sloan shouted. "These creatures lived in the oceans millions of years before Jesus Christ walked this Earth. They are, in every true sense, our gods. They are our fathers. Their presence brought the oceans to life. The same oceans that we would crawl from millions of years later. They are our creators and, if it is their will, we must honour them with sacrifices so that they may live."

"You gave it your wife, didn't you?" I said, suddenly realising I was facing someone crazier than Doug would ever be.

"It came to me." He said proudly. "It chose me to bring it those that would satisfy its needs."

"And as Careers Advisor..." I began.

207

"Yes," he interrupted, "I would be able to separate the no-hopers who were going to spend their lives shovelling shit, from the dreamers; brimming with hope and talent and ambition. I offered my wife as a symbol of my commitment."

"You're fuckin' nuts."

"Why?" he asked loudly. "Because I believe in a god that I can see? Because I serve a god that can reward me in *this* life? You're the one that's nuts, Norton. This isn't a Hollywood movie; you're not going to get a happy ending here. You know what happens to people who do good their whole lives? Nothing! They die alone and unloved in some fuckin' toilet in a nursing home. This life is all there is." He shot a glance at the window and made a break for it again. Doug swung the poker and caught him hard on his temple. Sloan dropped to the floor. I walked cautiously over to him. Blood was trickling from his head onto the carpet. I thought he was dead. The reality hit me. How the hell was I ever going to explain this? I tentatively pushed two fingers under his cheekbone and felt a pulse. I let out a breath of relief. I turned to tell Doug and saw him lift the poker above his head.

"What are you doing, Doug?"

Doug screamed and brought the poker down hard on the fireplace. The fire hadn't been lit in a long time by the looks of it, but soot and ash puffed up as he hit it again and again. Then he dropped the poker and started pulling at the brass fittings of the fire. He was like an animal, clawing with inhuman strength and pulling everything out in a few minutes. When he was done, he relaxed and turned to me. I walked over. The first thing I noticed was the smell of gas. Doug had broken the gas line. I was about to grab him and lead him out, when I looked down and saw Doug lift the fire grate to reveal a chamber under the house. I hadn't long to decide; the room was filling with gas, but there might be someone alive down there.

"OK, I need a torch. Look for a torch, Doug!" We ransacked the drawers and cupboards and found nothing. Doug lifted a scented candle and flicked open the lid of a Zippo lighter he had found. I grabbed his hands before he could strike the wheel and said quietly, "The gas." I don't know if he understood, he didn't look like he did. I looked down into the hole again and shouted, "Is there anyone down there? If you can't speak, try to make a noise." I listened intently and heard nothing. A light went on in the chamber under the house and I jumped back. I turned and saw Doug with his finger on a switch at the side of the chimney. I looked down again. It was about a ten feet drop to the ground. I thought I could see something at the very edge of my field of vision. A boot; a man's boot. I shouted again but it didn't move. The smell of gas was getting stronger. I pulled Doug over to the fireplace and put my hands on his shoulders, talking directly to his face. "Doug, I'm going down there. I'm going to have a quick look around to see if anyone's alive down there. You have to stay up here to help me get out again. Do you understand?" I met the same vague, non-committal look. "OK, lower me down." Doug took my hands and lowered me as far as his stretch would allow. It was a short drop to the floor after that. The stench down here was stronger than upstairs, but it wasn't gas down here; it was death.

I turned around and surveyed my surroundings. This wasn't just an underground room; it was the entrance to a tunnel. The lightbulbs that were crudely attached to the wall didn't throw enough light to see far down it. I gave a shout and the echo seemed to carry a long way. I turned back to where I had seen the boot; it was protruding from a pile of old canvas sacks. I walked closer. The stench got stronger. I pulled my T-shirt up over my mouth and nose. I drew my hand to the pile of sacks and hesitated, gathering courage. I threw them off to one side and saw Taffy's body propped against the wall. His face was almost completely caved in. He had been beaten repeatedly with something very solid and very heavy. Beside was the cause of the smell. Her skin was grey and decayed. Her eyes were milky and cold. Insects were crawling in and out of her mouth. Nevertheless, I recognized her as Sloan's wife. She had been lying down here for ten months. I stepped back in shock. My breathing was shallow and erratic. I wanted to get out of there.

From above, I heard Doug scream. I heard the scuffling on the floor above me. Sloan had woken up! I tried to jump up to the fireplace, but it was beyond my reach. All I could do was watch the little rectangle of light above me. I saw shadows moving fast. I heard screams and grunts. Then Doug's face filled the opening. He was bleeding badly. Sloan pulled his head out and I saw him slam Doug's skull against the inside of the chimney. Doug had lost all his strength. Sloan must have jumped him from behind and taken him by surprise. Doug collapsed.

Sloan looked down at me. "Now, Norton, you can watch as I bash this fuckin' halfwit's brains in." Sloan walked off and came back quickly with the poker in his hands. Doug cracked his eyes open and looked down at me. He moved his hand up to his face and showed me the Zippo still in his hand. I knew what he was going to do. I wanted to tell him to stop, but he had already flicked the cap open and had his thumb on the flint-wheel. I ran towards the tunnel.

4.

The thunderous sound of the explosion filled the tunnel. The lights died immediately. I felt the dirt falling on me in larger and larger quantities. I wanted to run but I had lost my bearings. It was completely dark; not the kind of dark in movies where a blue light somewhere off-screen shows the hero the way out, but total blackness. I stumbled about with my hands out until I found a wall, then moved back along that wall, away from where the majority of the roof was coming down. I could hear debris falling above ground, too. It sounded like the whole house was coming down. I kept backing along the wall until I reached its end. I had my bearings back now. This was the wall that the bodies were lain against. The smell of the collapsed earth was masking the stench for the moment. I just stood there until the cave-in stopped. I felt sure the weight of the house collapsing was going to bring this section of the tunnel down too. I would be buried alive. No one would ever know what happened to me.

The sounds of destruction quieted. My clothes were sticking to me with sweat. I didn't know if it was the fear or maybe the house burning above was slowly cooking me. I thought I should have been able to see the glow of fire around the grate but it must have been buried deeply under rubble. I wanted to cry, but I hadn't exhausted all the alternatives yet. I might still make it out. I tried to put the fear aside and think. My first thoughts were to get some light, to see the extent of the cave-in. Maybe it hadn't totally blocked the tunnel. Maybe there was a little corner that I could squeeze through. That tunnel had to come out somewhere. It suddenly clicked: Taffy was a smoker! I gently felt my way along the wall until I felt the body of Sloan's wife. I tried to step over her but tripped and fell on them both. The smell was unbearable at this distance and I vomited. I wanted to search him and get away as soon as I could. I stuck my hands out and felt a cold, decaying face under my fingers. I couldn't tell which of them it was. I moved my hands to the left and felt my fingers sink into another face. I was sick again. I remembered Taffy was on the left. I moved my hands quickly down his rough, tweed jacket and fished in his right-hand pocket. I felt his pouch of tobacco and pulled it out. I squashed the pouch in my hands, hoping he kept his lighter inside, but felt nothing. I put my hand in the pocket again and fished two matches out of his pocket. I ran my fingers up them and smelled their tips—they hadn't been used. Two matches weren't going to last a very long time and if Hollywood kept letting me down, no one would have abandoned fully-fuelled kerosene lamps down here. I felt my way across Taffy's chest and put my hand in my own sick. I shook off the vile substance and prised my hand between the two bodies and into his pocket, which only contained some rolled up paper and a few coins. I was about to retreat and burn the paper when it occurred to me that I should check Mrs Sloan as well. I ran my hands quickly over her body; over her breasts, over her hips to her pockets. I was almost sick again. There was a small hard rectangle in her pocket. I put two fingers inside her pocket and slid out a lighter.

I walked backwards from the bodies, slowly getting my composure back and hoping I didn't have to go near them again. I turned, put out my hands like antennae on an insect, and cautiously moved forward. When my feet tripped on the first earth of the cave in, I struck the lighter. I first looked at the lighter and saw it was a cheap, disposable one—that meant you couldn't keep it lit for long or the mechanism at the top got too hot and broke. I looked at the wall of mud. It looked solid. There were no convenient gaps for me to make my escape. I turned back and looked for the disregarded kerosene lamps or maybe a little bulldozer—it could happen in a Hollywood blockbuster! Unfortunately there was nothing of use that I could see. In a pinch I could burn the sacks that were covering the bodies of Taffy and Mrs Sloan, but that would only eat up the oxygen. The oxygen. That was something else to consider; if that wall of mud was sealed air-tight and so was the grate, I only had a limited amount of oxygen. The lighter clicked in my hand and went out. I tried to light it again but the wheel wouldn't turn. I put my thumb around and got it burned on the metal guard that surrounded the flame. I had left it on too long and now it was fucked. I was annoyed with myself—I knew that would happen. I was just so happy to be able to see again. Now, as the faint impressions of orange danced themselves to black before my eyes, I began to really worry. There was no way out.

Even if someone had known I had come here tonight, even if they knew about this underground chamber, even if they did think I was still alive, it could take them days to dig me out. I didn't have days. I might not even have hours. There had to be another way out. I dumped the paper I had found in Taffy's pocket on the ground and struck one of his matches on a coin. The paper was money; probably his wages for that week. I didn't care and lit it. As the money burned, I checked the walls of the chamber. There had to be something! There were three solid walls and the recently collapsed tunnel entrance made four. There were the lightbulbs on the wall, but I didn't see what good I could do with them, beyond breaking them and slitting my wrists. That thought crossed my mind and I smiled, then I thought it might actually come to that, and a shiver crept up my spine. At least that would be fast, but dying of suffocation would be slow, as would dying of dehydration or starvation.

The only plan I could form before the money burned out was weak, but it was the all I had. I went to Mrs Sloan and took off her high heels. I gripped one in each hand and went back to the collapsed entrance. I climbed up the ramp of earth as high as I could and started digging with the heels on my hands. I figured the wall would be thinnest at the top. I began to make progress. The heels were great for ploughing the earth and loosening it. I started to dig faster. Dirt started to trickle onto my face. I stopped digging. The roof collapsed again. I was covered in earth and stones and I was struggling to avoid being buried alive. I pushed myself free, rolled down the side of the mound and across the ground. Some earth came rolling after me, then it all settled again. It was only then that I noticed I had lost the high heels. They were buried somewhere in the darkness. I drew myself up into a sitting posture and brought my knees to my chest and rested my head on them.

I heard sirens above. Fire Brigade, Police and Ambulance. They had responded to the explosion—of course! I jumped to my feet and started shouting for help. I ran up the mound of earth and shouted. I ran to all the corners of the chamber shouting as loud as I could, in case they could hear me better in different places. I ran about and shouted for a long time. When I paused to get my breath back I heard how low and mumbled the shouts from up there sounded to me. It seemed unlikely that they could hear me with all the confusion above. I didn't give up. I kept shouting until I got dizzy. It was the oxygen, I was sure of it. I was nearly out. I felt so weak and disoriented. My legs disappeared beneath me and I fell against Mrs Sloan. I couldn't move, though the smell was worse than ever. I was going to die. The two bodies propped against the wall were going to have another companion for eternity. I couldn't draw a deep breath now. It seemed like my lungs had shrunk. I reached into my pocket and pulled out Taffy's last match. I felt around the ground and struck it on a stone. The match fizzed to life. I held it before my face and watched it burn. I was no longer interested in my surroundings, I just didn't want to die in the dark. The flame lessened as it made its way to the thumb and finger that were holding it. The flame reached my skin and burned me, but I held it until it went out. Again, the darkness. I didn't know if my eyes were open or closed. I began to feel an irresistible tiredness take me. The

213

ground above began to make noises; more earth falling, I supposed.

Suddenly light filled the whole chamber and blinded me temporarily. I put my arm over my eyes and heard a loud crash ahead of me. The light was so strong that it took me a long time to figure out what it was. The voices above were clearer now. My eyes finally readjusted to the light and I saw a police car in the chamber with me. All the cave-ins had weakened the roof to such an extent that when a car had been parked on the lawn above, the ground had given way below it. The car had slid down the same ramp as me and was now sitting perched at a forty-five degree angle with its headlights pointed at the ground. I heard the men above swearing in surprise at what had happened. I dragged myself to my feet and stumbled over to the car and collapsed on the bonnet. The officers all jumped back and drew their weapons when they saw me. I looked up and said, "Two more." I pointed back at the wall where I had been sitting and then passed out.

The police came to see me after three days in hospital. The most startling revelation was that Doug was still alive! The police said he jumped through the window just as the house exploded. He had been cut quite badly by the glass and suffered second-degree burns on his back. He wasn't in the same hospital as me, he was being held in Sycamore Acres' maximum-security wing. I guess we'll never really know how he got out of there for sure, but I imagine he somehow got the better of Sloan and struck the Zippo as he leapt for the window. Sloan hadn't survived. His remains had been recovered. Sloan's wife and Taffy had also been found and forensics had proved that Sloan had killed them both. When the inevitable question arose, "What were you doing there in the middle of the night?" I told them more-or-less the truth. Doug had come into my room in the middle of the night and led me to town. He had broken into Sloan's house, killed his dog, the two of them fought, Doug found the underground chamber, I went down, and boom! The lights went out. I didn't know anything about Sloan's motives or homicidal tendencies. They didn't seem entirely satisfied, but left saying they probably wouldn't need to talk to me again.

I was glad to get home. I had no need to be in hospital for three days. I hated the way they took me for tests and X-Rays in a wheelchair—I was fine, I could walk. I was rather unnerved when I didn't get a lecture from my parents. I knew they weren't going to let it go. If they weren't going to have a sit-down with me then they had another plan. I rang Emily and Toe-poke and told them the truth about what had happened. Toe-poke was mad; he said he was fit for duty and that the two of us would find this thing now and go Rambo on its ass. Emily was more scared and sympathetic. We talked for over an hour and even, somehow, got round to discussing Billy. She told me they had made a pact: she would keep quiet about their relationship and when he won the money from the Golf Club they would go on holiday together. I asked her if it didn't bother her that he would have to get jiggy with other girls to win. She said he had agreed to only kissing. Billy had said he could win without any big points at this stage. I wanted to shout IDIOT down the phone at her but I kept quiet. Maybe she was right, maybe that is all you can expect from a real relationship. Hollywood had weaned us on the idea of perfect partners and everlasting love and happy ever after. When I thought about everyone I knew, I realised no one had all three. Doug and Maxine were perfect and in love, but there was no happy ending. Maybe, as Mr Meat Loaf had said, two out of three *ain't* bad.

Chapter X - The Source

Some of Northern Ireland's most beautiful seaside resorts are located on the coast.

Holiday NI, Imogen Collins

- June, 1990 -

1.

For months I had been wracking my brains, trying to figure out what the source might be. When I did finally find out, it was by complete accident. Some people will tell you there are no accidents; that everything happens as it is supposed to, when it is supposed to. I didn't buy that. There were a lot of innocent people dead and if I had known where the source was earlier, they might still be alive. The idea that I was a pawn in a larger game just made me mad.

During June of your final year the teachers aren't so strict about school. They allow you to come in on the days you have exams and do as you please (officially we were studying) the rest of the time. Toe-poke and I weren't studying. He had missed too much school to even be entered in the exams and I didn't stand a chance of passing, so we searched during the days for the Siren's lair.

Imogen Collins had given up trying to get me to talk and was now following me most of the time. Her covert surveillance left a lot to be desired. Her bright yellow VW Beetle wasn't the most discreet car and the huge binoculars she used would have alerted even the most distracted subject. Toe-poke had suggested calling the cops on her, but I didn't need any more attention.

The Siren seemed to be Toe-poke's sole purpose in life. He was walking without crutches now, but his right leg had a pronounced limp. I think he wanted to take his anger out on the Siren. The doctors had now given up trying to restore his knee to its former glory and had told him that he was going to have to live with the fact that his knee would always be weak and he probably wouldn't be able to manage anything more than a gentle kick-about in the park. He didn't talk about what he intended to do now, maybe he didn't know. Maybe he only thought as far ahead as killing the Siren.

We walked along the beach that morning and saw the two Daves; Drake and Watt, huddled in the sand dunes rolling joints. They seemed to have developed a real liking for it. We stopped and chatted with them for a while. They had just taken their Physics exam and thought they deserved a treat. Toe-poke and I declined to indulge. The two Daves seemed amazed that anyone would refuse something so "mind-bendingly cool" as dope. They tried to argue the case intelligently, but were talking more and more crap as time went on. As Toe-poke put it: "I think they're tuned to a different station than us." They were harmless and funny in a stupid kind of way. Talking with them was like taking a break. I thought about coming to see them when I had killed the Siren. I might give it a try then. I might try a lot of things when this was over. We left the two Daves to their spliff construction and started down the sand dunes.

Dave shouted, "There's a gathering at the weekend if you change your mind."

I nodded a polite "OK."

The other Dave added, "We'll all be at The Source."

I stopped dead in my tracks and then ran up the sand dune again. "Where did you say you'll be?"

"The Source. You know, the car park at the end of the promenade?" Dave said.

"*That's* The Source?" I asked.

"Yeah," Dave said as if he'd given away a secret. "You can climb onto the rocks that overlook the sea. It's where a lot of ones go to smoke. There are a few water-tight hidey-holes up there, too, where people keep their stashes: that's why they call it The Source...I think."

"Let's go," Toe-poke said impatiently.

"Hey, man, you're not gonna fuckin' nark are you?" Dave asked.

I said no and Toe-poke and I ran off. That was why none of us knew where The Source was—it was stoner lingo. I would *never* have worked that out!

217

The promenade was on the other side of town, but we made it there quickly and ran all the way up to the car park that overlooked the harbour. It was full of cars because the sun was out and families had come to enjoy the seaside. We walked over to the rocks and looked down. It was easily a sixty foot drop to the sea and there were waves crashing below. There were a lot of little outshoots on the rocks that would be easy enough to get to and big enough for several people to sit on, though it didn't seem like the safest place to be if you were getting stoned. Toe-poke and I picked our way across and looked down at the giant inlet below. There was a cave right at the bottom where the sea met the rock-face. Toe-poke saw it, too.

"Can you feel it?" he asked in a low whisper.

"Yes, it's in there." I looked down the rock-face. It looked like there were enough footholds to make it to the bottom.

"C'mon, let's go get it," Toe-poke said, trying to edge past me.

I grabbed his arm. "No. First we get Emily. Then we get weapons. Then we come back and tear this fuckin' thing apart."

2.

When we got to Emily's, we noticed Imogen Collins parked a hundred yards up the road. She must have lost us in the town and waited here for us to show up. We stood on Emily's doorstep and waited for the bell to be answered. Her neighbour, Colin, with the broken heart, was kicking a ball against the wall. He looked at us with contempt. I didn't even try to talk to him this time. As soon as Emily opened the door I could tell she had been crying. We went to the kitchen and she put the kettle on. It hadn't even boiled when she ran out saying she'd be back in a minute. I got up and followed her.

I found her lying face-down on her bed, crying. I walked over and sat beside her. She kept crying. I lay down next to her and she rolled over and put her head on my chest and hugged me. Eventually the crying subsided and I asked her what had happened.

"They announced the Golf Club winner today."

"Oh, did Billy not win?"

"No, Danny Wells did."

218

"So you're upset because you and Billy can't go on holiday now?"

"No," she blubbed. "When Billy didn't win, he decided to come clean and say he didn't care because he had been cheating for months. He has a girlfriend."

"And what's so…"

"He wasn't talking about me! He's been seeing this girl that lives down the road from him. Cindy. She works in the supermarket. They're getting engaged!"

She started crying again. I let her cry because there was nothing I could say that would make it better. I don't know how long we lay there. When she got her composure back, I turned to her and looked her in the eyes. "I know this is probably the last thing you want to be thinking about now but, we know where the Siren's lair is. Toe-poke and I found it. We came to get you. We want to end this tonight."

Strength returned to her face and she sat up. "No, fuck it. I've got nothing to lose. I don't give a shit anymore. Let's go get it." She stood up and turned to me. The front door opened and we heard her father's voice. We ran to the kitchen and rejoined Toe-poke, just so Mr Matthews wouldn't get any ideas in his head about us alone in her bedroom.

Mr Matthews seemed glad to see us. I think he worried about Emily not having many friends. He insisted we stayed for dinner. We wanted to get away but he wouldn't take no for an answer. Emily made the dinner: steak and chips with all the trimmings; fried onions, mushrooms and peas. It was a meal fit for a king, or a prisoner on death row. That was what it felt like; our last supper. After we had all cleared our plates and thanked Emily, Mr Matthews told us to run on and he would take care of the dishes.

We stopped in the hall and had a quick discussion. I took the initiative and spoke first. "OK, first I think we should go to my place, steal the keys to my dad's shop and get some weapons."

"Is your dad an arms dealer?" Toe-poke asked sceptically.

"No, he owns More Than Gardens, but there's got to be some stuff in there that's sharp or pointy."

"To save time," Emily offered, "maybe we should check my dad's garage. He's got a lot of stuff for gardening and the like." We nodded agreement and Emily led us out to her dad's garage. It was indeed full of stuff both old and new. Something told me if he still had a wife, a lot of this would have been dumped a long time ago. There were bits of old cars, an old clothes-mangle, cast iron gates and God knows what was in all the boxes. Emily found a hand-sickle and Toe-poke armed himself with a hatchet. I found a sledgehammer with a broken handle. There was still about ten inches of the wooden handle intact; more than enough for me to hold onto.

I held it above my head and Emily and Toe-poke looked round at me. "Just call me Thor," I said. Toe-poke and Emily smiled.

Emily rubbed her thumb over the blade of the sickle. "These things aren't very sharp."

Toe-poke scanned the garage and saw the bench-grinder. "Does that work?" Emily shrugged. Toe-poke made his way over and turned it on and then off again. "Give it here and I'll sharpen it. I'll put an edge on my little hatchet while I'm at it."

"I spotted a rusty, petrol can and checked it; it was full. "We'll take this, too. Does anyone have a lighter on them?"

"I'll go in the house and get mine," Emily said and ran out the door. Toe-poke stood there in a shower of sparks from the grinder.

I suddenly felt the reality of the situation close in on me. This was really happening. We were really going out after this thing tonight, to kill or be killed. Emily returned just as Toe-poke finished sharpening the weapons. She had brought her hockey bag with her.

"It will look a bit suspicious walking through town with this stuff. I think it should all fit in here." We put the sickle, the hatchet, the sledgehammer and the petrol can in the bag. It was damned heavy and awkward to carry.

We stood there facing each other. "OK, I guess this is it," I said. "Are we all ready to do this?" Toe-poke and Emily nodded.

We all just stood there, none of us willing to take the first step, until Toe-poke spoke. "I've been thinking, Steve. If we could sense that thing today, maybe it could sense us, too."

"Yeah, probably," I agreed, not seeing his point.

"If it knows that we know where it is," he continued, "wouldn't it try to do something to protect itself?"

"Like make itself super strong by feeding on lots of people," Emily said.

I began to worry that if we ran to its lair right now it wouldn't be there. "OK, it would need a lot of people. A lot of people filled with hope. Where would it go to…?"

"Shit," Emily screamed and looked at her watch. "It's gone seven."

"So? What? What!" I asked.

"Rachel and Tony's engagement party is tonight."

"It's OK, it's not dark," Toe-poke said. "It won't be able to fool anyone."

"The party is in O'Neill's: it's right on the coast. If it's desperate enough it won't even try to fool anyone it'll just go in there and kill them all."

Toe-poke realised how much more urgent our mission had become. "That's miles away, we'll never make it in time."

A brilliant idea struck me. "I know someone who'll give us a lift."

3.

Imogen Collins was still in the same place when the three of us ran up the road towards her carrying a large bag. She put on her sunglasses immediately, so we wouldn't recognize her. I pulled open the passenger door and pulled the seat forward. Toe-poke and Emily jumped in the back. I put the seat down, sat down and closed the door. "You want to know what's been going on? You want to know what's been killing all those kids? Take us to O'Neill's and we'll show you."

"Are you serious?"

"I'm deadly serious, Ms Collins. But time is a factor here."

She nodded and started the car. She did a three-point turn in the road and we sped off towards the town. I was surprised by how quiet Imogen Collins was being. She didn't say a word for most of the journey, and then she ruined it by opening her mouth. "So, are you going to tell me what we're after?"

I considered her for a moment. "Remember when you asked me what was going on and I said you wouldn't believe me." She nodded quickly. "You said you would believe me, so let's see if you do. What we're chasing, what's been killing the kids of this town...is a Siren."

"A Siren. What's that?" she asked quickly.

"You never studied Greek, I take it." She shook her head. "It's a sea-monster that can make itself look like anyone who you have a picture of in your mind. It takes the form of someone who you will trust to get close to you, then it kills you."

A wide smile broke on her face. Her eyes danced with the thought of this worldwide scoop. "OK, I'm not saying I believe you, but I'm willing to go along with you and give you the benefit of the doubt. If you are telling the truth...this could be huge!"

"I'm telling the truth, don't worry about that."

"Ow!" she yelped. "This is the best thing that I could ever have hoped for." That one word suddenly made me think again. I turned to Toe-poke and Emily. They had both heard her say "hope" and now we all saw that she was brimming with it. She would be irresistible to it. She wouldn't be safe.

"Just pull over here," I said.

"What? Why? O'Neill's is still at least a mile away."

"Just here will be fine. Trust me." She slowed the car and pulled onto the grass verge. I leaned over her and opened her door. "Sorry about this, but it's for your own good." I opened the door and pushed her out onto the grass. I slammed the door quickly and locked it. Toe-poke climbed into the front with me and locked the passenger door.

"Do you know how to drive?" he asked.

"Sort of," I answered. "My dad used to let me drive round the supermarket car park on Sunday while it was empty." Imogen Collins was on her feet, banging at the window, tugging at the door handle, while screaming profanities and legal warnings. I put the car in gear and we jerked forward and onto the road. We raced towards O'Neill's. We were only a few hundred yards away—we could even see the partygoers through the large picture window—when all three of us felt the pull. Simultaneously we all put our hands on our chests, as the unnatural feeling called to us. The Siren was closing in on someone. But it wasn't ahead of us in O'Neill's, we felt drawn backwards.

We all knew what it meant, but Emily said it: "Imogen Collins. It's going after Imogen Collins." I swung the car around without slowing and skidded into a hedge and came to a stop. I put the car in gear again and gunned the accelerator. We saw Imogen Collins running up the road. She wasn't going to let go of the story and had obviously intended to make her own way to O'Neill's. When she saw us she smiled and raised her arms triumphantly, thinking we had had a change of heart and were coming back for her. Behind her the Siren crawled from the hedge surrounding the coastline. The long summer evening gave it no darkness to disguise itself. It moved quickly and stealthily across the grass towards Imogen Collins. I pressed hard on the horn and flashed the lights. Imogen Collins stopped running and looked confused. The Siren was racing towards her from behind. I pointed the car straight at her. She stood and watched us bearing down on her. We hurtled toward her; the Beetle from the front, the Siren from behind. I waved my arms frantically as we got close. At the last second she dove out of the way and I ploughed the Beetle head-on into the Siren. It cracked hard when we hit and it rolled over the roof of the Beetle and landed on the grass behind. I slammed the brakes and screeched to a stop. We all looked out the back window. The Siren got to its feet slowly. It was weak and we had hurt it. I grinded the gear-stick into reverse and slammed the accelerator again. The Beetle roared toward the Siren again. In the background I saw Imogen Collins fumbling with a camera and flashes going off. The Siren sized us up and ran up the road toward O'Neill's. I backed the car over to Imogen Collins and Toe-poke flung open the door and quickly put her in the backseat with Emily.

She was a gibbering wreck. "Did you?…it was a…what was?…it looked like nothing I've ever…"

We raced up the road and saw the Siren skulking on the big lawn at the side of O'Neill's. It didn't see us until it was too late. I hit it again at high speed, but this time it didn't go over the roof. At least one of its legs went under the wheels. The car bumped down and we heard a satisfying howl from the beast. I looked back and saw it get up and limp off slowly.

Emily screamed, "Steve, look out!"

I hit the brakes hard, but the car slid across the grass and crashed through the picture window. The front end of the Beetle sat on the dancefloor, the back end was still on the lawn. Thankfully we hadn't hurt anyone, though there was glass everywhere. I looked at my companions. "Everyone OK?" One by one, my shocked, but unhurt, passengers nodded. "Come on, this isn't over yet." I opened my door and got out. I popped the seat forward and everyone else got out. Toe-poke had the bag over his shoulder. Imogen Collins stood there dithering to herself.

"Steve?" Rachel's voice was unmistakable. I turned and saw her, dressed in a red silk dress. She looked beautiful. But more importantly, she looked well pissed off. I didn't have time to get into a whole discussion about my motives for smashing through the window in a car. I turned to walk away and saw Emily's eyes fixated inside, too. She was staring at Billy, in a tux no less, with a very pretty girl on his arm. I gripped her arm tightly and broke her stare.

"We have to go, Emily." She nodded dutifully. Toe-poke was already a few steps from the car and looking off to where the Siren had run. Emily and I joined him and the three of us started running towards town, and towards The Source.

4.

The Source was thankfully free of both tourists and stoners when we got there. We stared down the rock-face at the entrance to the cave. We all felt it. We all knew it was in there. And it was hurt and weak. There would never be a better time. We nodded to each other in silent agreement and started to make our way down the rocks. In the Hollywood movie, one of us would have a friend that was into abseiling and would lend us his equipment, which we would be able to use with little instruction. Another strike for the Hollywood team. We had to slowly pick our way down the precarious rocks. Toe-poke threw the bag ahead of us when he saw a ledge below that could hold it. We didn't want to drop it all the way to the bottom in case it alerted the Siren to our presence, but I feared it knew we were coming, anyway.

We finally made it to the bottom. I was second, after Toe-poke, to touchdown. We waited for Emily and then opened the bag. Emily took her sickle, Toe-poke his hatchet and I swung the sledgehammer by my side. The three of us stared into the cave. I looked at Emily and Toe-poke; focussed on the opening, and saw that they were just like me—pissed off at the world and with nothing to lose. We were in perfect condition to destroy this thing. I started walking and Emily and Toe-poke followed.

There was still enough light outside to illuminate a long way into the cave. We all felt the pull in our chests. The Siren was close and it knew we were here. We edged forwards into the dark. I wondered if we followed this tunnel far enough would it lead to the chamber under Sloan's house. There was a weird smell coming from ahead. We edged further on and I looked back at the entrance, getting smaller and smaller. As I faced forward again, the Siren pounced on me from above.

It pinned me to the ground. Its teeth were just inches from my face. I looked into those dead eyes and could have sworn I saw pure hate. Toe-poke whacked it on the shoulder with his hatchet and it fell off to the side. I swung the sledgehammer round and it thumped solidly into the sand. The Siren was on its feet. Toe-poke charged it again. The Siren swept its powerful arm and caught Toe-poke on the chest, sending him flying through the air and slamming into the wall. Toe-poke fell to the ground, winded and grabbing at his aching back.

I swung the sledgehammer in a large arc and caught the Siren full force on the back of the head as it watched Toe-poke. I ran to it, preparing to bring the sledgehammer down squarely on its face. One of its arms shot forward to intercept me. Emily brought the sickle down with all her strength and took its arm off below the elbow. The Siren screamed and dark yellow liquid spurted from the wound. It leapt to its feet and limped quickly away into the dark.

Emily and I looked at each other in excited terror. We ran to Toe-poke and found he was in real pain. He didn't care. He wasn't going to let us down and dragged himself to his feet. Emily handed him his hatchet. We looked into the distance and heard the Siren wailing.

"Bring the petrol can," I said. Emily ran and got it as I supported Toe-poke. We walked on, this time keeping an eye for attacks from above as well as from the front.

The weird smell got stronger the deeper we went. There was still some light and our eyes were becoming accustomed to the dark, but when we saw the cause of the smell, we didn't know what it was. It was huge and vaguely cylindrical. Maybe ten feet deep and twenty feet long, tapering off at the far end. In the end closest to us was an opening. I don't know what it was made of; it seemed organic, but like nothing I had ever seen before or since. It was a pale white colour with veins of blue through it.

"I think it's a nest," Emily said. "I think that's where it sleeps, maybe even hibernates."

"Let's burn the fuckin' thing," Toe-poke said coldly.

I didn't have to be told twice. I walked over and got the petrol can from Emily. She handed it to me and looked me in the eyes for a second before handing me her lighter. She didn't look scared. She looked proud of me. I nodded and walked forward and started dousing the nest in petrol. The nest hissed and spat where the petrol hit it and I had the feeling that this was not only organic, but also maybe alive. I looked back at the other two and they nodded that they were ready. I struck the lighter and lit it. The nest exploded in flames. The three of us positioned ourselves at the mouth of the nest. It sizzled and crackled with the heat. We tensed and kept our eyes fixed on the opening. Huge bubbles were rising and popping on the nest's skin.

The Siren burst from the opening and launched itself at me. Its back was partially on fire. It landed on me and closed its remaining hand around my throat and squeezed. I had dropped the sledgehammer on impact and my hand frantically skimmed the sand looking for it. The Siren bent backwards and I saw Emily standing behind it with her sickle stuck in its back. Toe-poke saw his opening and swung his hatchet into its chest. The hard shell cracked and bent inwards with the force of the impact. Toe-poke was close and the Siren grabbed him by the throat. It stood up and lifted Toe-poke above its head, crushing his neck. It turned and saw Emily and I running toward it and it threw Toe-poke against the wall again.

Though we had no plan, Emily and I seemed strangely co-ordinated in our attack. She grabbed the stump of its left arm and I grabbed its right arm and we pushed it to the ground. There was a rock sticking out of the sand about three feet, we pushed the Siren's back against it and bent its arms round each side. It was kicking and struggling furiously. Emily looked over at me as if to say "Now what?"

"Keep it on the ground," I shouted to her. "Bend its fuckin' arms back until they break off." Emily obeyed and we both pushed as hard as we could. The Siren's chest bent outwards from the pressure. I pushed the arm with all I had, my feet scrambling beneath me in the sand. Emily was getting covered in the blood from the severed arm, but was behind and pulling as hard as she could.

"All right, you fucker," Toe-poke said through gritted teeth. "That was a foul. Now I get a free kick." Emily and I watched as Toe-poke took three running steps and then drove his foot into the Siren's chest. The shell caved in completely and Toe-poke's foot buried itself in the chest wall. Toe-poke pulled his foot out, covered with that yellow blood, and stepped back. The Siren was having something resembling a seizure now. Emily and I held tight to it. Toe-poke lined himself up again. This was for the championship. Toe-poke took three steps forwards and drove his right foot under the Siren's chin and took its head off. The head flew backwards and slammed against the wall. The Siren twitched its last spasms of life in our grasp and then was still.

Toe-poke stood hopping on his left leg. "I think I've fucked my knee up again." He dropped to the ground gently and Emily and I went and sat beside him. The nest was still popping and burning behind us. We looked at the decapitated torso in front of us.

Something was moving inside the Siren. We could hear it. From the neck of the Siren a long black snake slithered quickly out and down the broken shell to the sand. Emily and I jumped to our feet.

...and the serpent was loosed.

I knew at once that the huge beast we had fought was only the vehicle. That snake was the real Siren, if it got to the sea it could find or grow another body and live on. Well, not on my fuckin' shift.

It slithered quickly towards the sea. I raced after it and stepped on it hard. It flailed wildly, biting at the leather of my boot and getting nowhere. I knelt down and waited for my chance, then grabbed it just below its head. A collar of spikes shot into my hand and I reflexively let go again. It slithered towards the sea again. Emily ran past me with her sickle. She edged forward with the snake, her sickle above her head, staying out of its bite reach, but trying to line up the edge of her blade at the same time. She was right above it, with one leg on either side of the snake, shuffling forward waiting for her chance. They were at the mouth of the cave now and I felt sure she would lose it. I heard the blade cut through the air. She brought the sickle down hard and impaled the snake through the head. She lifted the sickle and held the twitching, dying snake before her face. She walked back into the cave, past me, to the burning nest and threw snake and sickle into its midst.

I tied my hanky around my bleeding palm and walked back to Toe-poke. I collected the Siren's head and the severed arm on the way and threw them into the fire, too. Toe-poke still couldn't stand so Emily and I dragged the torso to the blaze and heaved it on as well.

We sat down with Toe-poke and watched it burn.

Toe-poke couldn't walk so he definitely couldn't climb out. It was decided that I would go and get help and Emily would stay with Toe-poke. I was exhausted as I climbed up the rock-face; emotionally and physically drained. As I neared the top a wave of pride began to fill me. We had saved, who knows how many, lives. The people of this town would be grateful that no one else would die by the Siren's hand, even if they didn't know who to be grateful to. The world would keep on turning because of us. Dreams could be pursued without consequence. I felt good for the first time in months.

I was close to the phone box I was going to use to call for help when I was shouted on. I turned and saw Tony, Billy, Justin, Scone and Bull all dressed in suits. All with their ties undone and their sleeves rolled up.

Tony spoke. "You pathetic, jealous little fuck! You think by spoiling our engagement party that I would change my mind about marrying Rachel?" They had formed a circle around me before I could speak.

"Listen, Tony, tonight had nothing…" Tony punched me straight in the face, breaking my nose. Blood spewed from my nostrils and as I lowered my head I felt punches coming from all directions. I remember falling to the ground and trying to stop highly polished shoes driving into my face…then nothing.

5.

My mum said I had been awake a few times, but it was nearly a week after that night, I actually remember being awake. The drugs they had me on were pretty strong. The sterile odour of the Intensive Care Unit is the first alien smell I remember. I had a broken jaw, a broken nose, a detached retina, four broken fingers, three broken ribs, thirty-nine stitches in my face and head, and a lot of bruising around my spine, which the doctors said was "worrying." Plus various other cuts and bruises that weren't so serious, but hurt nevertheless.

The first thing I asked my mum was if Emily and Toe-poke were all right. I had left them down there with no way out. My mum said Emily had been by a few times when I was out of it, but that's all she knew. At least she had got out. I had terrible visions that the tide had came in and filled the cave, drowning them both. Emily came in a couple of days later and told me that they had waited for hours for me to come back, during which time they had used the hatchet to carve the initials of everyone the Siren had killed into the wall. Emily said it was partially a memoriam, but also because she had to stop Toe-poke from passing out and between the two of them they remembered everyone. It was nice to know it was down there in the depths of the cave. Like all those initials were witnesses to the justice meted out to their killer. When they had finished carving all the initials and I still wasn't back, Emily had climbed out and brought the coastguard to get Toe-poke out of the cave. She said by that time the nest had burned itself out and since Toe-poke was waiting by the sea, the coastguard didn't have to go into the cave. She had told them that they had climbed down the rocks and Toe-poke had lost his footing and fallen, hurting his knee. She said Toe-poke's leg was strapped up again, but he was at home.

When I was nearly ready to come home my mum and dad dropped the bomb: they had sold our house and bought one in Ballymena, which was about fifty miles away from where we had lived. Dad was selling his business and reopening in Ballymena. They said Portstewart wasn't safe for us (meaning me) and we could make a new start in Ballymena. I argued with them that it was all over and would never happen again, but they said they had heard it all before, and to be honest, they had. And I couldn't guarantee that it wouldn't happen again. The Siren was dead, but there were plenty of angry young males who, for bad reasons or good, wanted me pulped. I told the cops I hadn't seen who beat me up—the law of the schoolyard still applied.

Imogen Collins was notable by her absence. I thought with me incapacitated and at the mercy of her questions, she would have been there round the clock. She never showed. According to Emily, she never reported anything that happened that night. Maybe it scared her too much or maybe she feared the ridicule. I doubt if her photos of the Siren were very clear; she was shaking a lot when she snapped them. Still, they were as good as any Loch Ness Monster picture I'm sure, and there's always someone willing to buy *them*. I guess she didn't want to be tarred with the loony brush.

The day I left hospital, to journey to the home I had never seen, was the last time I saw Emily. She came to my room as I was leaving and said she was going to France to work at a vineyard. She said she wanted to experience a little bit of life before she tied herself down to a 9to5. I wished her luck and we kissed. For the first time it wasn't about comforting her or satisfying the raging hormones in me, it was about love. She walked away; I didn't think she'd ever be back. I went home.

Epilogue

No, not at all, Tracey-Ann. Working for the Sofa Shopper Channel is the best job I've ever had. I've never been so happy. You should see the freebies I get; just look at these beautiful gold-effect earrings.

*Whatever happened to...*Imogen Collins

- August, 2004 -

This is the first time I've been back to Portstewart since all that happened. I never heard from Toe-poke and Emily. Like everyone else, I supposed they were getting on with their own lives. Even the people I was closest to at university have drifted away; letters become less personal and more factual, then they become postcards, then just a Christmas card, then an occasional email to point out something hilarious on the Internet. We all move on and maybe that's how it should be.

Maybe that was what eventually killed Toe-poke; he couldn't move on. Toe-poke was badly hurt killing the Siren and it took him a long time before he could even walk unaided. By that time he felt he had been out of education too long to go back to school. He did odd jobs (not all of them legal) around Portstewart and gained a bit of a reputation for telling tall tales when he was drunk. I wonder if those tales are really the height that some imagine. He drank more and more and worked less and less. He died a few weeks before his thirtieth birthday. Robert Taylor ended his days as the town joke, a drunk with some crazy stories. The official cause of death was Accidental Suffocation—to you and me that's choking on his own vomit. It's not how Hollywood would have shown the hero ending up.

I came back for the funeral. There was only his dad and I at the graveside. I went back to the house and talked with his dad over a few drinks. He still had all Toe-poke's football memorabilia on the walls. He said that was what killed him; having his dream crushed and thinking he wasn't good for anything else. He said Toe-poke had hit the bottle hard when he had gone to Scotland to get Mags back. He somehow thought she was the answer to all his problems. Of course, she

231

didn't want to know and Toe-poke had begun a drinking binge that would last the rest of his life. When I left the house his dad was pouring another and rested the bottle by his side and not on the table.

I went to Emily's house and found she didn't live there anymore. Mr Matthews was still there and he told me that Emily had married Colin, the boy who used to live next door. She was a sociology teacher and he was a solicitor, they both lived in London and only got back at Christmas. I felt happy for her. Despite Colin's attitude towards me, I think he had always loved her. Nevers and forevers fall easily from the lips of those who don't understand them. I'm glad Colin's dissolution of their friendship was just bullshit teenage posturing. Mr Matthews gave me their address and phone number in London. I took the piece of paper, though I knew I would never use it. Mr Matthews was also able to tell me that Rachel and Tony were still married, but Tony was in jail. Apparently he had been caught embezzling money from some charity he worked for. He denied all charges but was convicted just the same. Rachel still believed in his innocence and is dutifully waiting for him to get out. They have two kids.

I also went to Sycamore Acres and saw Doug. He's different now. He has a look of calm serenity on his face and meets everyone with the fascination and wonder of a child. I only stayed with him a few minutes. I don't think he recognized me. I don't know what happened to Doug in that bedroom all those years ago. Maybe the Siren had tried to take his hope and was interrupted, or Doug resisted it, so he didn't die. The doctor I spoke to said Doug still had nightmares sometimes that made him violent and unpredictable—he didn't think Doug would ever be released.

After everything that happened, my parents weren't surprised when I failed all my exams. I retook them the following year and did well enough to get into the university course that I wanted. I even learned to appreciate Dickens…eventually; though I still think he's the wrong thing to be forcing schoolkids to read. I'm a journalist now, which I know is ironic considering my experience with Imogen Collins, but I hope I'm nothing like her. My wife is a photographer. We both work for the same newspaper and are expecting our first child in November.

When I returned from Toe-poke's funeral, I rummaged around my mum's attic and found all my old stuff in a box: audio tapes from my tape recorder, Johnny's drawings, my short stories, old letters, even the video I had bought from Porno Bill, and I knew what I had to do.

I decided to take time off work to write this book because I wanted Toe-poke to be remembered as more than a drunk who told monster stories and ranted about how "he coulda been a contender" in the soccer world. Toe-poke was a hero. I hope after reading this, you know that. I remember him every day. Every time I look at the row of white dots across my palm, where the spikes from the snake stuck into me.

When I was back in Portstewart, I had to do one last thing before I left. I hired a boat and went to The Source. You can't climb down to the cave anymore; rock-falls over the years have left hardly any of the footholds that we used. I was nervous when I entered the cave. Teenage fear endures if you let it. I walked on, deeper into the dark, and switched on my torch. Nothing remains of the Siren or its nest, no doubt washed out to sea many moons ago. I found the sandstone wall where Emily had carved the names of the Siren's victims. I took out my penknife and added:

R T-P T

The Siren's last victim.

Printed in the United Kingdom
by Lightning Source UK Ltd.
112651UKS00001B/454-501